牡丹亭

THE
PEONY
PAVILION

The Peony Pavilion

A NOVEL

Xiaoping Yen

Xiaoping Yen
7/10/99

HOMA & SEKEY BOOKS
Dumont, New Jersey

ISBN: 0-9665421-2-6
Library of Congress Card Number: 99-90422

Publishers Cataloging-in-Publication Data
Yen, Xiaoping, 1956-
The Peony Pavilion: A Novel
Based on: Mudan Ting by Tang Xianzu, 1550-1616
1.   China—Fiction
2.   Love stories
I. Title   II. Title: Mudan Ting
PS3553.E   1999   813'.54-dc21

Published by Homa & Sekey Books
P. O. Box 103
Dumont, NJ 07628
Fax: (201)384-6055
Email: homa_sekey@yahoo.com
Website: www.homabooks.com (available soon)

Editor: Shawn X. Ye
Cover Design: Judy Wang
Cover Art and Illustrations: Qian Guisun

First American Edition
Printed in the United States of America
1 3 5 7 9 10 8 6 4 2

For my wife and daughters

ACKNOWLEDGEMENTS

I wish to thank all of those who have given me encouragement and support in writing this book. My special thanks go to Mr. Shawn Ye, my editor at Homa & Sekey Books, for his enthusiasm in classic Chinese literature and his determination to introduce its treasures to the English reading public. Without his unflagging support, this book would never be in existence.

The story in this book took place in the
Southern Song Dynasty (1127-1279) in China

Chapter One

THE BROWN earthen pot started to boil on the stove. As its lid popped up and down, steam came out, and the kitchen soon filled with the aroma of the stew.

The stew was her father's favorite, consisting of young bamboo shoots, salted pork, and fresh pork ribs. It needed one more ingredient, dried mushrooms.

"Are you going to put the mushrooms in, Kitchen Grandma?" Liniang asked.

"Wait, my child," Kitchen Grandma answered. She was a plump and short woman. Although she was almost eighty and a little slow in her movements, her hearing and eyesight were still good.

Liniang waited anxiously. After what it seemed to be a long time, Kitchen Grandma finally lifted the lid from the pot and stirred its contents with a pair of long chopsticks. She poured a small cup of wine into the pot and added some salt. Then, one by one, she dropped a handful of dried mushrooms into the pot.

The mushrooms floated on the surface for a short moment. Then they sank and disappeared in the turmoil of the pot.

"Are they going to work?" Liniang asked Kitchen Grandma.

"Yes," the old woman assured the girl. She then folded her hands in front of her, closed her eyes, and murmured a prayer.

Liniang had just turned sixteen. The day of her sixteenth birthday, she and her mother traveled to the Purple Light Convent for her coming-of-age ceremony. The mushrooms were a gift from the senior sister.

The convent sat half way up a steep hill in the Western Mountains. They started early in the morning. The ride was a long one, and the path to the convent was narrow and steep. The four young soldiers, who carried offerings, had to stop several times on the way up.

Sister Stone, who was her mother's friend, started the ceremony by bathing Liniang in an ancient wooden tub and dressing her in a coarse hemp outfit.

"Kowtow to the earth for giving you flesh and bone," the senior sister, her eyes closed, told Liniang when she came into the prayer hall after bathing.

Liniang kowtowed to the earth.

"Kowtow to the heaven for giving you spirit."

"Kowtow to your mother for giving you the completed form."

"Kowtow to your father for providing sustenance to your life."

"My father is not here, Reverent Sister," Liniang answered, her voice low and melancholy.

"Where is he?" the sister, who, according to legend, spent all her life sitting on the chair praying and never touched a bed, opened her eyes for the first time since they had arrived and looked at her sympathetically.

"Reverent Sister," Liniang's mother answered, "my husband is busy with government business, and he has asked me to receive the respect from our daughter."

"I know he is a government man, but he should at least make time for this important occasion," the sister complained.

"He had planned to come, but an urgent matter arose this morning," Liniang's mother lied.

"In this case," the senior sister turned to Liniang, "Kowtow to your mother again."

Liniang did.

The senior sister then waved her hand. Her mother and all the nuns retreated out of the prayer hall.

"You have grown into a very pretty young lady, my child," she told Liniang.

"Thank you, Reverent Sister."

"What is your wish for your life, my child?"

Liniang hesitated. Her mother had told her that she should wish for a good husband and a large family. "The sister has magic power, but she is only willing to use it on someone's sixteenth birthday," she had warned Liniang.

"I wish my father has more affection for my mother," Liniang answered.

The senior sister raised her eyebrows, looking surprised. "Think carefully, my child. You've got only one chance."

"I wish my father has more affection for my mother," Liniang repeated.

"Very well," the sister closed her eyes and started chanting. Although she looked ancient, her voice was surprisingly soft and sweet.

The other nuns, who had been waiting outside, filed into the prayer hall and joined in the chant. The rhythmic and mysterious voices filled the century-old wooden building, and they filled Liniang's heart with hope.

When it was over, Liniang and her mother thanked the senior sister and said good-bye to the nuns.

"Before you leave," the senior sister stopped Liniang, "I want to give you a present." She murmured to a young nun, who went out of the hall for a few minutes and came back with a small basket.

Opening the lid of the basket, Liniang saw a dozen of dried mushrooms. The mushroom the sister gave her had two heads from each stem, nestling against each other like lovers.

"They will do what you wish for, my child," the senior sister winked at her conspiratorially before closing her eyes again.

❀❀

It was a sleepless night for Liniang. As Liniang turned and tossed in her bed, the history of her family, as told by Kitchen Grandma, floated before her tired eyes.

Du Bao, Liniang's father, was born into a poor family. His father was a scholar, but he was not able to pass the government examination or get a government job.

At the age of forty, Du Bao's father saved up enough money to marry a girl from a nearby village. She gave him a son, and they named their son "Bao," which meant "treasure." Sadly, Du Bao's mother died of hemorrhage a few days after the birth of her son.

"I took pity on your grandfather," Kitchen Grandma told Liniang. "A poor scholar with a hungry baby. He was really desperate. So I offered to help."

Kitchen Grandma had just been widowed at that time. She had borne no children. Her parents-in-law insisted that she leave her husband's farm, but her parents refused to take her back. So it was a matter of relief to both families that Du Bao's father agreed to take her on as nurse and kitchen help.

Du Bao's father had a small farm, but his heart was not in farming. He struggled, living on meager rice and vegetables and on occasional handouts from relatives. When Du Bao was barely four, his father started teaching him classics. Day in and day out, father and son recited poems, essays, and official histories.

"Du Bao was the smartest boy in the village," Kitchen Grandma would tell everyone who cared to listen.

He took the provincial examination at the age of seventeen. Over two thousand people all over the province took the government test, but only seventy-six passed. Du Bao was one of them. His father was very proud of him, so was the whole village.

Success at the national level, however, came slowly. Every three years, his father would borrow money from his relatives, and he would trek to Hangzhou, the capital of the empire, for the big exam. At first, his relatives were eager and willing, encouraged by Du Bao's success at the provincial level. But as Du failed again and again, his relatives became skeptical, and his father found it more and more difficult to borrow the travel expenses.

Du Bao finally passed the national examination at the age of thirty-two. When his father, already old and frail by that time, received the letter from Du, he invited all his kinsmen for a celebration.

"Your poor grandfather," Kitchen Grandma's eyes would well up. "He was beside himself. He drank too much, he ate too much, he smoked too much, and he died the same night."

Du Bao waited in the capital for another two years before he received his royal appointment: Governor of Nan'an region in East China, two hundred miles east of his native village.

He returned to his village in a government carriage. He bought a marble tombstone for his father and spent seven days and nights at his father's grave fasting. The wake over, he made the rounds of his kinsmen, thanking them and giving them gifts he had brought with him from the capital.

Du Bao then sent a matchmaker to Liniang's maternal grandfather, a well-to-do farmer in the village. He wanted to marry his daughter, a very pretty girl of seventeen.

At first, the farmer rejected the proposal. Du Bao, at thirty-four, was twice the age of his daughter. Besides, he did not want his daughter to marry a bookworm who had no interest in farming.

"He is not a bookworm," the matchmaker explained. "He is a scholar."

"How is a scholar different from a bookworm?" the farmer asked skeptically.

The matchmaker dangled Du Bao's appointment letter before the farmer, "A scholar is a bookworm with this paper."

The bright red seal of the emperor impressed the farmer, and he agreed to the marriage.

The marriage celebration was held on the farmer's large estate because Du Bao's house was derelict and in danger of collapsing. The day after the marriage, Kitchen Grandma, then already in her early sixties, went to visit the new couple. Kneeling and with tears in her eyes, she said to Du Bao, "When you leave, I have no family here anymore."

The young bride raised the old woman to her feet. "Come to Nan'an with us, and I will take care of you," she promised.

"Your mother has a golden heart," Kitchen Grandma would repeat to Liniang whenever she had an opportunity. "Your father has a very smart head," the wrinkled old woman would add, "but his heart is cold."

Tossing in her bed, Liniang prayed that the mysterious chants and the two-headed mushrooms would finally warm her father's heart.

First, it was the proud voice of a single rooster from a farm house to the left of the estate, "cock-a-doodle-doo." Then, almost instantly, an army of roosters joined in from all directions, happily announcing the arrival of a new morning, "cock-a-doodle-doo, cock-a-doodle-doo, cock-a-doodle-doo."

Madam Du woke up. "What a nuisance," she complained. Turning to her husband at her side, she saw him sit up in the bed. She hugged him. "Please stay with me a little longer."

Freeing himself from his wife's embrace, Du Bao slipped off the bed. He walked to the wooden window barefooted and opened it. Immediately, a thin morning light spilled into the dark bedroom.

"You are going to catch a cold at the window," Madam Du warned her husband, who trembled slightly in the morning chill.

Her husband was fifty-one years old. He was a tall, well-built man. Although he was only wearing pajamas, he stood at the window erect and dignified, as if he were in his office, staring down at his obsequious staff. Sniffing at the crisp morning air, he coughed.

"Please come back to the bed," Madam Du pleaded.

Despite her entreaties, her husband remained motionless at the window.

Reluctantly, Madam Du rolled off the bed, wrapped herself in a sleeping gown embroidered with sunflowers and assembled her husband's official garment from a large mahogany wardrobe. A white cotton shirt, a black cotton pants, a purple brocade robe with golden girdles, and a black hat with two long flap wings at its sides. "Put them on," she urged.

Her husband put on his garment absent-mindedly.

Madam Du looked out the window. Dawn had broken over the tiled roof of the east house, but a thin white mist still hung over the courtyard. The mist, however, could not conceal the many shrubs in the courtyard dripping with crystal dews and blooming with colors.

In the distance, through the thin mist, she saw a carriage approach the wooden bridge in front of the estate. It crossed the bridge and pulled up at the stone gate. The driver, a uniformed army officer, got off his seat, patted his horses on the haunches, and lit a bamboo pipe stuffed with tobacco.

The officer was waiting to pick up her husband.

As Madam Du stood by her husband, memories of her married life flashed back. She and her husband had first lived in the governor's compound in the middle of the city after their marriage. Apart from the governor's apartment in the back, the compound also contained his office, the court, and living quarters for servants and soldiers.

Madam Du was soon pregnant. The couple found the official residence too small. Madam Du wanted privacy, and she missed the smell and the color of the country. Meanwhile, Du Bao wanted many children to pass on and proliferate the family name. So, with the dowry money from her parents, they bought a farm outside the west gate of the city.

The farm had a large manor house. It was walled in with a stone gate and thistle and hawthorn hedges and consisted of a main building and two smaller houses that formed two wings to the main building. In front of the manor house, a river flowed from west to east. Behind the house, a large garden encompassed a lotus pond, a meandering stream, and a green hill, which overlooked the farm and the city.

When Madam Du gave birth to a girl in the second year of their marriage, Du Bao named her "Liniang," which meant "a beautiful girl." He built a pavilion in the rear garden to commemorate the event, and planted peony shrubs around it.

"You give me a girl, I will build you a flower pavilion," Du Bao promised his wife. "You give me a boy, I will build you an ancestral shrine."

The peony shrubs bloomed, but not the couple's reproductive life. Having borne a daughter, Madam Du seemed to have become sterile. She consulted doctors and herbalists and visited temples and convents. Nothing worked. The peony pavilion remained the only structure in the huge back garden.

In the first few years of the marriage, Madam Du had ordered all her young female servants to wear plain clothes and to avoid unnecessary contact with her husband. Then, feeling the growing disappointment of her husband, she relented. For a year, she slept in her daughter's apartment.

"Pick any maidservant you like," she told her husband.

One year passed, but none of the maidservants became pregnant. When she asked them one by one whether her husband had invited them to sleep, they all shook their heads.

"Like father, like son," Kitchen Grandma told Madam Du. "All those years, his father was a lonely man. I was an attractive widow, and we slept under the same roof, but he never touched me."

Madam Du appreciated her husband's faithfulness. She knew well that any other man in her husband's position might have taken a few concubines. She felt inadequate, culpable, and guilty. She owed her husband a huge debt because she was only able to give him a daughter.

So Madam Du did not complain when her husband started to spend more and more time at the governor's compound and less and less time at the estate, leaving to her the management of the farm and the upbringing of their daughter.

In recent years, her husband had developed a rigid schedule. Every month, he would visit the estate on the fifteenth when the moon was full. He would spend one night, and on the sixteenth, his carriage would come to pick him up immediately after the first cockcrow.

While she and Liniang eagerly waited for his monthly visit, Du Bao rarely seemed to enjoy his visit. His face was grave and unsmiling, and he talked little. It was as if he regarded the visits more as a responsibility than a happy reunion.

"It is all my fault," Madam Du would tell herself tearfully.

It was an awkward night for Du Bao. For the first time in many years, after his usual quick sexual act with his wife, he could not fall into a sleep.

In the darkness, he smelled his wife. She was delicious. He visualized her as he had seen her the first night of the marriage, shy, reluctant, but seductive. Her black hair, her delicate curvature, her pretty face, everything about his wife, tempted him. He wanted to wake her up, embrace her, caress her, and consume her.

"What is wrong?" Du Bao was confused as he struggled to restrain himself from acting out his impulses.

Confucius, one of the ancient sages, once said that the key to a righteous life was to control unruly passions and to serve the best interest of the kings.

The Confucian saying had been Du Bao's motto in life. He had devoted his life to the study of classics, and after he was appointed Governor, to the administration of the region under his control. He was known throughout East China as an honest and effective official.

As to his private life, he had followed his father's advice. "It is the *essence* of your body," the old man had once told him, referring to the male bodily fluid. "Use it only for a worthy cause because every drop reduces your energy and your intellect."

When Du Bao married, he had used his essence unsparingly because the proliferation of family name, as his father had told him, was a worthy cause. But once it was clear that his wife was not able to produce any more offspring after the birth of Liniang, he had cut it back to a monthly event, and he was able to keep his passions under tight control.

But now his control seemed to be slipping. Du Bao felt embarrassed. "My discipline, my willpower, please help me," Du Bao silently prayed. Once dawn broke, he would leave immediately. He would re-read his classics, re-tool his mind, and re-focus his senses. Everything would be fine again, he assured himself.

Dawn broke. Du Bao got up, opened the window, put on his official garment, and saw the carriage coming.

"Take care of yourself, my husband," he heard his wife bid him good-bye.

Du Bao had not looked at his wife since he got up although he could feel her presence, alluring and tantalizing. He knew the right thing for him to do was to simply leave as he had always done. But he couldn't move his legs. Something inside him was holding him back.

"There is no reason why I should be afraid of looking at my wife," Du Bao told himself.

He turned abruptly toward his wife. Immediately, he was struck by the loveliness of her, her eyes, her hair, her nose, her mouth, and her ears. Everything about her was irresistible. He gazed at her with abandon. His face brightened, and his eyes glistened.

Madame Du gazed back at her husband. His lustful look surprised her. Her husband had never looked at her this intensely except in the first year of their marriage.

"Captain," Du Bao turned back toward the window and called out to the army officer who was smoking his pipe at the stone gate.

Hastily, the officer tapped his smoking pipe on his boots to empty the smoldering tobacco and ran through the courtyard toward the window.

"It is spring," Du announced his discovery to the officer when he came to a full stop at the window.

The officer seemed to be taken aback by the announcement. He knew fully well it was spring, but the governor had never talked to him about seasons before.

"I am taking a spring break before my trip to the capital. You and your soldiers too."

The officer was more surprised. The governor had never taken a spring break, or any break before. "Are you serious, sir?"

"I am not joking, at least not now. Why don't you go off before I change my mind?"

The officer grinned broadly, "Thank you. It's been a long time." He saluted and hurried off joyfully.

"It's been a long time," Du repeated while watching the officer running toward the carriage.

But Madam Du looked worried. It was so unusual of her husband to make abrupt decisions and to take days off from work. "My dear husband, are you ill?" she asked.

"No, I'm not ill, my dear wife. But it is spring."

"What about spring?" Like the officer, Madam Du was puzzled by her husband's new interest in the change of seasons.

"Spring is the season for love," Du answered. Impulsively, he took his wife into his arms and embraced her, "I am sorry, darling. I have neglected you."

No longer used to such attentions, Madam Du's body stiffened in resistance for a second. Then, slowly, she relaxed, and her body softened and responded to the embrace. She raised her head to kiss her husband, and her eyes glittered. "Let me close the window," she said softly.

The main house had a center hall and two apartments, one at each side. Liniang's apartment, like her parents', had a large window overlooking the courtyard, the stone gate, and the river that flowed slowly in front of the gate.

Every time her father came to spend the night at the estate, Liniang would get up at the first cockcrow, hide behind the window curtains, and unhappily observe the official carriage arrive at the stone gate and pick up her father.

Liniang had prayed that the carriage would for once not appear and her father would for once spend a day at home, but her prayers had never been answered. They seemed to be no match for the ineluctable routine of her father's life. Being of a sensitive nature, Liniang would throw herself in bed, feeling melancholy and depressed for a long time every time her father departed.

Watching her father finish up his favorite stew the night before had given Liniang renewed hope. In her dream, she imaged that dawn would never break, roosters would never crow, and her father would stay at home with her mother forever.

However, as always, dawn broke, and roosters woke up Liniang. She jumped out of her bed and went up to her window. She heard her father opening his window, and she saw the carriage arriving at the stone gate.

"Please, Reverent Sister," she murmured.

Miraculously, her prayers were answered. With great joy, she heard her father telling his driver that he wanted to take a spring break.

"It's been a long time, it's been a long time," Liniang repeated the driver's answer to her father as if it were the most delightful observation she had ever heard for a long time.

The husband and wife were still panting when they heard a tap on their door. Du Bao quickly put on his pajamas, picked up a book from a bookshelf, and hurried to his desk. Madam Du tidied her hair, smoothed her sleeping dress, and made the bed. Then she opened the door.

Liniang came into the room. She was smiling happily. In her hand, she had a tray with two glasses and a flask of wine.

"Why do you bring wine in the morning, my daughter?" Madam Du asked, a surprised look on her face.

"Blessings on you, father and mother," Liniang greeted her parents cheerfully. Putting down the tray on a desk, Liniang first bowed to her father and then to her mother. She poured the wine into the two glasses. "I am so happy that father is spending a few days with us," she beamed.

Du Bao had long noticed that his daughter had grown into a very attractive young lady, as attractive as his wife had been when he married her. But he had also thought that, unlike her mother, who had impressed him with her energy and vivacity, his daughter had a tendency to melancholy. In fact, as far as he could remember, Liniang had often looked forlorn and dispirited in his presence.

Now seeing Liniang so cheerful, Du Bao realized that his daughter had been unhappy because of him, because of his absence, his neglect, and his severity.

When his wife gave birth to Liniang in the second year of their marriage, Du Bao was disappointed. He had hoped for a son, a son he could teach and groom for prestigious government jobs just as his father had done.

When it was clear to him that his wife could not give him a son, the large estate house depressed him. Whenever he was at home, he could feel the dominance of "yin," or femaleness, in the air. He would listen to the voices of his wife, his daughter, and their staff of female servants, look at his collection of classic books handed down from his father, and silently complain that he had no sons to give the books to.

He was the source. He had made Liniang unhappy.

The realization pained Du Bao. He took a glass from the tray and finished it with one draft. "I am sorry, Liniang," he said gently. "I have neglected you."

Liniang burst into tears. For years, her father had scolded her and ignored her. For years, she had yearned for her father to say something tender and loving. Now she finally heard it. "I love you, father," Liniang knelt and put her head in her father's laps. "Mother loves you too."

A strong tide of remorse and love swept over Du Bao. Caressing her daughter's shiny black hair, he desperately wanted to express his feelings, but words failed him. He looked pained, and his voice choked.

"We know you have been very busy," Madam Du put her hand around her husband's shoulders and comforted him.

"Yes, we do." Liniang stopped sobbing, dried her eyes with a handkerchief, and smiled. She filled her parents' glasses again. "Enjoy," Liniang told her parents. Then she left their apartment, closing the door behind her.

Du Bao finished the second glass of wine, and a warm glow of affection filled his heart. He had felt disappointed that he did not have a son. Now, for the first time in many years, he felt proud, happy, and contented.

Du Bao loved his daughter, and he wanted to make up for his neglect. He decided that he would train and mold Liniang into a lady, an attractive and virtuous lady, suitable as a bride for the brightest young man in the employment of his majesty.

Winter sets in the west,
Spring arises in the east.
Like wild mountain flowers,
Love blossoms in flaming colors.

From Liniang's apartment came the rhapsodic voices of Liniang and her maidservant, Fragrance. They were singing a famous aria from a classical opera.

Du Bao and his wife had finished the whole flask of wine. Slightly inebriated and happy with his plan for Liniang, Du Bao took his wife's arm, "Let's go and talk to our daughter."

"What do you do everyday?" Du Bao asked Liniang when his daughter let him and his wife into her apartment and sat them down.

"I paint, I play music instruments, I embroider, and I read poems and stories. Do you want me to play some music for you, father?" Liniang asked merrily.

"Not now, my daughter," Du Bao answered. "I have some serious matter to talk to you."

"What is it, father?"

"Have you read any classics?"

Liniang had. A few years back, she had wandered into her father's library in the west house and browsed through some books on the shelves, but they invariably bored her. The sages from hundreds of years ago did not speak the language she understood, and they did not talk about things that interested her.

As she became an adolescent, her lack of interest in her father's library gradually turned into an active dislike. To her, it was a cause of her family's unhappiness. Every time her father came back, instead of spending time with her mother and her, he would rush through the dinner and then lock himself in the library. Liniang simply could not understand why the old books in the library were more attractive to her father than her mother was.

To vent her frustration, after her father's visits, Liniang would sneak into the library in the west house, pick up a book at random, and burn it page by page in the open stove in the kitchen. Kitchen Grandma was horrified, so was Liniang's mother. They tried to talk her into giving up her destructive behavior, but Liniang refused to listen and persisted. Afraid that Du Bao might find out if the losses accumulated, Madam Du finally put a lock on the library door, taking it off only when her husband came home.

Now her father was asking her whether she had read any classics. Liniang did not want to share her feelings with her father. He was in a very good mood, and she did not want to spoil it, so she simply shook her head, "No. I haven't read any classics."

"You are sixteen now. You need to study classics, especially those on maidenly virtues and wifely duties," Du Bao told his daughter.

"Mother has taught me well in these areas," Liniang protested lamely.

"Classics can prepare you for marriage to the most powerful family in the land just as they can prepare a man for the highest office of the empire."

"But I don't want to get married; I want to live with mother."

"You silly girl," Du Bao laughed condescendingly.

Liniang was dismayed by the prospect that she would be forced to spend hours on books she totally disliked. But she could not think of any other excuses without hurting her father, so she turned to her mother, her eyes pleading silently with her.

Madam Du used to despise the classics as well. She had inherited the attitude from her father, who believed that anyone who enjoyed spending his time on books instead of in the fields was a pathetic bookworm.

Now, having lived with her husband for seventeen years, she had a different view on the books. The books made her husband a good government official. He did not take bribes or give bribes, he never abused the people he governed, and the region enjoyed peace and prosperity.

But she did not understand why her husband needed classics to teach Liniang maidenly virtues and wifely duties. She had been teaching her daughter these things for quite some time, and she was sure that she was doing a better job than any classics could.

Like Liniang, Madam Du was loath to spoil her husband's good mood, so she considered her words carefully, "It is an excellent idea. But you don't have much time, and I don't have much understanding of the classics."

"I will hire a tutor," Du Bao told his wife and daughter.

Chapter Two

THE NEWS that Governor Du was looking for a tutor for his daughter spread quickly. The next morning, a dozen young graduates of the regional academy showed up at Du Bao's estate for the interview. Their horses and donkeys were tied to the wooden poles outside the stone gate, and they waited in the courtyard, chatting anxiously with one another.

The courtyard was a small square paved with bricks of a dark blue color, and it was dotted with blooming shrubs and flower. The young men, however, did not seem to notice the beauty all around them.

From the library in the west house, hidden behind a screen from the view of the young men in the courtyard, Du Bao and his wife inspected the candidates.

Standing with them was a shriveled old man with a bald head. He was Principal Lin of Nan'an Regional Academy. He was giving Du Bao and his wife a brief biography of every young man in the courtyard. He seemed to know all of them well, including their family history and details of their personal life. He was particularly enthusiastic about the qualifications of three young men in the crowd.

Governor Du, though, did not seem to be impressed. He listened quietly and nodded his head from time to time, but he never asked any question about any of the young men.

"Sir, here is a list of the three graduates I recommend highly." From the left sleeve of his gown, he produced a piece of paper with three names.

"How much did they pay you?" Governor Du asked. He knew Principal Lin's reputation for venality well.

"Not much," the principal gave a short embarrassed laugh.

Without glancing at the paper, Du Bao threw it into a wastebasket. He would have dismissed the old man a long time ago if not for the fact that he was one of the nationally recognized scholars on the poetry of the Tang dynasty.

The old man's face reddened. "Sir, it is not fair to assume that I would let any payment cloud my judgment," he defended himself.

Du Bao gave the old man a stern look.

Realizing that he was talking a little too vehemently, the old man abruptly stopped and retreated to a chair in the back of the library.

Initially, Madam Du had had her reservations about hiring a tutor. Apart from her skepticism about the usefulness of a classical education for Liniang, a tutor would cost too much money. She would have to pay him a salary, and she would have to provide him with three meals a day.

Unlike most government officials, her husband did not take bribes, so after his personal expenses in the city, Du Bao had little money left to give to her. Madam Du had to rely on the income from the farm to support the household, so she was reluctant to add one more employee to her payroll. Besides, a tutor was not an ordinary farmhand. She had to pay him a bigger salary in order to maintain the family's reputation in the local community.

"It's too expensive," she had told her husband.

However, after her husband had insisted that they needed to spend the money on their daughter, that a classical education would equip their daughter for a better marriage, and that they had already wasted some valuable years, Madam Du relented. After all, she thought, it was commendable for Du Bao to be finally paying attention to Liniang, and she should be supportive.

Now it seemed to her that her husband was having second thoughts about hiring a tutor. Tentatively, she remarked, "My husband, with your wisdom, surely you can find a tutor from the group of young men without relying on Principal Lin's recommendation."

Du Bao did not seem to hear.

As a matter of fact, Du Bao liked some of the young men assembled in the courtyard. He would like to hire them when the regional government had some job vacancies. But he felt none of them was an appropriate candidate to be his daughter's tutor. They were at an age when they were particularly susceptible to romantic passions. They might easily fall in love with his daughter, or his daughter might easily fall in love with them. This was something he wanted to avoid at all cost. He wanted to find a son-in-law for her daughter himself. His son-in-law had to be someone with a royal degree and a more important or prestigious government job than what he had. Du Bao believed that finding such a son-in-law required his personal attention, and that youthful love had no place in the process.

"Girls do not need to learn how to govern a country; they need to learn how to think and behave virtuously," Du Bao explained to his wife. Pointing at the young men waiting in the courtyard, he asked rhetorically, "Can any of these hungry-looking young men teach our daughter how to think and behave virtuously?"

Principal Lin, who was sitting in a chair in the back of the library and who only heard the phrase "hungry-looking young men," stood up to defend his students. "Sir, with all respect, they look hungry because the government has cut in half the stipends it pays the students of the academy."

Although he did not mention it, the principal was especially irked that the government had also cut his salary.

"Principal Lin, the country is at war with the northern barbarians. We all have to sacrifice for the war efforts," Du Bao explained. "Anyway, I used the word 'hungry' in a different sense."

Turning to his wife, he asked, "Do you want any of these young men to be with our daughter alone for ten minutes, now she is sixteen and curious about the ways of men?"

"What a jealous father," Madam Du thought. Her husband was not interested in interviewing the young men because he was afraid that Liniang and a young tutor might fall in love. Half in jest, and half seriously, Madam Du suggested, "My dear husband, now our daughter is sixteen, we may be able to find a man for her from this group."

"Nonsense," Du Bao rebuffed his wife vigorously. "None of them has passed the national examination. I definitely don't want to have a son-in-law without a royal degree and without a respectable government job."

"Some of them will one day," the principal pointed out.

"My dear husband, you did not pass the national examination until thirty-two," Madam Du gently reminded her husband.

"Both of you are right," Du Bao conceded, "but Liniang can't wait until one of them passes the royal examination."

"Who do you want to hire then?" Madam Du asked.

"I am interested in an older graduate," Du Bao answered.

"How much older?" the principal asked.

"A graduate in his fifties or sixties."

The old man frowned. By his definition, a graduate who was looking for a job at that age was a failure. He, as the principal of the academy, had only contempt for those graduates and did not want to have anything to do with them.

"I am sure you have such a graduate?" Du Bao pressed the principal, who appeared to be reluctant. He liked old tutors because he believed they had better control over their passions. Moreover, remembering his father who had never passed the royal examination and who had struggled all his life, Du Bao felt a strong affinity with them.

"I do have such a graduate," Principal Lin hesitated. "He graduated the academy forty-five years ago. Since his graduation, he had taken the royal examination fifteen times and never passed it."

"What is his name?"

"His family name is Chen, and his full name is Chen Zuiliang, *Chen the Most Virtuous*."

"Chen the Most Virtuous," Du Bao repeated to himself. "There must be a reason for a man to have this name. What does he do now?"

"He runs a drug store started by his grandfather."

"So he is a medical man as well. That must be useful sometimes." Calling for a servant, he ordered, "Dismiss the young men in the courtyard, and deliver a letter of invitation to Chen the Most Virtuous immediately."

Feeling sorry for the young men who had been waiting in the yard since early morning, Madam Du went out into the courtyard, gave two *taels* of silver to each of them, and thanked them for their time before dismissing them.

Chen the Most Virtuous was sitting at the high counter in his storefront. He had a mare of white hair and a wizened face. His robe was worn and frayed at the sleeves, and he smelled an indescribable mixture of the herbs he handled everyday. On the counter, Chen had an old yellowing text before him. Like him, the text smelled of herbs, and many of its pages were missing or broken.

Although Chen the Most Virtuous was gazing at his book, his mind was focusing on his dinner. It was already early afternoon. His breakfast, a bowl of thin rice porridge, had already disappeared from his stomach. His wife, who had gone to her brother's house to borrow some rice and meat, had not returned yet. From time to time, Chen felt the sharp pangs of hunger and tried to stop them by bending over his body.

The streets started to get busy. Farmers with baskets of vegetables, eggs, and meats sat on the sidewalks, showing their wares and bargaining with shoppers. Right in front of his storefront, a young woman with a baby girl in a cloth bundle on her back was hawking eggs. Chen gazed at her and her eggs for a long while, took a deep breath to muster courage, and then walked up to the young woman.

"Greetings, farmer lady."

"Greetings, sir. Have a look at my eggs. They are fresh and they came from young and pretty-looking hens."

"How many kids do you have?" Chen the Most Virtuous ignored the sales pitch.

"I just have one girl," the young woman tapped the girl on her back with one hand.

"What a pretty girl," Chen glanced at the baby girl cursorily and continued, "but of course you want a boy next time?"

"Sure," the woman nodded.

"I have a herbal powder in my store that will help you get a boy next time."

"I never heard of such a herbal powder," the woman looked up at the disheveled old man and was skeptical.

"Trust the doctor," Chen assured her. "I have satisfied clients all over the city. Madam Lin, Madam Wang, Madam Zhou, Madam Ge, Madam An, and so on." Chen the Most Virtuous started to recite the names of all his neighbors, although none of them had ever bought the powder from him.

The young woman looked impressed. "How much does the powder cost?"

"Usually, I charge a dozen eggs for a *tael* of the magic powder. Since you are such a charming farmer lady, I only ask for ten eggs."

"Ten eggs?" The young woman appeared to be hesitant. She needed to sell the eggs to buy a new cooking pot. The baby had tipped over the old one and broken it, she told Chen the Most Virtuous.

"Nine eggs then," Chen bargained.

"Eight," the woman countered.

"Eight then. It's a deal."

Chen headed toward his store and came back shortly with some black powder wrapped up in an oily piece of paper.

While the woman was counting her eggs, a few young boys from the neighborhood, who had been playing on the sidewalks, gathered around them and watched the woman silently.

"Go away," Chen the Most Virtuous shouted at them.

The boys refused to go away, so Chen pushed them away. The boys moved to the other side of the street and started to chant:

> *Chen, Chen, Chen,*
> *Liar, liar, liar.*
> *The magic powder,*
> *A pack of dirt soil.*
> *The medicine man,*
> *Has no daughter nor son,*
> *Because he fed his wife*
> *Too much black powder.*

The woman stopped counting her eggs. "Is it true that you don't have any offspring?" she asked Chen.

Chen's face reddened. Furiously, he threw his powder on the sidewalk and dashed after the boys. The boys scattered around a corner. When Chen the Most Virtuous came back to his storefront, panting and hungrier than before, he saw that the young woman had already moved to the other side of the street and was eyeing him warily.

"A meal gone," Chen sighed to himself. He picked up the wrapped powder he had thrown on the ground and went back to his counter, praying that his wife would come back with something for dinner.

"Congratulations, Doctor Chen!" a loud and cheerful noise woke him up from his daydreaming.

Raising his head, Chen the Most Virtuous saw a middle-aged man on a walnut-colored horse, beaming at him. "Congratulations on what?" he asked grumpily.

The man dismounted from his horse. "Governor Du is seeking a tutor for his daughter. He has rejected all the young applicants recommended by the principal of the academy because he wants a mature and responsible man. I recommended you to the governor, and now the governor has invited you for an interview."

"Who are you?" Chen the Most Virtuous glared incredulously at the man who, although in possession of a fine horse, dressed like a lowly household servant.

The man seemed to know what Chen was thinking. "Doctor Chen, do not look down upon a menial servant. Here is the letter of invitation." He waved an official-looking document in front of Chen.

"Give it to me," Chen, still disbelieving, demanded.

"I will give it to you if you promise to give me one tenth of your salary on the fifth day of the fifth month and on the ninth day of the ninth month." He waved the letter again in front of Chen's face.

Suddenly raising his arm, and surprising the messenger with his agility, Chen seized the letter the middle-aged man was waving. Afraid that the man might come after him for the letter, he ran into the back room of his store, slammed the door shut, and opened the letter. As he read the letter slowly, his face brightened.

When Chen the Most Virtuous came out of the back room, his steps were light and his voice excited. "My friend, thank you for bringing me the letter." Pointing at the wrapped powder on the counter, he offered, "Take the magic powder. It will give you lots of sons."

The middle-aged man regarded the oily package for a long while. He then opened it, sniffed at the black powder, and felt it between his thumb and forefinger. Convinced of its usefulness, he re-wrapped the powder and put it into his sleeve. He had too many sons to feed already, but he could give it as a gift to a relative or a friend who needed it.

Chen the Most Virtuous had never been to the governor's country estate, but the messenger had given him directions before he left.

In quick succession, Chen the Most Virtuous shaved, combed his hair, dusted his long and dirty garment, wrote a note for his wife, and shut down the store.

Because Chen had no money to hire a horse, or a donkey, and because he had eaten nothing in the whole day except for a thin rice porridge in the morning, the trip was a long and tiring one. When he reached Governor Du's family estate about two miles outside the city gate, he was out of breath.

"Graduate Chen the Most Virtuous presents himself before your honor," a servant led him into the library and announced.

Chen dropped to his knees and prostrated. He was older than the governor, so there was no need for him to prostrate, but he did it anyway, partly out of respect, and partly out of exhaustion. His legs were tired, and his stomach was cramping.

Governor Du, who had been reading, turned around and saw a gaunt and haggard man at his feet. He was taken aback, but gained his composure quickly when he realized that the man at his feet was the candidate he had summoned. "There is no need for this formality, Doctor Chen." Du Bao got up from his chair, "Please arise and seat yourself."

"Sir, can I have some water please?" Chen stood up slowly and asked. "It was a long walk."

Seeing the pitiable state Chen was in, Du Bao smiled sympathetically. He asked the servant to take the old man to the kitchen in the east house for some refreshment and to summon Madam Du to the library for the interview.

When Chen came back from the kitchen, his spirit revived. The governor and his wife were at the entrance of the library to welcome him. The governor was a tall and well-built man, and his wife a slim and very beautiful woman. They were smiling at him amicably and respectfully as if he were their old friend.

In a corner of the library, Chen the Most Virtuous saw the old snooty principal of the academy staring at him with hardly-concealed contempt. He seemed to have just woken up from a long and uncomfortable nap, and he seemed to be in a bad mood.

"I have long been aware, sir, of your scholarly endeavors and your family history of medical practice," Du started the interview. "May I ask what classic you would start with my daughter if you are hired?"

"Of the six classics, *The Book of Songs* is the essence." Chen chose the book because it happened to be the book he had been reading earlier that afternoon and for the past few weeks.

"May I know why?"

For all his inadequacies and failures, Chen the Most Virtuous was a quick thinker. It only took him a few seconds to come up with an answer he thought would please the governor. "In every verse, there is an edifying homily to teach the virtues of maidenhood and wifely duties."

"Very good," Du was impressed. The poor man seemed to know exactly what he wanted to instill in his daughter. "Now may I ask how you would discipline my daughter if she does not make necessary progress?"

From the question, Chen the Most Virtuous instinctively knew that the girl he was going to teach, if he got the job, might have a less than obedient personality. He had to show Governor Du that he knew how to discipline without alienating his wife or his daughter by being too insensitive or too harsh.

"May I ask whether the young mistress has a maid to accompany her in her studies?"

"Yes, she is going to be accompanied by her maid, Fragrance," Du answered.

"Sir, I wouldn't dare to discipline the young mistress, darling to your lordship and her ladyship. Instead, I would lash her maidservant as her substitute with a whip my father used against my flesh. The young mistress, who I am sure has a sensitive nature, would feel the pain her maidservant feels and would work harder."

"Excellent," Du Bao was again impressed. He turned to his wife, who was sitting beside him, "What do you think about our candidate?"

"I like his answers, but I don't like his smell. I can smell him even from ten feet away," Madam Du whispered in his ears.

Du Bao laughed good-humoredly, "You are hired, Professor Chen. Now, sir, take a drink with me and with Principal Lin in the back garden to celebrate. But before you come to work tomorrow, please wash yourself and put on a new robe. I'm sure Principal Lin has a few scholarly robes which you can borrow."

Lin, who had been watching the performance of his former student, was impressed with Chen's skillful answers as well. To him, the fact that even one of his least successful students could stand up to the occasion reflected well on his skills as an educator. Pleased with himself and with Chen the Most Virtuous, he answered magnanimously, "Professor Chen can choose whatever robes I have. He can even take a bath in my humble residence."

Chen the Most Virtuous belched. What a fulfilling breakfast! For the first time in his life, he ate his breakfast at Governor Du's kitchen, with a young kitchen woman at his beck and call, and for the first time in his life, he clearly felt his belly stretched and fulfilled to capacity.

Now it was time to teach, he told himself. He wiped his mouth with a tablecloth, picked up his old book and his leather whip, and walked out into the courtyard. Chen ambled across the courtyard toward the library in the west house, enjoying the sound his new silk robe made as he walked. When he got into the library, he hung his whip on a bookshelf and sat down on the chair Governor Du had sat on the day before. He closed his eyes and soon started to snore; he had eaten too much.

After a long while, some raucous birds, fighting over corns the young kitchen woman was feeding them, made a loud burst of noise. Chen the Most Virtuous woke up with a start. He looked out the window. The sun was high over the river that ran in front of the estate. After his long breakfast and after his long nap, it must be quite late, but the library was still empty, and there was no sign of his student.

"She must be a badly spoilt girl," Chen the Most Virtuous concluded. "I must deal with her sternly today to set an example." Chen picked up a bell on the desk and rang it forcefully several times.

Through the library window, Chen saw two girls leisurely step out of the main house and walk toward the library side by side. Chatting and laughing, they did not seem to show any guilt for having to be summoned to the class, nor did they appear to be nervous in any way before meeting him. Chen the Most Virtuous was annoyed.

The girl on the right had a radiant face, a pair of enchanting eyes, a sweet smile, and a tall and shapely figure. Her jet-black hair was held back in two buns with golden lace and ivory head-pieces. She wore a pink embroidered dress that almost reached the ground.

The girl on the left was slightly shorter, but just as pretty. She was dressed in a plainer outfit, and her buns were combed side-ways. She had a mischievous look on her face.

The two girls entered the library.

The taller girl bowed and introduced herself. "I am Liniang, your student. My best respect, esteemed sir."

The shorter girl followed. "I hope you are not tired, esteemed sir. I am Fragrance, young mistress's maidservant. I'm the person you are going to whip if mistress is naughty."

For a brief moment, the proximity of two beautiful girls and the light but distinct fragrance they were wearing dazzled Chen the Most Virtuous. Instead of greeting them, he stared at the two girls, his mouth open and his eyes wide. Sitting at his counter day in and day out for almost forty years, Chen had seen girls of all classes decked out in all finery, but he had never seen girls as lovely as the two standing before him in the library. He was speechless.

The two girls exchanged an amused look. Then they made a little cough and repeated their greetings.

His face flustered, Chen the Most Virtuous stammered a few words of introduction, but the words were so mumbled that even he himself could not hear what he said.

Liniang and Fragrance tried hard not to laugh.

Chen the Most Virtuous finally managed to snap out of his embarrassing stupor and regain his composure. Sitting back in his chair, and putting on an air of annoyance, he said sternly to Liniang, "According to the classic *Rites*, a daughter should get up at the first cockcrow to wash, to dress, to pay respects to her parents, and to eat breakfast. She should start her work once the sun is up. You are now a student and your work is to study. You need to be here earlier than now."

"I shall not be late again," Liniang answered.

"We understand," Fragrance added. "Tonight we won't go to bed so that we can present ourselves for our lessons in the middle of the night."

Chen the Most Virtuous glared at Fragrance. The servant girl had no respect for his authority. It did not bode well for the class. Instinctively, he looked back at the shelf where he had hung his leather whip. He felt the urge to grab the whip and give the mischievous servant girl a good beating.

But Chen managed to control his impulse. He did not want to make a noisy fuss on the first day of his class, which might give Governor Du and his wife the wrong impression that he could not exercise proper control over the two girls without resorting to harsh measures.

So he ignored Fragrance. Addressing Liniang, Chen said, "Today we are going to start with the first poem in *The Book of Songs*."

"Of course, sir," Liniang went over to the shelves. She knew where the book was, but she pretended that she didn't, and took her time before taking the book out of the shelf.

Chen looked admiringly at the clean and tidy book Liniang put on the table. With self-conscious embarrassment, he opened his own dirty-looking book. He should have borrowed a new book from Principal Lin when he borrowed his silk gown. He made a note to himself that he should do so after the class.

"Now read the first poem. Slowly, and with feelings." Chen closed his eyes and moved his head sideways to show what he meant.

Liniang and Fragrance grinned at each other while their tutor was shaking his head in an exaggerated manner.

When Chen finished, Liniang opened the book and started to read the poem.

"Gwa, Gwa," cry the ospreys
On the islet in the river,
So precious the virtuous maiden,
A befitting mate for our prince.

"Not bad," Chen commented, "but you need more feelings." He then closed his eyes and started to recite the poem himself. "Gwa Gwa, Gwa Gwa."

"Well done, Professor Chen," Fragrance interrupted. "You sound exactly like a female osprey. The only imperfection is that you sound more like an old spinster than a young maiden."

Slapping Fragrance on her arm in disapproval, Liniang asked Chen the Most Virtuous, "What is so great about this poem, Professor Chen?"

Chen explained earnestly, "An osprey is a bird. An islet is a small island. 'Gwa, Gwa' is the sound it makes when it cries."

"Young mistress knows all these," Fragrance interrupted again. "She asks for the moral of the poem."

"Do not interrupt me," Chen gave Fragrance a stare. "Anyway, the moral of the story is a virtuous maiden should never talk to men and should never think about men."

"Are you a man or a woman?" Fragrance asked.

"Professor Chen is different," Liniang stopped Fragrance. "He is our tutor."

Chen the Most Virtuous continued. "The bird is an image that introduces the thought of 'the precious virtuous maiden,' who is a nice, quiet girl waiting for the prince to come seeking her." He stared at Fragrance, repeating and emphasizing the words "nice" and "quiet."

"What is it that the prince is seeking from the precious and virtuous maiden?" Fragrance was undaunted by Chen's stares.

"Now you are being prurient," Chen the Most Virtuous turned around in his chair and pointed at the leather whip hanging from the bookshelf. "You know what the whip is for."

Slapping Fragrance again on the arm, Liniang asked, "Sir, the first poem is definitely an edifying lesson. Do all the poems in *The Book of Songs* talk about the same matter?"

"There are three hundred songs in the Book. They talk about different matters, but their meaning can be summed up in one sentence."

"Just one sentence?"

"Yes."

"What is it?"

"Set aside all amorous thoughts," Chen answered slowly, pronouncing each word distinctly.

"And wait for the amorous prince?" Fragrance blurted out.

"You impudent slave," Chen exploded. Jumping out of his chair and grabbing his whip from the bookshelf, he shouted at Fragrance, "On the floor, on the floor."

Fragrance jumped up from her chair as well. She ran to the other end of the table, facing Chen the Most Virtuous. She grimaced at the angry professor and lowered her body as if she was ready to race him around the table.

"You wicked girl, kneel at once for such rudeness to Professor Chen," Liniang scolded her maidservant. Liniang disliked the class as much as Fragrance did. But she felt that Fragrance went too far. After all, Chen was older than her father, and he deserved respect.

"There is a saying," Liniang continued. "*A tutor for a day is a father for a lifetime.* Professor Chen really has the right to beat you or me. Now beg for mercy."

Reluctantly, Fragrance came up to Chen the Most Virtuous, knelt before him, and apologized.

"Since this is her first offense, please spare her, sir," Liniang pleaded on behalf of Fragrance.

Professor Chen flexed his whip at Fragrance menacingly. "This time I let you go on account of your mistress' entreaties. Next time, I will have blood on your ass."

"Now get out of the library and let Professor Chen have a moment of peace," Liniang told Fragrance.

Happily, as if she had been released from a prison, Fragrance leapt out of the library and into the courtyard. She reappeared at the window with a mischievous grin, "Professor Chen, you are holding the wrong end of the whip."

Chen looked at his whip. Indeed, in his anger, he grabbed the wrong end of the whip. He realized his mistake and his face went purple with embarrassment.

Laughing triumphantly, Fragrance disappeared.

"Next time, I will have blood on your ass."

Liniang felt sorry for Chen the Most Virtuous. It must be torture to him being taunted repeatedly by Fragrance. In order to make him feel better, Liniang smiled her most charming smile and addressed him in her most gentle voice, "Sir, you have taught me enough today. I want to do something for you in return."

"You don't have to," Chen mumbled in gratitude.

"I want to," Liniang insisted. "May I ask how old your wife is, Professor Chen?"

"She is exactly sixty."

"I would like to embroider for her a pair of slippers with sixty stars."

Chen the Most Virtuous was moved. At the beginning of the day, when he first saw her in the courtyard, Chen the Most Virtuous had thought of Liniang as a beautiful but spoilt girl, a typical product of a prominent family. Now he started to like Liniang. To him, she was no longer just a girl of astounding physical beauty or a girl with a powerful father, but also a person endowed with a sensitive and loving heart.

Chapter Three

THE RIVER that ran through the farm came down from the Western Mountains and flowed east toward the Yangtze River. The river ran slowly, and the water was chilly, clear, and almost transparent.

In front of the estate, a wooden drawbridge spanned the river. About twenty yards downstream from the bridge, a platform built with slabs of limestone slanted into the river. The platform was primarily used as a loading dock for boats, but the servants also used it to wash clothes. Else where, the banks were covered with tall reeds.

It was a cool but sunny morning. A large freshly painted boat parked at the dock, and on its flagpole, a yellow pennant embellished with a red coiling snake flapped in the wind. The calligraphy on the pennant read "Governor of Nan'an Region."

Liniang, Fragrance, Kitchen Grandma, Chen the Most Virtuous, the head farmer, and an assortment of Du's household employees bid farewell to Du Bao and Madam Du. They wished the couple a safe and pleasant journey, and they waved as they watched the boat depart for Hangzhou, capital of the empire.

As the boat disappeared beyond the walls of Nan'an city, Chen the Most Virtuous hurried back to the kitchen. He had finished his breakfast before he came to the dock, but standing outside, saying good-byes, and waving his hands had made him feel hungry again. He wanted to replenish himself with some snack and a pot of jasmine tea before starting the class.

"We need a break from that Professor Chen," Fragrance told Liniang as they watched him rush into the kitchen. "We have spent five days in the library, and I am bored to death," she yawned.

Liniang was bored with the classes as well. Professor Chen's relentless harping on maidenly virtues made her very sleepy everyday. However, she had to go to the class. "Father told me before his departure to attend the class everyday without fail," Liniang sighed.

"Don't worry," Fragrance assured Liniang. "I know how to arrange it."

"What are you going to do?" Liniang asked curiously. Fragrance was two years older than Liniang, and she had proven to be resourceful on many occasions.

"Let's get back to our apartment and wait there."

It was a long wait. Chen the Most Virtuous spent more time in the kitchen to finish his snack than it would take other people to finish their dinner. Finally, they saw him come out of the kitchen. He walked to the library in an easy gait, a satisfied look on his face.

They heard the small brass bell start to ring once Chen got into the library.

"He forgot to take his after-breakfast nap," Fragrance joked.

"Shall we go to the library?" Liniang asked.

"Ignore him," Fragrance answered.

The bell rang again. This time it took on an insistent and impatient tone.

"Ignore him," Fragrance told Liniang again.

Chen the Most Virtuous soon emerged from the library. He walked quickly toward the opened window of Liniang's apartment, his face red and angry. Fragrance pushed Liniang behind the curtains.

"Good morning, sir. I hope your second breakfast was satisfactory." Fragrance greeted Chen the Most Virtuous from inside the window.

"Where is young mistress? Why are you two not in the library?" Chen the Most Virtuous barked at Fragrance.

In the past few days, Chen had restrained himself because he did not want to give Du Bao and his wife a bad impression. Now with Du Bao and his wife gone to Hangzhou, he felt that he had more freedom to reign in the rude and rebellious servant girl.

Fragrance was undaunted by Chen's aggressive questions. "Quiet, Professor Chen. Don't wake up young mistress. She is not feeling well today and cannot go to the class."

"What nonsense!" Chen bellowed. "A few moments ago, she was sound and well."

"She was at the platform because she did not want her parents to know that she was ill."

What a transparent and pathetic lie the rude servant girl was telling him. "Why not?" Chen the Most Virtuous demanded loudly.

"The good-hearted young mistress did not want to get you into trouble. That's why."

"This is ridiculous," Chen yelled at Fragrance.

"Professor Chen, you have no idea how angry Governor Du will be with you when he comes back," Fragrance's voice took on an ominous tone.

"For what reason?" Chen still did not believe what Fragrance was saying, but his face clouded.

"Why, that *Book of Songs* of yours, you have been singing a bit too sweetly, and my poor young mistress has been thinking too much of your young gallant prince."

"How is it possible? I told her not to think about men."

"How can she wait for her prince without thinking about him?"

Chen the Most Virtuous paused. On reflection, he remembered that Liniang had become less and less attentive as the classes progressed, and her eyes had taken on a more and more distant look. He had thought that she was bored, but now it appeared that the poem had affected her in a way that he had not intended or expected.

But Chen would never admit that the poem he taught might have produced some unintended consequences, not to the servant girl, nor to anyone. So he said, "It has nothing to do with the poem. It's the Spring Illness."

"What is the Spring Illness?" Fragrance asked skeptically. She had never heard of it before.

Behind the curtains, Liniang perked her ears. She had never heard of it before either.

In fact, Chen the Most Virtuous had just invented the illness on the spur of the moment. Since he was a quick-witted man, he had no trouble in describing the symptoms and the etiology of the newly discovered ailment.

"As trees and flowers come into bloom, the air is filled with minute particles that can affect the balance of bodily humors of susceptible boys and girls. The affected persons become lethargic, restless, and disoriented."

"But it only started after you asked her to read that 'Gwa, Gwa' poem," Fragrance countered.

"I told you already that it has nothing to do with the poem."

"I think it does," Fragrance insisted. "I hope young mistress gets over her illness before Governor Du and Madam Du come back," she continued in a threatening tone. "Otherwise, Professor Chen, you'll be in big trouble."

Chen's face twitched involuntarily. His job was not an easy one, especially because he had to deal with the belligerence of Fragrance. However, it was much better than sitting in his store-front, not knowing where the next meal was coming from. As a tutor, he had three meals a day plus a very good salary. He wanted to keep his job if it was at all possible.

"I will browse through *The Compendium Medica* in the library to come up with a remedy," he promised Fragrance in a conciliatory voice.

"How about the class?" Fragrance pressed Chen.

"Young mistress can have a few days off," Chen answered. "When she feels better, we'll read something different."

"Have a good day, Professor Chen," Fragrance chuckled to herself as Chen walked back to the library, a worried expression on his face.

"Let's play a chess game," Fragrance urged Liniang once Chen the Most Virtuous was out of sight. "We haven't played a single game since your father hired that Professor Chen." Liniang was not very excited about the idea. "It's such a beautiful day. Don't waste it."

"We can't play in the courtyard," Fragrance warned. "Professor Chen is in the library, and he would see us if we played in the courtyard."

Liniang thought for a while. Then she had an idea. "Come with me," she told Fragrance.

The two girls went to the back of their apartment. Liniang pushed open the window and pointed at the lush, green hill in the back garden. "Let's climb to the top of the hill," she told Fragrance excitedly.

Liniang had never been into the garden. A wall of thistle hedges separated the house from the garden. More importantly, her mother had forbidden her from visiting the garden, saying the garden was for adults only. But Liniang had always been attracted by the singing of the birds in the garden and by the pond, the pavilion, and the lush hill.

When Liniang was barely able to walk, Kitchen Grandma began to regale her with stories of mischievous goblins that lurked in the garden, ready to beguile innocent young girls.

The stories had made the garden a mysterious and enchanting territory to Liniang. In her dreams, Liniang often played with the little spirits, hopping around in grass, bushes, shrubs, and trees. The goblins were naughty fun-loving creatures, but they never harmed her in any of her dreams.

Fragrance, who had never visited the garden either, was tempted by Liniang's suggestion. However, her enthusiasm was immediately dampened by her fear of goblins. "There are goblins in the garden," she reminded Liniang.

"I am not afraid of the goblins," Liniang answered. "Don't tell me you are afraid of them," seeing the hesitation on Fragrance's face, Liniang goaded her.

Maybe she shouldn't be afraid of the little creatures, Fragrance told herself. Kitchen Grandma often visited the garden to collect wild mushrooms, bamboo shoots, and other delicacies. Besides, Garden Boy spent all his days in the garden, clearing its winding paths and maintaining the pond. When it was the season, he also picked beautiful flowers for Madam Du and Liniang. Although the garden goblins were reputed to love to play tricks on people, nothing bad had ever happened to them. They never lost a limb, they never became crazy, and they never even caught a bad cold.

"I am not afraid of goblins," Fragrance told Liniang, "but Madam Du forbids you and me from visiting the garden. I don't want to get into trouble."

"I am sixteen, and you are eighteen," Liniang answered. "Besides, my mother is not here."

"But she has asked Kitchen Grandma to watch over us."

"We don't have to let her know. Even if she knows, I know how to deal with her."

Fragrance considered it for a while. Then she looked across the hedges into the garden. As her curiosity grew, her fears of goblins and of Madam Du ebbed. "Let's go," she finally made up her mind.

The glory of spring was everywhere. Red, yellow, blue, green, purple, and a myriad of other colors greeted Liniang and Fragrance as they unlocked the gate to the back garden and let themselves loose in the forbidden luxuriousness of nature.

"What a beautiful place!" Liniang exclaimed.

"Imagine we have never come in here before," Fragrance echoed excitedly.

Immediately inside the back garden, there was a large pond. Green lotus leaves floated on the water, and flocks of wild ducks quacked and chased each other. A pebble path circled around the pond, with flowering shrubs dotted along the path. On one side of the pond, plum trees gently swayed in the breeze; on the other side, wavy willow trees. A pavilion stood where the plum trees and the willow trees met on the side of the pond away from the houses.

Liniang and Fragrance walked around the pond and stepped inside the pavilion. They looked admiringly at the gold gilded trellis of the wooden structure. "This must be the pavilion your father built on the occasion of your birth," Fragrance told Liniang.

"This is my place," Liniang nodded, looking at the peony plants surrounding the pavilion. She knew that her father had hoped in vain to build many more pavilions and shrines to commemorate the births of his sons and daughters.

"Let's go to the top of the hill," Liniang told Fragrance. She did not want to stay too long in a place that was as much a reminder of her father's disappointment as a symbol of his love for her.

The hill was about two hundred yards northwest of the pond. It was covered with trees and undergrowth. A small stream came down from the hill into the pond where the willow and plum trees met.

The two girls trotted along a narrow dirt path that wound its way alongside the stream. As they penetrated the undisturbed depth of the garden, surprised birds flew into the air, noisily protesting the unexpected intrusion.

"Are they goblins?" Liniang looked at the scattering birds and joked.

"Don't joke about goblins," Fragrance hushed. She looked around fearfully. "Goblins don't like to be disrespected."

"Fine, no more jokes," Liniang assured her maid laughingly.

The dirt path stopped at the foot of the hill, so the two girls followed the stream that came down from the hill. The stream was a slowly rising bed of rocks and boulders. Amid the thousands of rocks, water gargled down and gently flowed toward the pond.

In high spirit, Liniang and Fragrance hopped from rock to rock as they ascended the hill. Although it was a day in early spring and the temperature was moderate, they soon started to sweat. Half way up the hill, they stopped at a little pool of water to cool down and rest.

"Hello, Young Mistress and Miss Fragrance," a voice boomed from behind a maple tree at the edge of the stream.

"Goblins," Fragrance jumped up.

Surprised, Liniang looked up in the direction of the voice, shielding her eyes with her hands from the shining sun.

A bony, tall, and dark-complexioned young man appeared from behind the tree and jumped effortlessly onto a large rock at the edge of the water pool from which the two girls were drinking. He was in his early twenties and had been working as a gardener for Madam Du for many years. He was simply called "Garden Boy."

"Young Mistress and Miss Fragrance, what are you doing here?" Garden Boy beamed at them from atop the rock. He was happy to see Liniang and Fragrance because his job was a very lonely one. He came to work at sunrise and went home at sunset. During the day, he talked to birds, to foxes, to squirrels, to trees, to flowers, but he hardly had a chance to talk to any human beings.

Moreover, the gardener was especially happy to see Fragrance. He had liked Fragrance since he came to work for Madam Du as a young boy, and as both of them grew up, he found her to be more and more attractive and irresistible. Unfortunately, Fragrance was a difficult girl to approach, and his job did not allow him much contact with her.

"You should have a beating, sneaking around in the garden scaring us," Fragrance grabbed his leg, pulled him off the large rock, and pushed him into the water.

"Miss Fragrance, I work here in the garden," the young man retorted, his eyes fixed on Fragrance playfully. "It's you who are sneaking around in the garden with young mistress."

"Please don't tell my mother," afraid that the garden boy might cause trouble for them, Liniang pleaded with him.

"Well, it depends." The gardener was noncommittal. He liked Liniang, and he loved Fragrance. He would never tell on them, but he did not want to promise them so easily. He wanted to get something out of the two girls. If he played it right, the young man hoped, Liniang might give him a silver coin, or better yet, Fragrance might treat him with some new affection.

"It depends on what?" Fragrance demanded.

"I was wondering whether you could sit with me side by side for a while," he pointed at a flat rock.

Fragrance gave him a slap on the face. "Don't be smart with me, young man."

"Miss Fragrance, I think I deserve better than a slap from you."

"What makes you think so?" Fragrance asked.

"You know I like you very much." Undaunted by the rebuff, the young man continued to gaze at Fragrance brazenly.

"If you like me very much, I have a question for you," Fragrance grinned mischievously.

"What is your question, my young princess?" the man asked in a flirtatious manner. He was glad that the unexpected encounter was turning in a favorable direction.

"Do you pick two bunches of flowers some mornings, one for Madam and one for young mistress?"

"Yes."

"Why don't you pick a bunch for me?" Fragrance demanded.

"I'm sorry, Miss Fragrance, but I have a poem here to make up for my oversight."

"Well, if it's a good one, I'll let you off your beating."

"All right. Listen, Miss Fragrance." The gardener cleared his throat and started to recite.

> *Flowers I have picked*
> *Day in and day out,*
> *But you are the juiciest*
> *I have no doubt.*
> *Let's have some fun today*
> *While we still may.*

"You lascivious lad," Fragrance was embarrassed. Her face blushing, she slapped the young man again.

"Lascivious?" The young man was puzzled by the word. He came from a poor family, never had a day of education, and could neither read nor write. He had bought the poem from Chen the Most Virtuous, who told him that the poem could win the heart of any girl. However, instead of helping him, the poem seemed to have backfired on him.

"Miss Fragrance, I don't know what you mean by *lascivious*," he groaned.

"It means bad. B.A.D. Bad." Fragrance hissed at him.

The young man felt humiliated. "I paid Professor Chen two coins for the poem. I'll get them back from him." Abruptly, he turned away from the two girls and hurried downhill.

"If you say anything about our outing to anyone," Fragrance called after him, "I'll report your lascivious poem to Madam Du once she comes back and make sure you have trouble day in and day out."

❀❀

"You are a very bad girl, the way you scared Professor Chen and Garden Boy," Liniang remarked when the young gardener disappeared out of their sight.

"The old skeleton is a pompous fool, an ignoramus."

"Don't be so disrespectful," Liniang admonished her.

"He deserves it," Fragrance answered. "Why did he tell your parents that he would beat me if you misbehaved?"

"He didn't mean it," Liniang tried to abate Fragrance's anger against Chen the Most Virtuous. "He probably just wanted to please my parents."

"But I like the gardener," Fragrance changed the topic.

"Why then did you treat him so rudely?"

"What do you suggest, my young mistress?" Fragrance retorted. "Should I say to him, 'Thank you very much for your compliment and for your interest. Let's have some fun today'?"

The two girls giggled.

Liniang and Fragrance continued to climb uphill. Soon, the rock bed narrowed, and the stream became a dribble of water. Finally, it led them to a small and dark cave.

Liniang and Fragrance peeked into the cavity. It was totally dark. They could see nothing. The only sound they could hear was the incessant dripping of water inside.

"Let's see how far we can get into the cave," Liniang suggested.

"Maybe we should leave it alone," Fragrance answered cautiously. "If goblins live anywhere, they may be living in the cave."

Liniang thought about it for a while and agreed reluctantly, "We will come to explore when the god of gardens is on duty."

Above the cave, the climb became more difficult. The slope was steeper. There was no waterbed to follow and the dense undergrowth hampered their progress. They had to use their hands as well as their feet to negotiate the difficult terrain. When they finally reached the top, they were both panting heavily.

The top of the hill was a gray rock surface the size of their kitchen, slanting slightly toward the east, broken in several places into small crevasses. It was barren and devoid of any growth. The wind was blowing harder here than it was near the pond.

To their west and north, a long distance away, rugged, rocky mountains rose over the horizon. Although it was spring already, snow still capped some of the taller peaks. To the east, the city of Nan'an, with its ancient walls and clusters of brick and wooden buildings, bathed in the bright sunlight.

Between the mountains and the city and extending east and south beyond the city was flat, green, and well-irrigated farmland dotted with forested hills. The river, like a glimmering silver ribbon, wound its way from the snowcapped mountains through the farmland to the great Yangtze River in the distant east, passing on its way many farming estates and the city of Nan'an.

Liniang felt exhilarated. The hilltop gave her a grand view of Nan'an region she had never experienced before. She suddenly felt older, wiser, and more in control of the world she was living in.

Then she heard Fragrance sobbing beside her. "What is wrong?" Liniang was puzzled.

Fragrance continued to sob.

Liniang sat Fragrance down on the rock, "Tell me what is bothering you, Fragrance. Is it the goblins?"

Fragrance raised her head to look at Liniang. "I wanted to see my village," she pointed at a cluster of villages in the southerly direction. "But I don't remember which one is my village."

For a long time, Liniang had thought that Fragrance was her big sister. They had worn the same dress, slept in the same room, ate at the same table, and played together.

However, on the day Liniang turned ten, after the big birthday party, their relationship changed. Madam Du had Fragrance's bed moved to a smaller bedroom in the apartment and taught Fragrance to comb her pigtails sideways like a servant maid. She also asked Fragrance to start addressing Liniang as "young mistress."

"Why?" Liniang asked her mother.

"I'm sorry," Madam Du explained, "but from today on, Fragrance is not your big sister anymore; she is your maidservant." Madam Du then narrated to both of them how Fragrance came into the family.

Madam Du bought Fragrance when Liniang was four years old. It was in the depth of winter, several days before the New Year.

A fresh snow had fallen, and a bitter wind was blowing. Madam Du had gone to a tailor's in the city to fit for a new dress. When the tailor was working on her measurements, she heard a young child wailing piteously in the street. Peeking out of the store window, she saw an unkempt man in a tattered cotton coat standing at the street corner. At his foot was a young girl couched in a large basket case. She was covered with an old blanket. Her hair was disheveled and her face was swollen with cold. Tears hung on her face, almost frozen.

A small crowd had gathered around the man and the girl. A middle-aged woman in a thick fur coat was bargaining with the father.

Madam Du got out of the store and walked up to the crowd. She felt miserable for the child and for the father, whose eyes were blood-shot and whose face was a sickly blue.

"Give me a hundred, madam," the father pleaded with the woman in the fur coat.

"Fifty," the woman answered.

"Ninety, please."

"Fifty," the woman insisted firmly.

"Eighty, please," the man almost begged. "I have two more kids to feed. I have a debt to settle before the New Year. Please give me eighty."

"Listen," the woman replied sullenly. "I take this girl home, you get fifty silver coins, and you have one fewer mouth to feed. Is that not a good deal for you?"

The man knelt before the woman. He was on the verge of crying. "Have pity, madam. I owe a moneylender eighty coins. I have to pay him back before the New Year. Or he will take away my land."

"Fifty is the best I can give," the woman answered without emotion.

Madam Du looked at the young girl. She had stopped crying, and she had closed her eyes. Her mouth was blue, and she was shivering uncontrollably in the bitter cold.

A strong gust of wind blew a piece of yellow paper off the basket. Madam Du picked it up. The paper said the girl's first name was Fragrance, she was six, and she was pretty and cute. The asking price written on the paper was two hundred.

Madam Du felt sick. The man sickened her, the woman sickened her, the suffering of the child sickened her, and the weather sickened her. The girl was only six, two years older than Liniang. Maybe Liniang would like some company, a girl she could play with and a girl who could serve her when she grew up, she told herself.

But Madam Du hesitated. She did not want to take the girl away from her father and her family. Then she thought, if she didn't, others would. Her father was willing to sell her for the wretched price of eighty silver coins to anyone. Uneasily she took out two silver bars from her coat, which was worth one hundred coins each, and gave them to the man.

The man patted his daughter on her head, kowtowed to Madam Du, grabbed the two bars of silver, and walked away abruptly.

"Do you still remember your family?" Liniang asked Fragrance.

Fragrance nodded her head piteously. She remembered the cold morning when her father put her in a basket and told her that she was going to a family with three meals a day and new clothes for every new year. She remembered her mother holding onto the basket, begging her father not to take her daughter away, her father pleading with her mother in a loud voice, then finally hitting her in the face. She remembered her two kid brothers hiding under their bed, wailing, "I want big sister, I want big sister," and her father yelling, "shut up, or I'll take you too." She remembered her neighbors, disturbed by the commotion, gathering at their door, shaking their heads, and one of the women wrapping an old blanket around her cold body. It was a nightmare that had been haunting her ever since that blustery winter day.

Fragrance wanted to forget. It was too far away, too long ago and too painful. She was still young and she should think about her future.

"I want to find a man," Fragrance told Liniang suddenly.

Liniang was surprised by the vehemence of Fragrance's sentiments. "Are you not happy with me?" she asked.

"I am very happy with you, young mistress, but I want to set up a family of my own. I want children. I don't want to be childless and lonely when I'm old."

Liniang nodded sympathetically. "How about the gardener?" she asked. "He loves you."

Fragrance shook her head forlornly. "I like Garden Boy, but he can never afford to buy my freedom from your parents. I want a man who has money."

"A man with money may not love you," Liniang cautioned.

"I have no choice," Fragrance answered sadly.

"Once I marry and set up my own household, I will let you go," Liniang promised. "You can marry whomever you like, and he does not have to pay anything."

"But does that depend on the will of your future husband?" Fragrance was skeptical.

"I am sure I can persuade him," Liniang assured her maidservant.

"Thank you, young mistress," Fragrance burst into tears. "I hope your father finds a good man for you as soon as possible."

"Oh, no," Liniang protested, "I want to find a man myself." Liniang would not trust her father on this issue. Her father wanted for her someone with a royal degree and a prestigious government job, but he never thought about whether she would like the man.

Fragrance sighed. She explained carefully to Liniang that although it might be acceptable for a servant girl like her to look for a man on her own, it was unheard of for a girl from a prominent family to do so.

"I want to marry someone I like and someone who likes me," Liniang answered with determination.

"Your father will never let you," Fragrance predicted gloomily. "Then you will die as a spinster, and I will never be free."

"Don't be so pessimistic," Liniang told her. "I'm sure I can convince my father."

Fragrance knew very well that Du Bao was a man of tradition and a man of strong will, and she doubted Liniang would ever be able to prevail over her father, but she sincerely hoped Liniang would.

"I will pray for you," she told Liniang.

Chapter Four

LINIANG SAT back in the bench, soaked her feet in a large basin of warm water, and let a young maid slowly massage her aching soles.

She felt happy and free. For the first time, her father and mother had gone to Hangzhou together, and for the first time, she had been able to play in the back garden and climb up the hill. She was tired from the day's activities, but she felt mentally invigorated.

Fragrance sat opposite her, her feet in the same basin. She looked happy and contented as well.

"Let's see whose feet are larger?" Liniang suggested.

The two girls raised their feet out of the basin and matched them one on one over the basin.

"My feet are larger," Liniang cried out happily.

"Just by a little bit," Fragrance answered. "Anyway, you're not supposed to have large feet."

According to Kitchen Grandma, Liniang was supposed to have a pair of tiny feet. "Only three inches long," Kitchen Grandma would always tell Liniang.

Many years ago, when Liniang was still a toddler, her father came back from a trip to Hangzhou. He carried Liniang up into his arms and asked his wife to measure the length of her feet.

"Three inches," Madam Du answered.

"It's the right size," Du Bao told his wife. "We need to bind her feet and stop them from growing anymore."

"But why?" Madam Du was perplexed.

"It is the new fashion in Hangzhou," Du Bao answered and told Madam Du the story.

A few months before Du Bao's trip to Hangzhou, the emperor and his wife had a big argument in his court. The queen was unhappy that the emperor had been spending days and nights with a concubine with a pair of very small feet, neglecting her and other concubines.

"Why are you so crazy about that woman? Her feet are so deformed that she can hardly walk," the queen asked.

"I am crazy about her precisely because of her feet," the emperor answered. "I love a woman who can barely walk. How delicate, how vulnerable."

The imperial idiosyncrasy soon caught on. First, the emperor's ministers started to bind their daughters' feet, then the army generals, then the judges. Now even rich merchants, who were forbidden by law to imitate the fashions of the court, started to hide their daughters in the houses and bind their feet in private.

"How awful," Madam Du exclaimed after Du Bao finished the story.

"I know it's awful," Du Bao answered, "but if we want Liniang to marry someone powerful in Hangzhou, we have to do it."

Madam Du did not like the idea. "I don't want Liniang to marry anyone in Hangzhou if we have to disable her feet in order to do so."

"What a lack of ambition," Du Bao scolded his wife. "Besides, the fashion is spreading to other cities as well. Pretty soon, everyone with a social position or some wealth is going to do it."

Madam Du still did not like the idea. She came from a farming family with a profound attachment to the fields, forests, and rivers. Although she had never worked on her father's farm, she had been an active girl and loved to play. After her marriage, with the help of her father, Madam Du learned to manage her farm since her husband was too busy as a governor and showed little interest, and she enjoyed it.

Madam Du knew that her daughter would love to hop, to jump, and to run in the courtyard once she was able to. She did not want to deny Liniang such simple pleasures. Besides, Madam Du wanted to pass on the family tradition to Liniang. She could not image what Liniang's life would be like if her feet were deliberately disabled.

Nevertheless, after struggling with herself for a few days, Madam Du reluctantly started to bind her daughter's feet.

"For all her doubts, your mother was an obedient woman," Kitchen Grandma told Liniang. "She did not want to disrespect your father."

The trouble was whenever she bound Liniang's feet too tightly, Liniang would cry for hours without stopping. Madam Du cajoled and threatened, but the crying never stopped.

So one day, Kitchen Grandma told Madam Du, "Why don't you loosen the clothes a little bit?"

Madam Du heeded Kitchen Grandma's advice. She still bound her daughter's feet, but the cloths were only wrapped around her feet loosely. They were more like a piece of footwear than a bone-constricting tool.

When Liniang was seven or eight, she started to ask questions. Her mother did not wrap her own feet with some cumbersome clothes. Nor did Kitchen Grandma, Fragrance, or any servant in the household.

"Why do I have to?" she insisted.

She was the daughter of a governor, Madam Du told her. She would look more attractive, and she would be able to marry into a well-connected family in the capital.

"I don't care to marry someone in the capital," Liniang told her mother. "I want to live in Nan'an with you forever."

Madam Du smiled. Her daughter had such a way with words that it was almost impossible for her to get angry.

Madam Du agreed to let Liniang take off the cloths, which had had no effect on the growth of Liniang's feet anyway, but she exacted a promise from Liniang. Whenever Du Bao came to the estate, she should wear long skirts to cover her feet and should walk in very small steps to suggest that her feet were bound.

"No jumping, no running, and no big steps when your father is here."

For many years, the deception worked. It was simple for Liniang to pull it off since her father seldom came to the estate, and even when he came, he would come at night and leave early in the morning.

Her father finally discovered the deception when he came home unexpectedly one day and caught Liniang chasing a cat in the courtyard. Du Bao exploded.

"It was my fault, son," Kitchen Grandma told Du Bao. "I loved the girl too much to allow her to suffer."

Du Bao was disappointed and angry. However, since Liniang was already twelve, and her feet had almost grown to full size, there was nothing he could do about it.

There came a knock on the washroom door.

"Who is it?" Liniang asked.

"It's me," Kitchen Grandma answered.

Hurriedly, Fragrance withdrew her feet from the basin.

But before she had time to dry them, Kitchen Grandma pushed open the door and wobbled into the washroom. She looked at Fragrance disapprovingly.

"Why are you washing with young mistress?" Kitchen Grandma demanded.

Fragrance quickly dried her feet, put on her shoes, and stood up from the bench.

"Kitchen Grandma, come and sit with me," Liniang tried to pacify the old woman. "I asked Fragrance to wash with me."

"It doesn't matter what young mistress says," Kitchen Grandma admonished Fragrance. "You should always wash after she does."

"I'm sorry, Kitchen Grandma," Fragrance grimaced an apology.

"Why are you here, Kitchen Grandma?" Liniang sat the old woman beside her affectionately.

Kitchen Grandma waved her hand at the young maid who had been massaging Liniang's feet. The maid left the washroom and closed the door.

"Where did you go today, my child?" Kitchen Grandma asked Liniang, a tender and anxious expression on her wizened face.

Liniang hesitated.

"We didn't go anywhere," Fragrance answered. "We…"

"I didn't ask you," Kitchen Grandma stopped Fragrance with a stern glare.

"We…" Liniang wavered. She wanted to affirm what Fragrance had said, but she had never told Kitchen Grandma a lie before, and she did not want to start now. Besides, she was not sure whom Kitchen Grandma had talked to already.

"Tell me the truth, my child."

"We went to the back garden," Liniang confessed in a low voice.

For a short moment, Kitchen Grandma's shriveled face blanched with alarm, and her coarse hands trembled visibly.

"There are goblins in the garden," she said fearfully.

"We didn't see any," Liniang took the old woman's hands into hers and tried to calm her down.

"You can't see goblins because they lurk behind trees and bushes."

"But you go there everyday, Kitchen Grandma," Liniang reminded the old woman.

"I am too old," Kitchen Grandma answered. "Goblins are no longer interested in me."

"What do goblins do anyway?" Liniang asked curiously. "Why should I be afraid of them?"

"They play all sorts of tricks," Kitchen Grandma whispered to Liniang. "They especially like to make nice girls fall in love."

"What's wrong with falling in love?"

"Hush, my child," Kitchen Grandma put a hand on Liniang's mouth to silence her. She looked around the washroom to make sure that there was no one else in the room.

She saw Fragrance standing beside them. "The water in the basin is getting cold," she told Fragrance. "Why don't you go and get some hot water?"

"Nice girls never fall in love," Kitchen Grandma told Liniang as Fragrance left the room.

"Did you ever fall in love?" Liniang asked.

"Yes, but I was not a nice girl," Kitchen Grandma dabbed at her eyes with a handkerchief. "I married my husband because I loved him. My parents did not like it, his parents did not like it, and God punished us for our misdeeds. My husband died young, very young," Kitchen Grandma sobbed.

"After he died, his parents drove me out, and my parents refused to take me back. Your grandfather took me in and saved me. He was a good man. May he rest in peace," the old woman prayed.

"But your grandfather refused to marry me because I was not a nice girl," the old woman started to sob again.

"I'm sure there was a different explanation," Liniang tried to comfort the old woman.

"Here I am, old and childless," tears ran down her cheeks. "This is what I get for falling in love, my child."

Liniang embraced Kitchen Grandma tightly. "I am your child, Kitchen Grandma, and I love you."

"Promise me you will never go to the back garden again," Kitchen Grandma pleaded with Liniang.

Liniang hesitated. She loved the old woman, but she could not promise something she knew she would not be able to keep.

"Please, my child. I want you to have a good life." Kitchen Grandma went down on her knees.

Hurriedly, Liniang raised the old woman to her feet. "Don't, please don't," she said in a troubled voice.

Liniang and Fragrance went to the class the next day.

"Are you feeling better, my student?" Chen the Most Virtuous asked Liniang solicitously.

Liniang shook her head. She had felt happy and exhilarated when she visited the garden the day before, but Kitchen Grandma's story and her entreaties depressed her. Coming to the class only worsened her depression.

Chen the Most Virtuous took out a paper bag of herbal mixture out of his sleeve. "I went through *The Compendium Medica* yesterday and concocted this remedy for your Spring Illness."

"Thank you, Professor Chen." Turning to Fragrance, she said, "Ask the young kitchen woman to prepare the remedy." She knew that she was not going to take the concoction, but she did not want to hurt Professor Chen.

"Boil it with three bowls of water over a slow fire for three hours," Chen the Most Virtuous instructed Fragrance.

Fragrance grabbed the bag from Chen and threw it to the other end of the table. "What Spring Illness? Young mistress is ill because you have asked her to wait for her handsome prince to come seek her."

"Don't be rude, Fragrance," Liniang chided her maid.

"I don't want to tell the kitchen woman to prepare the useless remedy," Fragrance answered.

Liniang picked up the bag of herbs, stepped out of the library, and went to the kitchen herself.

She walked slowly, and she took time to explain to the young kitchen woman what to do with the herbs. On her way back to the library, she heard Chen the Most Virtuous and Fragrance arguing heatedly about the poem they had studied on the first day of their class.

She made a little cough before she entered the library.

"Well," Chen the Most Virtuous cleared his throat. "Today, I want to clarify the concept of waiting in a more understandable fashion," he told Liniang. "In this family, as in all respectable families, you don't wait for men to come looking for you. You wait for your father to find a right man for you."

"Can I refuse to marry him if I don't like the man?" Liniang asked.

"No," Professor Chen shook his head. "It is the duty of a daughter to accept her father's choice."

"What if I don't like the man?" Liniang persisted.

"You learn to like him after the marriage."

"What if I can't learn?"

"When there is a will, there is a way. The key is your attitude toward your parents."

"What should be my attitude toward my parents?"

"Absolute obedience," Chen the Most Virtuous answered without any hesitation. "This is one of the four fundamental principles of ethics."

"Are you sure, Professor Chen? I've never heard of it before." Fragrance asked skeptically.

"Neither have I," Liniang echoed.

"I'm not inventing this," Chen the Most Virtuous answered. As if hurt by the girls' disbelief, he got up and went over to the bookshelf. He rummaged through the books, picked up a thick volume on history, and opened its pages.

"The first emperor of the Han Dynasty gave a most coveted honorary title to a young woman in the Kaifeng region," he started to read.

"For what?" Liniang asked.

"For filial obedience. Her father decided to marry her to an old village leper because the leper agreed to give the father a piece of his land," Chen the Most Virtuous continued the story. "The girl wedded the leper without any complaint and devoted herself to the care of the dying leper. After he departed, the young woman refused to remarry because she wanted to be true to her husband."

"What a selfish father," Fragrance cried out unhappily. She remembered how her own father had torn her away from her pleading mother and crying brothers and sold her for two hundred *taels* of silver.

"What a silly woman," Liniang exclaimed. She had been in a low spirit when she came to class. Now her spirit sank even lower.

"No more of this insolence," Professor Chen threw the book on the table in desperation. "You must show proper respect to an imperial degree honoring a most virtuous woman."

The class continued for a few days, and the two girls became restless.

Happily, one day, after his breakfast, Chen the Most Virtuous came to the library to announce that he had to leave early because his wife was ill.

"Take a few days off," Liniang told him.

"I'll be back tomorrow," Chen answered.

"Oh, no," Fragrance was visibly disappointed.

Chen the Most Virtuous assigned the girls homework and then went to ask the young kitchen woman to prepare for him some pork ribs and vegetables he would come to pick up the next day.

"Professor Chen," Fragrance cried out of the window, "you don't have to come for them tomorrow. Garden Boy can deliver them to your store."

"Let's go to the back garden again," Liniang told Fragrance when Chen the Most Virtues disappeared out of sight.

"I can't," Fragrance told Liniang glumly. "Kitchen Grandma told me that she would break my legs if I go to the back garden again."

"She would not," Liniang assured her.

"She would," Fragrance insisted. "I know the old woman well enough."

"Then I'm going alone," Liniang told her maid.

"Come back soon," Fragrance reminded Liniang. "You don't want Kitchen Grandma to know."

"I'll just take a stroll along the pond," Liniang promised.

When she opened the gate and stepped onto the pebbled path along the pond, Liniang was momentarily seized with a fear of the famed goblins, but the fear soon passed.

"Come out and meet me, you little creatures," Liniang challenged them whenever she passed a tree. Amid the trees, birds fluttered, and in the grass, squirrels scurried, but no imaginary goblins came out from behind trees or out of grass to greet her.

Where were the goblins Kitchen Grandma warned her about? Why were they not lurking behind trees, ready to entice girls into love? It was all a myth, Liniang told herself.

Even if goblins did exist, Liniang wondered, what was the harm of falling in love? Would it be any worse than marrying someone her father would pick for her and spending her whole life with him?

Liniang relaxed and breathed deeply. She stooped down to admire a white daffodil, she threw a pebble into the pond, and she imitated the singing of an oriole. The sound and the smell of spring soon overcame the depression she had felt for the past few days. A sense of youthful optimism came over her.

Liniang soon reached the pavilion. It was an open wooden structure built on a brick foundation surrounded on all sides by peonies with white, pink, and dark red flowers. Liniang sat down on a bench and gazed at the flowers. "Let my father yield to my wishes, and let my life bloom like the peonies," she prayed hopefully.

The sun was brilliant, the sky was cloudless, and the pond glimmered in the sun. Over the Western Mountains, however, thick and dark clouds started to accumulate, and thunders roared in the valleys of the mountains.

Liniang felt tired and drowsy.

She had told Fragrance that she would return shortly, and she saw the ominous clouds spilling out from the mountains, but she felt a short break would not delay her for too long. So she leaned her back against a pillar and closed her eyes.

Immediately, in the imaginary landscape of her mind, she saw dozens of goblins, men-like creatures the size of squirrels, hopping around on the trellis of the pavilion and busily gesturing to one another.

"Little fellows, what are you gesturing about?" Liniang asked genially. She had no fear, no apprehension of the creatures, but only curiosity and good will.

The little creatures smiled at her, waved, and then disappeared. Before Liniang's eyes, colors of infinite variety started to float and dazzle. Then music began, tender, sensual, and intoxicating, like the sound of love Liniang had never experienced before.

Excited, Liniang stood up and danced on the floor of the pavilion. Gradually, as the tempo of the music increased, Liniang let herself go. It was delightful and delicious. She became weightless, her body and soul melted and merged into the boisterous spirit of the spring.

"Liniang, Liniang, where are you?" a male voice came from a distance. Liniang was annoyed. It must be Garden Boy looking for her.

Liniang hid behind a pillar of the pavilion. She wished that the young gardener would not come close to the pavilion. But he was persistent, and he seemed to walk toward the pillar behind which she was hiding.

Liniang crawled into a bush for cover.

But it was useless. The gardener had no trouble finding her.

"So this is where you have been hiding—I have been looking for you everywhere," he came to the side of the bush and spoke in a sonorous voice.

Embarrassed, Liniang backed out of the bush slowly and stood up. Then she realized that the man grinning at her was not the gardener. Liniang had never seen him before. He was neither a member of the domestic staff, nor a member of the farming team.

"Who are you, and what are you doing here in my garden?" Liniang asked.

"I am as much a willow as you are a peony," the young man answered enigmatically.

What a strange answer! Liniang was intrigued. She stared at the man again and noticed that the young man was wearing a garment woven entirely with willow branches, and his head was covered with a crown made of them as well. What a strange attire for a man! She had never seen a man, or a woman, or a child dressed in this way. Liniang was even more intrigued.

"Where are you from?" Liniang asked curiously.

The man pointed at the willow trees.

Liniang looked. Through the gathering darkness of the impending storm, all the willow trees seemed to be waving at her in greeting. The willow trees were definitely friendly, Liniang thought. She smiled and waved back at the willows in return.

"Liniang, did you say you wanted to find a husband yourself?" the young man asked.

Liniang was surprised. A few days ago, as they came down the hill, she had told Fragrance that she wanted to find a husband herself. She had never told anyone else.

"Did you eavesdrop on our conversation?" she asked him suspiciously.

Ignoring her question, the young man continued, "Liniang, I am the man you have been waiting for."

Liniang examined the young man closely. He was tall, handsome and well built, and he had a charming and endearing smile. Liniang blushed.

"Come with me to a place where we can get to know each other better," the young man invited.

Liniang gave him a shy smile and blushed more, but she refused to move. He walked up to her and drew her by the sleeve.

"See the plum trees over there?" the young man pointed at the plum trees that ringed the east half of the pond.

"Yes, but, young sir, what do you mean to do?" Liniang asked hesitantly and in a low voice.

"I will open the fastening at your neck, and loosen your girdle at your waist. There may be some pain. But if you bear with me, I promise you will enjoy it."

Liniang turned away from the man, sprang onto the pebble path, and raced toward the house. What a lascivious thing for him to say, she thought indignantly. She wanted to get a few men from the house and throw this impudent intruder into the river.

Liniang had never run a race but had always wanted one. With her long and lithe limbs, she had imagined that she could outrun all the servants and farmers in the estate. However, to her chagrin, she found out that the stranger was a better runner than she was, and he caught up with her before she was able to reach the gate of the back garden.

"No," Liniang cried.

The young man grabbed her from behind, took her into his arms and, despite her protest and struggle, carried her off the pebble path into the depth of plum trees. He stopped at a small clearing in the woods where the soil was covered with green and soft grass. Putting her gently on the grass, he tried to kiss her on the lips.

"Please no," Liniang pleaded, panting from her exertion.

The young man gazed into her eyes tenderly for a long while. Then he softly whispered, "You are a very beautiful girl."

"Thank you," Liniang was flattered. "You are a very handsome man as well."

"I love you," the young man continued in a soft voice.

"But we are complete strangers," Liniang protested, wedging her hands between her lips and the young man's.

"You are a peony and I am a willow," the young man answered.

"What on earth do you mean?" Liniang was perplexed.

Without explaining, the man moved her hands gently off her face and kissed her.

Liniang wanted to scream, but her voice failed her. She wanted to kick, but her strength vanished. As the young man embraced her tightly and kissed her repeatedly, passion started to stir in her young bosom. Every minute, it grew stronger, more potent, and more overwhelming. Finally, it took over her whole body and soul.

Liniang closed her eyes and let go of herself in the intense pleasure of union. The plum trees, the pond, the houses, the hill, the river, and the city all disappeared. There were only peony and willow in this new world of love. Time stopped.

Liniang closed her eyes and let go of herself in the intense pleasure of union

Then, out of the blue, without any warning, a tremendous thunder exploded over her head. Large drops of cold water splattered on her face.

Liniang jumped up. To her surprise, she saw herself on a bench of the pavilion instead of in the clearing amid the plum trees. She looked around her. The willow-clad young man, who had been so loving and tender, had disappeared.

Liniang looked at the willow trees from where the willow man had emerged, but there was no sign of him. She looked at the plum trees where the willow man had carried her, but he was not there either.

The rain was raging, and the wind was howling. Amid the terrifying storm, Liniang heard a gentle voice, "Wait for me, my love. Wait for me, my love." Then the voice was gone, drowned out by the fierce outburst of nature.

Rain poured down from the sky. Water flowed into the pond in all directions. The stream from the hill, usually a trickle of water, suddenly became an enlarged torrent. The pond soon overflowed.

Liniang shivered. She was wearing only a cotton dress and a light coat, and they were dripping with water. She might soon catch a bad cold, Liniang warned herself.

Liniang sat down at the marble table in the center of the pavilion. The building sheltered her from the punishing rain, but it did not protect her from the wind that came in through the open structure. She shivered more and felt very cold.

The rain had no sign of stopping. As Liniang waited, it only became heavier and noisier. "I don't want Kitchen Grandma to worry about me," Liniang reminded herself. "I must go home right now."

Liniang drew a deep breath and dashed into the torrential rain. The pebbled path around the pond was already covered with an inch of water, and the rain beat against her face, blinding her from time to time. She covered her face with her hands and kept running. Unable to see the waterlogged path clearly, she tripped on a broken tree branch, lost her footing, and fell into the pond.

Liniang was immediately submerged in the surging mass of water. She kicked frantically to come to the surface, and when she succeeded, coughed violently to expel water from her lungs and nostrils. Then she noticed with horror that she was being carried away from the bank of the pond to its center.

"Oh no," she panicked. "I am going to die."

At that time, a large broken tree branch floated by. Liniang grabbed it and held onto it with both hands. Catching her breath and calming herself down, she kicked hard to propel the branch toward the bank. It took her a long time and a lot of energy, but finally she reached the bank. With her last strength, she maneuvered herself onto the bank and then collapsed on the pebble path. All she could do was to raise her head in the air so that she could breath.

After a few minutes, Liniang tried to stand up and struggle back to the house, but her body was trembling uncontrollably and her leg muscles were cramping and in extreme pain. She collapsed onto the path.

She thought of yelling for help, but decided against it. After all, no one in the house would be able to hear her in this storm, and she did not want anyone to see her in this humiliating situation. She would rather just take a break, gain her strength, let her legs recover, and struggle back to the house on her own.

Then she saw Fragrance and Garden Boy appearing at the gate of the garden. Fragrance was carrying a large umbrella made with dark yellow oilcloth. However, the gushing wind was too strong for her, and the young man had to help her to control the umbrella. They inched along the path slowly.

"Fragrance," Liniang cried out at the top of her voice and with all her remaining strength.

Liniang only vaguely remembered what had happened next.

After hearing her cry for help, Fragrance looked up and saw her struggling in the rain. She threw the umbrella down. A violent gust blew the umbrella into the air and then dropped it into a thicket of wild bushes.

The gardener rushed over to her with Fragrance, pulled her unto his back and carried her step by step through the mud and water into the house. Kitchen Grandma ordered young maids to wash her, clothe her, feed her chicken soup, and put her into bed.

She felt cold and trembled wildly. Fragrance covered her with more blankets. After a while, she started to feel hot. Kicking off the blanket, she tossed and turned. Kitchen Grandma applied cold towels to her forehead.

Liniang remembered the young man she had met in the garden walked into her bedroom, sat down by her bed, and told her, "Liniang, I'm the man you have been waiting for," "Liniang, come with me to a place where we can get to know each other."

She blushed in her sleep. What a handsome man! He was tall, he was strong, and he was gentle. She felt sweat break all over her body.

Was it just a dream? She asked herself. If it were a dream, how could she remember his tender touches so vividly? How could she feel so much excitement? It must be a vision, a vision of the man she was going to marry, and a vision of the happiness of her married life.

Then she remembered waking up in the middle of the night. A candle was burning on a table, and Kitchen Grandma was dozing off on a chair by her bedside.

"Kitchen Grandma," she called.

The old woman woke up, her eyes red and watery.

"Kitchen Grandma, please go back to your room," Liniang told the old woman. She felt very guilty.

Kitchen Grandma stood up from the chair unsteadily. She put her hand on Liniang's forehead. "You're still running a high fever, my child," she said sorrowfully.

"I'll be fine soon," Liniang comforted the old woman.

"Wait," Kitchen Grandma left the room.

She soon came back with a bowl of noodles. "Eat it," she told Liniang. "It is cooked in chicken soup."

Liniang shook her head. "I don't have any appetite."

"Let me feed you," Kitchen Grandma said.

"No," Liniang shook her head again. "I'll eat it later."

Kitchen Grandma put down the bowl on the table, her face tired and worried. "It's all my fault," she said.

"It is my fault, Kitchen Grandma," Liniang struggled not to cry. "You told me not to go."

"I gave your mother the idea," Kitchen Grandma started to sob. "If I hadn't, you would have a tiny pair of feet, and this would never have happened."

"Kitchen Grandma," Liniang held the old woman's hand in hers, "I love my feet, and I love you for giving my mother the excellent idea."

Chapter Five

IT WAS Madam Du's first trip to the imperial city. It was also her first trip anywhere with her husband. Madam Du was excited and elated.

The couple lodged at the imperial hotel, a short distance away from the royal palace. At dawn the second day after they arrived in Hangzhou, Du Bao went to the palace with his written report for the emperor.

Before Madame Du had time to finish washing, combing and dressing, her husband was back from the palace.

"What did you talk to the emperor?" Madam Du asked her husband, surprised by the brevity of the meeting.

"I didn't see the emperor," Du Bao answered. "A eunuch said the emperor was too busy and he would pass on my report to the emperor later."

"Did you see the emperor last time?" Madam Du asked curiously.

"I have never seen the emperor," Du Bao lamented with a hint of bitterness in his voice. "It is always the same story. The eunuch would ask what gift I had for the emperor. I would tell him I had nothing but the report, and the eunuch would then say the emperor was too busy."

According to the tradition of the Song Dynasty, the emperor was supposed to use the audience to evaluate the work of his regional officials, to promote, demote, or transfer them based on their performances. Madam Du was surprised at the emperor's disregard of the tradition.

"Maybe he was really too busy," Madam Du answered.

On his previous visits, Du Bao had felt a deep sense of disappointment. He had worked hard, and he had wanted promotions. The emperor's lack of interest in him and in his work had rankled for a long time.

This time, however, his disappointment only lasted for a short while. With his pretty wife on his side, he quickly regained his sense of equanimity. "I don't care whether or not he is really busy."

"I'm happy to hear it, my husband."

"Let's go to the West Lake," Du Bao told his wife enthusiastically. He was eager to show her around the imperial city.

The lake was a wondrous place. In the morning sun, it glimmered quietly. Lush hills surrounded the lake on three sides, and Buddhist and Taoist temples stood atop the hills. On the east bank of the lake, a tree-lined, flower-bordered boulevard extended the length of the city from the South Gate to the North Gate.

Du Bao and his wife took a long walk alongside the lake, ate lunch at a lakeside restaurant, and hired a boat in the afternoon.

When dusk descended, they went to a fashionable restaurant at the center of town and ordered plentiful wine and seafood. Red lanterns illuminated the dining hall, and young girls sang and danced on the stage. Very soon, they were pleasantly intoxicated.

The next morning, Du Bao and his wife were planning for another day of tour when a royal messenger arrived at the hotel.

"His Majesty wants to see you immediately."

Du Bao rode with the messenger to the palace, not sure why the emperor wanted to see him after so many years of neglect.

The emperor was two years younger than Du Bao, but his hair was totally gray, and he looked tired, drained and enervated even in the morning. The emperor must have lived a very indulgent life for him to look so worn out, Du Bao thought critically.

"I am sorry I didn't have time to see you on previous occasions," the emperor apologized, "but I did read your report every time."

"I hope you are happy with my work."

"I'm very happy with your work," the emperor answered emphatically. He invited Du Bao to his private office and offered him tea.

"Tell me," he asked Du Bao, "why Nan'an seemed to be the only region in East China that had no peasant uprisings and the only region that paid its taxes every year to the central government?"

Du Bao's face lit up.

Since he became governor of Nan'an, Du Bao had set up a chain of grain depots throughout the region, and he had encouraged rich farmers to contribute to them by publishing a yearly list of donors and by honoring them on various occasions. In times of famines, the grain depots opened their doors to the poor, thereby discouraging them from banding together to plunder.

Du Bao had set up a local militia force. He recruited young vagabonds and the homeless, the people who were most likely to make trouble in times of crisis. He fed them, clothed them, and trained them. The militia, along with his regular soldiers, kept the region free of bandits.

Du Bao also ran a clean government. He did not take bribes, and he punished harshly those subordinates who were caught asking for or accepting bribes.

"Anyone with a grievance or an important matter can come and see me without paying a gift," he told the emperor.

Embarrassed, the emperor coughed.

A eunuch came up to pat him lightly on his back. A second eunuch gave him a cup of Ginseng soup on a silver plate.

The emperor finished the soup slowly. When he was done, a third eunuch came up with a warm towel to wipe his mouth.

The Ginseng soup helped the emperor to regain his composure. Clearing his throat, he ordered, "Get a map."

Two eunuchs opened a large map of China in front of the emperor and Du Bao.

Pointing to the Yangtze River that separated South China from North, the emperor said solemnly, "Beijing is gone, Kaifeng is gone, and Nanjing is gone. Now the northern barbarians are trying to seize Yangzhou. If they succeed, I will have no city left north of the Yangtze River, and the whole southern China will be exposed to the attacks of the barbarians."

"Your Majesty should defend Yangzhou at all cost," Du Bao advised. "Later, you can use the city as a springboard for counter attacks against the barbarians."

"The barbarians are spearheaded by a band of local rebels led by a renegade called Li Quan," the emperor continued.

"He is better known as Li the Bandit," Du Bao told the emperor. "Your Majesty must try to destroy the rebels to deprive the barbarians of local support."

"You're absolutely right," the emperor nodded his head enthusiastically. "If you do not object, I am appointing you to be Pacification Commissioner for Yangzhou, in command of all the civil and military authorities north of the river."

Du Bao hesitated. While he was happy that the emperor, after so many years, finally recognized his ability, his devotion, and his achievement, Du Bao knew it was a responsibility fraught with personal risk and dangers. Besides, he had no experience commanding a large army that was stationed in the region to combat the rebels and to stop the advance of northern barbarians.

"Yangzhou is the last defense against the barbarians," the emperor stressed. "I need someone as able and loyal as you are."

Du Bao was moved by the emperor's trust in him. He had always wanted to excel himself in the service of the empire. Now the opportunity had finally come.

"Your Majesty," Du Bao knelt in front of the emperor and promised, "I will do my utmost."

"I'm sorry," Du Bao explained to his wife, who had been waiting at the hotel in anticipation of another day of sightseeing. "The emperor wants me to leave for Yangzhou immediately."

Madam Du was not happy about her husband's new job. The Yangzhou region had been impoverished by years of famines and peasant uprisings and local rebels supported by the northern barbarians.

But Madam Du did not show her unhappiness. She always believed that her husband's career should come first. "I'll go back to Nan'an to pack. I will join you with Liniang as soon as possible."

"Don't come now," her husband shook his head. "I'll send for you and Liniang when the situation is safer."

"But I don't want you to be alone," Madam Du protested.

"I'll be fine," Du Bao embraced his wife and said good-bye.

"Take good care of yourself, my dear husband."

The journey back to Nan'an took a few days. Madam Du sat in the boat cabin alone. Worried about her husband, she was melancholy. Gone was the high spirit she had felt on her way to Hangzhou.

On the evening of the sixth day, when the sun was setting into the Western Mountains, she finally saw her own house. Its chimney, like those on other houses and cottages, emitted curls of white smoke into the evening sky. It was dinnertime and Madam Du felt hungry.

As her boat approached the estate, a domestic servant noticed it. Quickly, Kitchen Grandma, Fragrance, Professor Chen, and other employees of the household lined the bank to welcome her.

"Where is Liniang?" Madam Du quickly noticed the absence of her daughter.

Before the boat was securely tied to the dock, Madam Du jumped onto the platform. "Where is Liniang?" she asked Kitchen Grandma uneasily.

"Young mistress is ill," Kitchen Grandma answered in a sad voice. Her face was puffy, and her eyes were swollen.

Madam Du hurried toward the stone gate, through the court-yard, and into the main house.

Liniang had been running a fever, and Kitchen Grandma had insisted that she stay in bed. When she heard her mother come into her room, Liniang sat up in her bed and greeted her mother, "Welcome home, mother. But where is father?"

Madam Du was shocked by Liniang's sickly condition. Her face was gaunt, her eyes were tired, her lips were cracked, and her breathing was labored.

"Where is father?" Liniang asked again.

"The emperor has sent him to Yangzhou," Madam Du answered.

"Is father going to be there for a long time?"

Madam Du nodded.

"Is he going to visit us once a month?"

"No, Liniang. It's too far away, and there is a war going on there."

"Oh, no," Liniang's face clouded, and she started to cough. It was a long and painful cough.

Kitchen Grandma quickly handed her some warm water.

Waiting for her daughter's cough to subside, Madam Du asked, "How did you get so ill, my daughter?"

Liniang hesitated. She was afraid to tell her mother that she had been caught in a storm while visiting the garden. On the other hand, everyone on the estate knew it and any one might tell her mother later. "I was caught in a rain and got a bad cold," she finally told her mother.

"Why were you in a rain?"

"I was…" Liniang faltered.

Without waiting for an answer, Madam Du felt Liniang's forehead and took her pulse. "Rest well, my daughter. I'll get you a doctor tomorrow morning."

❀❀

When dawn broke the next morning, Madam Du went to Liniang's apartment to see how her daughter had been doing. She knocked gently on the door.

Fragrance opened the door. "Madam," she seemed to be surprised to see Madam Du so early in the morning.

"How is young mistress?" Madam Du inquired.

"She is..." Fragrance stuttered.

Madam Du was puzzled by Fragrance's response. Fragrance was usually clear-headed and direct. She was never so hesitant. "Are you ill as well?"

"No, I am fine, Madam. Thank you for asking."

"Let me in," Madam Du pointed at the door Fragrance was holding half open.

Fragrance's face twitched nervously. But despite her obvious hesitation, she opened the door completely and stepped aside to let Madam Du into the apartment.

Madam Du walked into Liniang's bedroom. Her daughter was not in the room.

"Where is young mistress?"

"I... I don't know." Fragrance lowered her head and stared at the floor.

Madam Du was annoyed. From Fragrance's hesitant demeanor, she knew immediately that Fragrance was not telling her the truth and that there was something wrong with Liniang not being in the apartment. She sat down at a table by the window and thought for a while. Then she asked, "Fragrance, how many years have you been here?"

"Twelve years," Fragrance answered, not sure why Madam Du asked. The mistress knew how long she had been at the estate.

"Have I treated you well since you came here?"

"Yes, you have treated me like your own daughter," Fragrance hastened to answer. She wanted Madam Du to know that she was grateful to her and appreciative of her good life.

"Then why don't you tell me where Liniang is and what is wrong with her?"

Fragrance faltered. Liniang had asked her not to tell Madam Du what had happened. She did not know what to do, so she continued to stare at the floor.

"How old are you?"

"Eighteen," Fragrance answered, again not sure why Madam Du asked.

"Now you are of marriageable age," Madam Du said in a deliberate voice. "I can sell you or give you away to any man I want if you don't tell me the truth."

"One man I have in mind," Madam Du continued as Fragrance remained silent, "is Professor Chen. He has a wife, but no offspring. I think he needs a concubine."

"Please, Madam, I beg you," Fragrance was on her knees. "I would rather serve young mistress all my life than to live a moment with that old skeleton."

"Then you must not hide anything from me if you want to live in this family," Madam Du answered sternly.

Fragrance burst into tears.

Madam Du gently put her hand on Fragrance's shoulder.

"Tell me, where is young mistress and what is she doing?"

"She is in the garden," Fragrance sobbed.

"In the garden? When she is ill?" Madam Du could not believe her ears. Since Liniang was very young, Madam Du had forbidden her from visiting the garden.

With her eyes still on the floor, Fragrance continued, "It all started when young mistress visited the garden a few days ago in a storm."

"What happened?"

"She met a young man and slept with him under the plum trees."

"She did what?" Madam Du jumped up and yelled in disbelief.

"It was all a dream," Fragrance hastened to explain. "She had a dream in the pavilion. She slept with the man in the dream."

"Oh, it was a dream," Madam Du was relieved somewhat and sat down.

"Young mistress has since been visiting the pavilion every morning hoping to see the man again."

"Does young mistress know that it was all a dream?"

"She yells at me every time I tell her that it was a dream," Fragrance sobbed.

"Oh, my dear," Madam Du muttered. "Some mischievous goblins must have befuddled her senses."

Madam Du rushed to the garden and to the pavilion, but Liniang was not there. "Liniang," she called out several times.

"Yes, mother," Liniang walked out of the willow woods, her eyes glassy and transfixed. She looked as if she had just come out of a trance.

"What are you doing here, Liniang?" Madam Du asked, a worried expression on her face.

"I'm getting some fresh air, mother," Liniang lied.

"The man you dreamed of in your dream is a goblin," Madam Du confronted her daughter.

Liniang looked surprised. Then she realized Fragrance must have told her mother everything. "He is not a goblin," she protested vehemently. "He is my love."

"If you come to the garden again," Madam Du told her daughter, "I'll call Sister Stone here to exterminate all the goblins."

"Please do not harm the goblins," Liniang was horrified by her mother's threat.

"But the mischievous creatures have beguiled you."

"It has nothing to do with them," Liniang defended the goblins.

"It has everything to do with them," Madam Du answered firmly. "Promise me, or I will send someone for Sister Stone right now."

Liniang balked. She loved the garden, the pavilion, the hill, the pond, and the woods. And she had promised to wait for the handsome young man at the pavilion. But she knew her mother would carry out her threat if she did not promise. Not wanting the innocent goblins to get hurt, she nodded her head reluctantly.

"Let's go home now," Madam Du urged.

"Move my bed into young mistress's room," Madam Du told a servant when they got back to the house. She wanted to be with her daughter day and night to make sure that Liniang did not visit the garden again.

Chen loved his job. Fragrance was a pain, but the salary was good, and the meals were even better. Moreover, he didn't even have to teach much. His student seemed to be ill most of the time. He felt lucky that he was able to land such a job after a life filled with disappointments and failures.

But Chen was smart enough to realize that if his student was ill for too long, he might not be able to keep his job. Besides, he wanted to impress on his employers that he was not only a tutor, but also a doctor. Perhaps they would even give him a raise.

As Chen sipped tea after his long breakfast, he saw Madam Du come out of the main house with a worried expression. He immediately went out of the kitchen to greet her.

"I'm sorry I didn't have a chance to say welcome to you last evening, Madam Du."

"It was my fault, Professor Chen."

"I didn't see Governor Du come back last evening."

"The emperor has appointed him Pacification Commissioner for Yangzhou."

"Congratulations on your husband's promotion."

"Thank you," Madam Du replied politely, but her tone betrayed a hint of impatience.

"I'm sorry, Madam, but I'm sure I can help cure young mistress's illness."

Madam Du remembered that Chen ran a herbal store and was a doctor as well, but she had never used Chen before and did not know how good he was at medicine.

"Give me a chance," Chen promised. "Young mistress will be up and running in no time."

Madam Du considered it for a while. Then she invited Chen into Liniang's apartment.

❀❀

"My student, I have been worried about you," Chen greeted Liniang as he entered her bedroom.

"Please accept my apologies for my absence, Professor Chen."

"Tell me, my student, what are the symptoms of your illness?"

"I am running a fever, and I cough a dry and painful cough."

"What else?"

"I have no appetite for any food. I cannot fall asleep at night, and I have no energy."

Chen nodded his head, "What is the reason for your sickness?"

"Why do you need to ask?" Fragrance interrupted. "It is those poems you were teaching, 'So precious the virtuous maiden, A befitting mate for our prince.' The young mistress is love-sick."

"Do not interrupt," Madam Du told Fragrance.

"Let me feel your pulse, my student."

Liniang freed her left arm from under the blanket. She was wearing a short-sleeved sleeping gown. When Chen saw her bare arm, his face reddened.

"Wait a minute," Madam Du took a handkerchief and wrapped it around her daughter's wrist. According to tradition, even a doctor could not directly touch a maiden.

Chen took Liniang's handkerchief-wrapped wrist and tried to concentrate, but he was too flustered by the sight of Liniang's bare arm to notice that he was feeling the back of her wrist.

"Oh, there is no pulse," he was alarmed.

"Professor Chen," Fragrance told him contemptuously, "maybe you should turn her hand over and feel her pulse on the wrist!"

Chen was embarrassed. "My family has practiced medicine for generations, and I know how to feel a pulse anywhere," he defended himself.

"Why don't you feel young mistress's pulse on her toes then?" Fragrance countered.

"Now you are being rude, Fragrance," Madam Du admonished Fragrance.

Chen took Liniang's pulse again. Then he stood up, put on a deliberative air, and paced the room for a few minutes. "It is a case of the Spring Illness aggravated by exposure to inclement weathers," he finally gave his diagnosis.

"What is the Spring Illness?" Madam Du asked. She had never heard of it before.

"As trees and flowers come into bloom, the balance of bodily humors fluctuates. A person is afflicted with the illness when the fire in his body becomes dominant."

"What is the cure?" Madam Du asked.

Chen again paced the room for a few minutes.

"I need to use a laxative," Chen answered.

"Why a laxative?" Liniang asked.

Pointing at Fragrance, Chen told Liniang, "Ask you servant girl to prepare a big chamberpot, because I will give you a strong laxative to flush out the fire in your system."

Liniang was embarrassed, "Oh, dear."

Chen tried his laxative for several days, but Liniang's fever persisted, and she became weaker by the day. Madam Du then invited a string of famous doctors from Nan'an. They all had their own diagnoses and herbal concoctions, but none seemed able to help Liniang.

Liniang ate little, she slept little, and she often spent her days sitting at the back window in her apartment, gazing at the garden and listening to birds singing and chirping.

Madam Du at first did not want to disturb her husband. He had enough to worry about in Yangzhou. But as Liniang deteriorated slowly despite the best efforts of all the doctors, she became increasingly worried. Finally, she decided to send a messenger to Yangzhou with a letter on Liniang's illness.

The messenger came back in sixteen days with a letter and the best doctor in Yangzhou.

"My dear daughter," Du Bao wrote Liniang, "I'm very distressed to hear of your long illness. I wish I could be with you, but military and civil responsibilities make it impossible for me to journey back at this time. Please get well soon. I eagerly await news of your recovery."

The doctor examined Liniang immediately. Then he spent one full day in the library going over all the medical treatises. He spent another day preparing his herbal medicine in the kitchen himself.

After about a month, the doctor gave up ruefully. "I'm very sorry, Madam Du. I've done my best, but nothing seems to be able to cure an ailment of the heart." He left the estate and went back to Yangzhou.

By fall, Liniang had become totally emaciated and extremely weak. She lay in bed day and night, her breathing was shallow and labored, and her eyes seldom opened.

One morning, Liniang opened her eyes and looked at her mother guiltily.

"Is the Mid-Autumn Festival coming up?" she asked.

"It's coming up in half a month," Madam Du answered.

Liniang knew that on the holiday, when the moon was fullest in the entire year, couples should be together no matter how apart they were from each other during the rest of the year.

"Mother, please go to Yangzhou so you can be with father on that day."

"No," Madam Du patted her daughter on the shoulder. "We'll go together when you recover."

"I'm not going to recover, mother."

"Don't talk nonsense," Madam Du stopped her daughter. "You're going to recover."

The Mid-Autumn Festival soon arrived. But in the Du household, there was no banquet, there were no traditional moon cakes, and there was not even a mention of the holiday.

In the early evening, a large and bright moon started to climb up the cloudless sky.

"Mother," Liniang struggled up in her bed, "let's sit at the back window."

Madam Du helped Liniang out of the bed and to the window. The mother and daughter sat down and gazed at the moon and at the desolate back garden.

"Mother, I'm truly sorry that you cannot be with father tonight because of me."

"I'm happy to be with you."

Liniang held her mother's hands, tears welling up in her eyes.

Night soon deepened, a wind started to blow. In the moonlight, they could see leaves falling onto the ground and being blown around in the garden.

"Leaves fall, flowers shed, and grass wilt. It is the season to die," Liniang whispered to herself.

"Don't be so pessimistic," Madam Du answered. "It's time to go to bed."

"Let me wait here for my love tonight," Liniang pleaded with her mother.

"He will not come," Madam Du answered in a pained voice.

"He loves me and he will come."

"If he does not come tonight, will you give up on him?" Madam Du asked hopefully.

"He will come," Liniang insisted.

"I'll let you wait tonight," Madam Du told her daughter. "If he does not come tonight, I will get Sister Stone tomorrow."

"Thank you, mother. Can you and Fragrance sleep in your apartment tonight?"

Madam Du hesitated.

"Please."

Madam Du looked at her daughter's pleading eyes and nodded her head.

Madam Du did not sleep in her apartment. She sat at the dining table in the center hall. She wanted to be near if Liniang needed help.

The center hall was the largest room in the whole house. At one end of the hall, a large oak door opened onto the courtyard. At the other end, a portrait of her husband's late father hung on the wall, looking down sternly on the square dining table in the center of the hall.

Madam Du went up to the portrait, lit some incense in her late father-in-law's memory, and prayed. "The benevolent spirit of the Du family, please help Liniang overcome her illness. She is your only offspring. I will prepare the best dishes for you when Liniang gets better."

The night dragged on slowly. Some time after midnight, Madam Du fell into a tortured sleep.

She was woken up by a low sobbing sound from Liniang's apartment at dawn. Opening the door gently, she stepped into the apartment.

"The moon is gone," Liniang cried piteously as she saw her mother coming into the apartment, "but he has not come."

"He never existed," Madam Du told her daughter gently. "It was a naughty goblin playing a trick on you."

"But he promised."

"You need to get some sleep," Madam Du helped her daughter to her bed.

Sister Stone and Madam Du had been good friends ever since Madam Du invited the sister to her estate to conduct a seven-day memorial service for her father when he passed away.

Sister Stone arrived at Madam Du's estate in the afternoon. Without eating lunch or taking a break, she went directly to Liniang's apartment.

Sister Stone was shocked by Liniang's condition. She was drifting in and out of consciousness, and she barely opened her eyes when her mother told her that Sister Stone had come to visit.

"Am I dying?" she asked almost inaudibly.

"You're not dying," Madam Du held her daughter's hands and assured her.

"After I die," Liniang told her mother, "let Fragrance free."

"You're not dying, young mistress," Fragrance sobbed.

"Please bury me in the back garden among the plum trees," Liniang continued in a whisper.

"Don't talk nonsense, young mistress," Sister Stone said firmly. "You'll be fine soon."

"Are you not here for my memorial service, Sister Stone?"

"No, young mistress. I'm here to conduct an exorcism session."

"Exorcism?"

"You're ill because goblins have possessed you."

"Leave them alone, Sister Stone."

"Young mistress, did you meet a young man in your dream?"

Liniang nodded her head. Her eyes were still closed, but a smile had come upon her face.

"How does he look like?"

"He is a handsome young man."

"I'm sure he is."

"He is tall and strong."

"And?"

"He is gentle and tender."

"Very good, young mistress. Continue."

"He is a willow man."

"A willow man?" Sister Stone raised her eyebrows. "Why do you call him a willow man?"

"He wears a willow crown and a willow garment."

"How interesting," Sister Stone exchanged a look with Madam Du.

"He is handsome, he is tender, he is a willow man, and he is my love," Liniang droned faintly, a sad smile on her face.

"Very good," Sister Stone stood up. "You take a rest, young mistress, and I'll see what I can do."

❀❀

After Sister Stone had left her room, Liniang fell into a tormented delirium.

Where is my love? Liniang asked. He promised he would come, but she has waited for him for four months, all in vain. He did not even come last night, the night of the fullest moon and the night of reunion for lovers and families. Has he forgotten her? Has he found another love?

Or was it just goblins playing tricks on her? Fragrance, Kitchen Grandma, her mother, and now Sister Stone all said it was. Why would goblins play tricks on her? They loved fun, but they would never harm her, a friend of theirs.

"Where is my love then? Has he forgotten me? Does he have another girl?" Liniang asked repeatedly in her delirium.

As if in answer to her questions, a chant came from the courtyard. It was a female voice, but it was an aggressive voice. Condemning, demanding, and threatening, the voice undulated and surged in the air.

Liniang opened her eyes and looked at her mother inquiringly.

"Go back to sleep, Liniang."

"Who is making the noise?"

"No one."

"Let me go to the window," Liniang became suspicious and agitated.

"It is only Sister Stone," Madam Du told her daughter reluctantly.

"Why is she chanting in the courtyard?"

"She's doing an exorcism ritual."

"Let me look."

"You're too weak. Sleep."

"Please, mother, let me look."

With a sigh, Madam Du helped Liniang out of the bed and to the window.

Pushing open the window, Liniang saw Sister Stone dancing around a burning pyre of willow branches. She was brandishing a yellow wand in the air and chanting secret curses.

"The willow man!" Liniang cried out. Her head started to spin, and her heart started to cramp. She opened her mouth wide and gasped for air.

"Liniang, Liniang," Madam Du cried as she held her daughter in her arms.

Struggling for breath, Liniang begged, "Stop burning the willow man."

"Sister Stone," Madam Du called out of the window, "please stop."

"We can't stop now," Sister Stone answered.

Madam Du looked at her daughter. Her eyes were tightly closed, and her mouth wide open. Her face was ghostly pale, and beads of cold sweat were breaking out on her forehead.

"Stop the ritual. Extinguish the fire. Immediately." Madam Du yelled.

Liniang smiled faintly as her mother and Fragrance carried her back to her bed. She rested for a while, trying to catch her breath. Then she pointed at her chest of drawers.

Fragrance opened the top drawer and took out two boxes; one made of mahogany, the other rosewood.

"Open the mahogany box," Liniang told her mother.

Madam Du opened the mahogany box. In the box, there was a scroll. It was a self-portrait of her daughter. The portrait captured her daughter at her merriest, prettiest and most innocent moment.

"This one is for you and father," Liniang whispered. "The other one is for the willow man."

Madam Du started to sob.

Liniang gazed at her mother, her eyes full of anguished love. She had been ill for a few months, but her mother seemed to have aged for more than ten years. Mother, mother, you have given me birth, cared for me, and loved me. But now I am leaving you, all alone in the world, childless and hopeless.

A strong wave of guilt swelled up in Liniang's chest, gnawing at her failing heart, suffocating her and obliterating her.

Before Liniang succumbed, she gathered all her strength and gasped out her last words, "I love you, mother."

"Don't leave me, Liniang, please, please, please, come back," she heard her mother cry piteously. But she floated away, and the wailing became more and more distant.

Sister Stone sat down with Madam Du at Liniang's bedside and prayed silently for a long time.

"Young mistress has departed," she finally told Madam Du.

"She is only taking a nap," Madam Du replied, her eyes fixed on Liniang's pale face.

For the whole night, Madam Du sat at her daughter's bed, without taking a break. From time to time, she felt for Liniang's pulse on her wrist and her temperature on her forehead, hoping that her heart would beat again, and her face would become warm again.

By next morning, Madam Du was worn out and heart-broken, but she still refused to accept Liniang's death.

"We need to make funeral arrangements," Sister Stone told her friend.

Madam Du screamed, "Liniang is not dead, she is not dead."

"We are not burying Liniang," Sister Stone held her friend in her arms and comforted her. "We are just moving her to a new place in the garden. Liniang loves the garden."

After the burial, Kitchen Grandma, teary-eyed, told Madam Du, "Go to Yangzhou."

"I'm staying here with Liniang," Madam Du refused.

"I'll take care of Liniang," the old woman replied. "You go to your husband. May god give you a baby again," she prayed.

Madam Du shook her head.

In resignation, Kitchen Grandma sent a messenger to Yangzhou.

Everyday, Madam Du visited the grave, burning incense and saying prayers.

Then the messenger came back from Yangzhou. With him were four young soldiers. They carried a marble tombstone from the boat into the back garden and set it up at Liniang's tomb. On the stone, Du Bao had chiseled the following words:

To My Only Daughter, Rest in Peace Forever

After the ceremony, the soldiers told Madam Du that Commissioner Du wanted her to join him immediately.

Reluctantly, Madam Du bid good-bye to Liniang's grave and left for Yangzhou with Liniang's portrait.

Chapter Six

IT WAS spring and the middle of the plowing season.

About a thousand miles to the south of Nan'an, near the southern city of Guangzhou, three farmers were taking a lunch break in the shadow of a willow tree. One of them, a young man, quickly finished his meal, leaned against the willow tree, and soon fell into a slumber.

The other two farmers finished their lunch and got up.

"Wake up," the oldest of the three farmers bellowed at the sleeping young man.

The young man did not wake up.

The third man, who was the son of the old farmer, shook the sleeping man several times.

Liu Mengmei, the daydreaming farmer, woke up with a start. Opening his eyes, he saw his uncle and his cousin staring at him.

"Did you sleep enough last night?" his uncle asked.

Well, he did not sleep enough the previous night. He had worked in the rice paddies until the stars began to shine in the sky. Moreover, he had not been able to sleep well. Dreams had kept waking him up.

"A working man never sleeps in broad daylight," his uncle admonished him.

Guiltily, the young man told his uncle that he had not intended to sleep. He had just sat down against the willow tree to give his aching back a short break. "Then I saw a white thin mist drifting out of the forest. Then I had a very strange dream."

"A white mist in the middle of the day?" his uncle and cousin scoffed incredulously.

Liu Mengmei went back to work. As he pumped water from an irrigation ditch into rice fields, the dream kept coming back to him.

What a strange dream!

In his dream, he flew past mountains and rivers and landed in a grand garden. There he met a very beautiful girl under a pavilion surrounded by peony flowers. They made love in a plum grove and promised each other that they would meet again.

His heart pounding, his head aching, his whole body sweating profusely, Liu Mengmei felt deeply disturbed. He had been content so far in his life, but now he felt unhappy with his life. He wanted to escape, to look for his girl, and to start a new life.

Liu Mengmei stopped working, went over to the willow tree, and sat down again.

"What's wrong?" his uncle yelled.

"I'm sick," Liu Mengmei told his uncle.

"No one gets sick in the middle of the plowing season," his uncle shouted angrily. "Get back to work."

Liu Mengmei had no memory of his parents. According to his uncle, his father had been a magistrate in Guangzhou, a major city in Southern China. When Liu was three years old, a bloody uprising swept through the city. After the soldiers put down the uprising, his uncle went searching for Liu Mengmei's parents in the ruins of the city.

He found his father's decapitated body in the courtyard of his official residence, but he could not find his mother and their two children.

His uncle spent two days digging through tons of debris to a secret cellar under the burned-down house. In the cellar, he found Liu Mengmei, Liu's kid sister, and Liu's mother. Only Liu was breathing. He was able to survive, his uncle told him, because his mother had placed him closest to ventilation.

His uncle raised him on his farm outside the city. His uncle had his own children, a son and two daughters. When the two boys grew older, his cousin went to a local academy while Liu stayed home to help in the fields.

Once, Liu overheard an argument between his uncle and his aunt when he woke up in the middle of the night and went to the kitchen to get some water. Under a dim candle, his uncle and aunt were sitting at the long wooden dining table, counting gold and silver coins.

"We should send Liu Mengmei to school as well," his uncle told his aunt. "All this money came from the cellar."

His aunt said no. "It's good enough I agreed to raise him. Besides, the money is only enough to pay for one person."

Liu Mengmei was not a person to hold a grudge. He yearned to go to school like his cousin, but he also understood his aunt's point of view.

His cousin did not like school. "Whenever the first emperor of the Han Dynasty saw a scholar," he liked to tell Liu Mengmei, "he would order his soldiers to take down the scholar's hat and piss into it."

But Liu Mengmei liked books. He started to read books his cousin had brought home whenever he had a chance. In farming seasons, he read books at night. In winter, when there was not much farm work, he would go to the school and stood outside the classroom, listening to what the schoolmaster was saying.

The schoolmaster drove him away several times, but Liu Mengmei always went back. After a few days, the schoolmaster took pity on him and let him into the classroom.

Liu Mengmei excelled in his studies. But he was the poorest kid in the school, and he was the only part-time student. His schoolmates picked on him constantly and mercilessly. Only when he grew into a big-muscled young man, no doubt helped by his work on his uncle's farm, and broke the nose of a particularly vicious kid, did his schoolmates stop tormenting him openly.

His cousin failed to pass the provincial examination. The schoolmaster suggested to his uncle and aunt that it would only be a waste of money for their son to try again. "Let Liu Mengmei have a try. I'm sure he will be able to pass it."

His aunt exploded. She threw a book at the schoolmaster and cursed at him. She withdrew her son from the school and ordered Liu Mengmei not to go there anymore.

Soon after the unhappy incident, his uncle and aunt married off their two daughters. Then they found a pretty bride for their son.

Liu Mengmei started to feel lonely. One day, he told his uncle, "I want to marry as well."

His uncle discussed the matter with his wife and told Liu Mengmei, "You can marry, but you cannot stay on the farm." The farm was too small to support two families. Liu Mengmei needed to find a girl whose parents were willing to give him land to start a family.

It was impossible for Liu Mengmei to find such a bride. In the neighboring villages, there were families with only girls, but their parents wanted men with either wealth or government jobs for their daughters. When the village matchmaker told them that Liu Mengmei was a hard working orphan, they simply shook their heads and closed their doors.

Night fell. Liu Mengmei, his cousin, and his uncle washed themselves in a river and plodded back to their house. At the dinner table, Liu Mengmei told the whole family about his dream.

His aunt burst out laughing as if it were a hilarious joke. "Goblins must have beguiled you and befuddled your senses."

"I want to find the girl," Liu Mengmei announced.

"It is just a dream," his uncle said. "Besides, even if it is true, you don't know where she lives."

"Even if you know where she lives," his cousin asked, "do you think her parents will let you, a penniless laborer, marry her?"

"Better stay with us," his aunt stopped laughing. "At least you have three meals and a place to sleep." She did not want to lose a strong and skilled farmhand.

"I want to find the girl," Liu Mengmei insisted.

"Now you're being stupid and willful," his aunt rebuked him.

His cousin did not want to lose Liu Mengmei either, but he had grown up with him, liked him, and felt sorry for him. He felt especially bad when he sometimes saw Liu Mengmei absent-mindedly gazing at his young wife at the dinner table.

"You are very smart," he told Liu Mengmei. "Go and take the royal exam. If you pass it, you can have whatever girls you dream of."

"We have no money to send him to Hangzhou," his aunt interrupted her son.

"Look for a sponsor," his uncle told Liu Mengmei. "When it is not busy on the farm, go and talk to people with money. Tell them how good you are at scholarship. Some good fellows might agree to pay your expenses. Who knows?"

"Now all of you are dreaming!" his aunt slammed her chopsticks on the table and left the kitchen in disgust.

It was a hot afternoon. Although it was already early fall, the sun was still sizzling in Guangzhou, and the air was very humid.

Inspector Miao, a plump, middle-aged government official, sat in his office, sweating and feeling listless.

"What absurd weather," he complained.

As a royal inspector of jewels, Miao collected precious stones for the emperor and his family. He did not pay money, but he gave out minor government positions or commercial concessions to anyone who had an unusual stone or two.

His office had been a busy place. In recent years, however, as the Song Dynasty seemed to be losing its war with the northern barbarians, his office had fewer and fewer visitors. His customers, Miao guessed, were just waiting to see who was finally going to win the war, the southern court or the northern barbarians, before they decided to part with their stones.

Miao opened up a folding bamboo bed. He lay down on the bed, ready to take a nap.

"Go away," he heard his bodyguard yelling in the courtyard.

He stood up and looked out of the window. His bodyguard, a burly and muscular soldier, was pushing at a rustic looking young man who tried to poke his head inside the gate. The young man had a shabby shirt and an unshaven and sweaty face.

"What is going on?" Inspector Miao shouted.

The bodyguard came to the window, his face red from the heat and from the argument. "Sir, this beggar at the gate calls himself a scholar and insists that you receive him."

The man certainly did not look like his usual types of customers, who were mostly local gentry and merchants and traders from overseas. However, since he hadn't had a visitor for many days, he decided he might get some entertainment out of this unusual visitor.

"Show him in."

"Show him in?" the bodyguard thought he heard it wrong.

"Yes, show him in," Miao repeated.

The bodyguard turned back toward the gate, his face grew redder. Indignantly, he led the visitor into Miao's office and stared at him menacingly.

Miao waved his bodyguard away and looked at his visitor curiously. He was young, in his mid-twenties, well built, and ruggedly handsome. His face, however, was haggard and gaunt as if he had not been eating or sleeping well for some days.

"Respect to you, Your Honor. My name is Liu Mengmei, and I was a student of a local academy." The visitor held his hands together in front of him and made a slight bow.

"Why do you want to see me, young man?" Miao asked.

"I would like to have a look at the jewels you have collected recently," the young man answered.

Miao became suspicious. He looked hard at his visitor again. He was definitely destitute, but he did not look like a robber, nor did he seem to hide a knife on him. "The jewels are the property of the court and are not for public viewing," he answered.

"I am a scholar, and I happen to know a few things about fine jewelry," Liu assured him.

Miao slowly poured a cup of tea from his pot. He was hesitating.

"After you show me your treasure, I have something to show you as well," the young man promised.

"You do?" Miao became animated.

"Yes."

Putting down his teacup, Miao stood up and took Liu Mengmei into the library to the left of his office. The walls of the library were lined with shelves made of lacquered wood and the shelves were filled with books, memorabilia and curios. Miao pushed a shelf stuffed with miniature stone animals. The shelf creaked sideways, revealing a hidden door in the wall. He lit a lantern, unlocked the hidden door, and went down a flight of stairs into the cellar. He then unlocked another door and led the young man into a dark room.

In the darkness of the room, reflecting the light from the lantern, rows of colorful stones were shining and glowing on a felt-covered table.

"Sir, I must say you have an excellent collection," Miao's visitor seemed to be impressed.

Miao's face brightened up in the darkness. He always loved it when people praised his collection. Tenderly, he picked up his stones one by one, showing them to his visitor from different angles and telling him stories about where they had come from. The emeralds came from Persia, the rubies from India, and the diamonds from Africa.

"Sir, although you have an excellent international collection, you have not acquired the best treasure in this region," his visitor told him as they walked up the stairs to the library.

"What treasure do you have, young man?" Miao asked eagerly. He offered a seat to his visitor and poured a cup of tea for him.

Liu Mengmei slowly sipped his tea. Between his sips, he looked at Miao intently as if he could not decide whether to show him the treasure or not. Finally, after a long suspenseful moment, he said, "I'm not sure whether you are able to appreciate its value."

"Do not insult me," Miao answered. "I have been at this job for over ten years."

Liu Mengmei stood up and stepped to the middle of the office, his body erect and his head held high.

"Sir, the treasure is standing right before your eyes."

"Where?" Inspector Miao looked at the young man. His clothes were frayed and dirty, his face was rough and oily, but his expression was sincere.

Slapping his chest with his right hand, the young man said in a solemn voice, "Sir, I am the treasure."

Miao realized that the young man had no stones to show him. He was annoyed and summoned his bodyguard.

"Yes, sir," the burly bodyguard appeared at the door.

"Show this young man out," Miao ordered.

"Let's go," the bodyguard grabbed the young man by his arm and pulled him to the door.

"In all honesty, sir, I am a gem among men, and I am able to serve the emperor well," the young man struggled free and addressed Miao again.

Inspector Miao burst out laughing, "I'm afraid the emperor has all too many gems of your sort already."

"Sir, give me a chance," Liu pleaded.

"If you have something for me that I can appreciate," Miao pointed in the direction of his underground cellar, "I can arrange some government job for you here and now, but since you have nothing but you, I am sorry I cannot do anything for you." He fished for a silver coin in his pocket and threw it on the desk. "Take it and leave now."

The young man did not even look at the coin on the desk. "Sir, if you have a few minutes, I will discuss with you in detail my plan to repel the northern barbarians and to rebuild the country. If I don't impress you, throw me out of your court anytime."

Miao hesitated. He looked at the young man intently as if appraising a piece of jewelry. He surely talked well and had a contagious self-confidence. What if this young man really had the talent he claimed? He might be doing the court a good service by sending him to the capital, Miao thought.

"Have you passed the provincial examination?" Miao asked.

"No, but I have a letter of recommendation from my schoolmaster."

Miao glanced at the letter quickly. The schoolmaster said that Liu Mengmei was his best student. Liu could not take the test because he did not have money. The schoolmaster hoped that some benevolent sponsor would allow his student to demonstrate his talent at the royal examination.

Miao sat down and wrote a short letter on a piece of official stationary and put it in an official envelope. "Take this letter to the commissioner for royal examinations. He will take care of you."

"Thank you," the young man bowed, "but I have nothing to meet the expenses of a long journey."

"He is trying to cheat money out of you, sir," his bodyguard raised his voice angrily.

Miao looked the young man up and down again. He might be a cheat; he might not be a cheat. Miao really could not tell. What the hell, Miao finally told himself. He had made enough money for himself in this job, and he could be charitable once in a while. He stood up, went into the library and came out with two bars of silver worth two hundred *taels*.

"This should be enough to cover your traveling expenses," he told the young man.

Liu Mengmei knelt, his face full of gratitude. It had been more than two years since he had had his dream under the willow tree and since he had started looking for a sponsor. He had visited local government officials, rich landowners, and wealthy merchants. Some of them had listened to him patiently and got rid of him with a few *taels* of silver. Others had simply turned their vicious dogs on him.

"Stop daydreaming," his aunt once scoffed at him. "No one will be stupid enough to throw money at you."

Liu Mengmei, however, was not discouraged.

Now his persistence finally paid off. "I will not disappoint you, sir," he promised Inspector Miao.

Liu Mengmei woke up with a start. He looked out the window of the small inn. The snow had stopped. The sky was cloudless. He opened the window. A cold wind blew into the room. He sneezed. But the cold air energized him. It swept away the stale air in his lungs and filled him with a yearning to be out and moving.

He looked at the calendar on the wall. He had stayed in this inn for twenty days now. The night he arrived at the inn, it started the first snow of the year, and it went on and off, never stopping for long. The roads were treacherous, the inn owner told him, and it would be wise for him to wait out the snow.

The inn owner was a grumpy old man, but his wife was a gentle woman. She prepared nice meals for him everyday. She talked to him about her two sons who had been drafted to fight the northern barbarians. It was colder in the front, she would sob, but her sons had no warm beds to sleep on and no warm meals to fill their stomachs.

"Don't worry, ma'am," Liu Mengmei would comfort her. "They'll take care of themselves and be back sound and safe."

The sun rose, and the day brightened.

He had to leave, Liu told himself.

It was early fall when Liu Mengmei took his leave of Inspector Miao and bid farewell to his uncle and family. Now it was winter, but he had only traveled about a thousand miles to the outskirts of Nan'an, and if he let snow and ice stop him, he could well be spending the whole season in this inn. He could not stay here until spring came. He had to leave.

Liu assembled all his belongings, which were not many, into a bundle.

He walked into the dining room. The hostess had already prepared the breakfast, a steaming pot of rice porridge and a plate of pork dumplings. Seeing his bundle, she was surprised, "You want to leave today?"

He nodded.

"But the roads are treacherous."

"It will be treacherous until spring."

"Stay with us until spring. You pay whatever you can afford," the hostess told him earnestly.

"Thanks, ma'am. But I have to get to the capital as soon as possible."

"What's the hurry?"

"I want to prepare for the national examination."

"You can study here. I promise I am not going to bother you anymore." The woman thought she had talked to the young man too much, and she seemed to be on the verge of tears. For some reasons, she regarded her guest as a substitute for her two sons who were fighting the barbarians in the northern front.

Liu put his arms on her shoulders and embraced her. "No, you are not bothering me, ma'am. I just need to go to a library and read some books."

The hostess nodded her head. She understood that he had to use a library, she said. Wiping away a few tears with her sleeve, she yelled toward her bedroom, "Get up, old man. The young scholar wants to leave today. Bring that old coat of yours and give it to him."

"He must be crazy," the old man grumbled as he walked out of his room in his sleeping gown, a coat in his hand.

"Thanks a lot, old guy," Liu slapped him on his potbelly. From his wallet, he counted twenty silver coins.

"Take care of yourself," the old man took the money. "If you change your mind, come back here." Then he went back to his room and his bed.

"Eat your breakfast while I prepare you a lunch," the woman told him.

Liu Mengmei quickly finished his breakfast, put his lunch in his coat pocket, and said good-bye to his hostess.

"The city of Nan'an is about fifteen miles away. Be sure to find lodging there."

"Take care, my woman," Liu took his leave and was on his way.

As far as Liu could see, snow and ice covered the fields all the way across the plains to the high mountains in the north and west. Except for a few leafless tree trunks, it was a bland whiteness. Liu followed the wooden signposts on the roadside. Between the posts, it was difficult to know where the road ended and where the fields started.

The road was deserted. Only a few gray wolves followed him at a distance. Liu knew they were waiting for him to drop dead.

No way, he shouted at the wolves and waved a stick in the air. Ignoring him, the wolves followed him patiently and silently.

He had started out in high spirit, encouraged by the beautiful scene and the fresh air. As the journey wore on, he became tired. The lunch, two corn cakes and two chicken legs the inn hostess had prepared for him, boosted his energy, but not for long. By mid afternoon, he was staggering and stumbling, pulling his baggage behind him in the icy road.

Liu stopped at a wooden post to take a break. He looked at the wolves behind him. They had edged closer behind him. "These beasts seem to have more foresight than I do." He bit his lips and struggled on.

Then he saw the city of Nan'an on the horizon. It was a small city. Its walls and houses were not as high as those of Guangzhou, and its outskirts were not as populous as those of Guangzhou's. However, with white smokes rising from its many chimneys and with hungry wolves behind his heels, the city looked like a heavenly place to Liu Mengmei at that moment.

Spitting at the wolves following him, Liu trudged on. It did not look like a great distance, but Liu was tired and the road was covered with snow.

When darkness started to descend on the white plains, Liu Mengmei had finally reached a frozen river that came from the west and wound its way east to the city of Nan'an about two miles away and beyond. Here, the road turned and ran alongside the river. Immediately across the river, an estate house stood silently.

Liu contemplated the darkening sky and the menacing wolves behind him. He didn't know how long it would take him to cover the final distance and whether he had the stamina to complete it before the wolves were upon him.

Liu Mengmei gazed at the estate across the river. It was walled in with hedges and a stone gate. Behind the gate, three houses half enclosed a large courtyard. White steam and gray smoke slowly drifted out of a chimney from the house in the east. Liu could almost smell rice and cabbage being cooked.

He had to seek shelter at the estate, or he would fall somewhere between here and the city of Nan'an and become dinner for the hungry wolves.

Liu surveyed the river. A dozen or so yards to his left, there was a wooden drawbridge, but the bridge was half way in the air. He thought of yelling for someone to lower the bridge, but he was afraid his yelling would lead the wolves to fall upon him. He looked behind him. The wolves were stalking him from three sides. They were so close now he could see their red beady eyes in the semi-darkness and smell their stinky breaths.

There was no time to wait, Liu told himself. Grabbing at the roots of withered reeds and carefully lowering himself onto the frozen river, he tested the ice. Feeling that it was solid enough, he started to inch across the river. Then he heard a crack, and before he knew where the crack came from, his body slid into an icy hole. Water rushed to embrace him. After a few minutes of panic and struggle, he calmed down. His legs peddling, he tried to hold onto the ice and to pull himself out of the hole, but the ice was too slippery and his hands quickly became numb.

"Help!" he yelled.

Before leaving for Yangzhou, Madam Du asked Chen the Most Virtuous to help the head farmer keep books. "He knows much about farming, but not much about keeping books."

Chen happily agreed.

Then Madam Du asked Sister Stone to live on the estate and help Kitchen Grandma take care of Liniang's grave and the house.

Sister Stone hesitated. She had lived in the Purple Light Convent for many years, and she preferred the communal living of the convent.

"Please do it for me," Madam Du pleaded with her friend.

Sister Stone finally agreed. "I'll see to it that the grave site is properly maintained, the incense is burnt everyday, and services are performed on proper occasions."

Madam Du left with Fragrance, who insisted on accompanying her to Yangzhou despite her offer to set her free. After Madam Du left, Kitchen Grandma promptly dismissed all domestic servants.

"Kitchen Grandma," Sister Stone cautioned her, "you may want to keep one or two servants to help around the house."

"I've been a servant all my life. I don't need another servant around," the old woman answered stubbornly.

Every morning, Kitchen Grandma would visit Liniang's grave. She brought dishes she cooked, burned incense, and scattered paper money. She would tell Sister Stone again and again how she had witnessed the birth of Liniang, taken care of her, seen her grow up, and felt pride in her beauty and vivacity.

Winter came, but Kitchen Grandma kept up her daily visit. Sister Stone pleaded with the old woman, "Please don't go to the grave anymore. It's getting cold out there."

"I'm too old to be afraid of anything."

One morning, during the depth of winter, Kitchen Grandma came back with a chill and took to her bed. Her condition quickly deteriorated.

"Bury me in the garden," she told Sister Stone as she realized that she was not going to live long.

"I'll bury you next to Liniang," Sister Stone promised the old woman.

The old woman rolled her head from side to side. "I'm a servant. I can't be buried next to young mistress. Bury me a distance away from her, but not too far."

After the death of Kitchen Grandma, Sister Stone was alone on the estate. Although she was a nun, she was not used to a solitary life, and she craved for company.

Chen the Most Virtuous came to visit occasionally. The head farmer sometimes came to complain about Chen, whom he considered to be ignorant in farming matters, and unreasonable in demanding rents. Sister Stone visited the Purple Light Convent from time to time. She also invited her fellow nuns to visit. All these helped to relieve her solitude and made her life less boring.

But in winter, when rivers froze and snow made roads almost impassable, very few visitors ever came to the estate, and life became very dreary and monotonous to Sister Stone. She thought of going back to the convent, but decided against it, remembering her promise to Madam Du.

She just wished that a visitor, any visitor, might suddenly knock on the gate.

That day, Sister Stone had spent the whole afternoon sweeping the snow from the courtyard. Since she lived in a room next to the kitchen, there was really no need for her to sweep the snow. But Sister Stone liked to be in the open air and enjoyed the work. It made her cheerful and made her forget her solitude.

When dusk descended, Sister Stone put away her shovel and broom, went to the kitchen, and started cooking rice and cabbage on the stove.

Then Sister Stone heard someone yelling for help from a distance. Who could be out there in this weather? She opened the kitchen door and heard the cry again. It seemed to be coming from the river outside the stone gate.

"This is the opportunity for a good deed," Sister Stone told herself. She put on a heavy coat, pushed open the gate, and hurried to the riverbank.

In the river, she saw a young man struggling in an ice hole, trying to climb out, but the ice was too slippery for him to hold onto, and the man seemed to be losing strength. On the riverbank opposite the estate, a few wolves were watching the struggling man silently.

Sister Stone hissed at the wolves, but they remained motionless on the bank, staring at the man.

"Hold on," she yelled at the young man. She ran back to the kitchen, found a rope, came back to the river and threw one end of the rope to the man. With the help of the rope, Sister Stone pulled the man onto the bank.

"Thank you, ma'am," the young man stammered.

"I'm a nun. Call me Sister Stone."

The young man was surprised that a nun should be living in a large estate house, but he was too cold and hungry for a conversation or for self-introduction.

"Sister Stone, my luggage bundle is still in the water," the man muttered through clenched teeth.

"Forget about your bundle. Let's get inside and warm up first."

Sister Stone led the way to the gate. The young man tried to follow her. However, his legs were too frozen to move easily on the slippery ground. He struggled and fell on the icy ground with a thud.

Sister Stone turned around and saw the young man floundering awkwardly on the frozen ground. She laughed, put her hands under his arms and dragged him toward the gate.

"My, you are strong," the man muttered. He was embarrassed that he was being pulled along by a nun, but at the same time was appreciative of the sister's manly strength.

At the gate, they looked back at the wolves. They were still standing on the bank, as if they could not decide whether they should wait for him to resume his journey tomorrow.

"You have to strip off all you wet clothes," Sister Stone told the young man once they were inside the kitchen.

He fumbled with the buttons of his coat in an effort to take it off. But his fingers were still too numb, and they started to sore in the warmth of the room.

"I guess I have to do it for you," the nun laughed again. "You have a nice body," she complimented the young man as she ripped off his last undergarment.

The young man looked extremely embarrassed. He thought of telling the nun to leave him alone, but he decided against it because he thought it would be rude to say it to someone who had just saved his life.

"I will get something for you to wear," the sister announced after she had stared at his naked body for a while.

He relaxed.

Sister Stone returned in a few moments and gave him a blanket. "Sorry, I don't have any men's clothes here."

The young man wrapped the blanket around him.

Sister Stone spread his wet coat before the stove and reassured him, "We will get your baggage from the river tomorrow."

Relieved, the young man sat down by the fire and looked hungrily at the steaming pots on the stove.

"You haven't introduced yourself," Sister Stone grinned at her unexpected visitor.

"My name is Liu Mengmei," the young man answered apologetically. "I'm from Guangzhou, and I am on my way to Hangzhou for the royal examination."

"In this weather?" Sister Stone asked incredulously. A southerner simply did not appreciate the power of winter.

Glancing out of the window, Sister Stone saw it started to snow again. "No one travels in this weather, my southern friend," Sister Stone told the young man with unconcealed glee. "I'm afraid you'll have to keep me company here for a long time."

Chapter Seven

THE UNDERWORLD was a horrifying place. Every day after the bugle blew three times, guards would come into the prison with a list. They opened cell doors and dragged out people whose names were on the list. The prisoners who were dragged out beseeched, implored, and pleaded with the guards, but the stony-faced guards never let go of anyone.

Those dragged out of their cells were hauled into a cave painted blood red at one end of the corridor. Then from the cave would come blood-curdling screams that could last for hours. No one ever came back from the cave.

"Are we all going to end like that?" Liniang asked her next door neighbor one day, pointing at the cave.

"Pray we go to the other cave," the elderly woman pointed to a yellow stone gate on the other end of the corridor.

"What's the difference?"

"If you go through the yellow gate, you're going to live again."

"Live again?" Liniang asked incredulously.

"Yes," her neighbor nodded her head, her eyes filled with a glimmer of hope.

"As humans?" Liniang asked hopefully.

"As humans, or as animals, depending on the way you lived your last life."

"But I haven't seen anyone go through the yellow door. Everyone went to the red cave there."

"Pray, young lady, pray."

Liniang had spent almost three years in her cell praying. Then finally, one day, after the bugle blew three times, a guard with a list came to her door.

Fear and hope rose simultaneously in her.

"Let me go to the yellow cave," she prayed her last prayer and readied herself.

The yellow cave was very large. Candles flickered on many ledges, giving the cave a bright look compared with the gloom in the prison cells.

Judge Hu of the Tenth Circuit Court was a bony old man with a sparse beard. He had just come back from a very long vacation, but he was already depressed by the prospect of work.

"How much of a backlog do I have?" he asked his chief clerk impatiently.

"Your Honor," the chief clerk, a short man as bony as the judge, answered, "over the three years when you were away, our officers snatched four hundred fifteen sinners. I have already disposed of those sinners with a history of mortal transgressions."

"Very good," the judge nodded his head.

"Now we have one hundred fifty-six sinners left. Since they have committed only venial offenses, I am awaiting your decision as to what form of reincarnation to give them."

"One hundred fifty-six cases for me to decide?" the judge frowned. "I will handle four cases today."

The chief clerk thumbed through his file. "Of the first four prisoners, three are male and one female. The male prisoners have been making all sorts of protests in prison."

"Call the male prisoners," the judge ordered.

"Call the male prisoners," the clerk blew a bugle and repeated the judge's order.

From a narrow tunnel behind a protruding rock in the left of the courthouse came out two fiends, one with a horse-head and the other with a buffalo-head. They were followed by three totally naked prisoners. For a short moment, the candlelight dazed the prisoners, so they covered their eyes. When their eyes adjusted, they filed before the judge, and bowed.

"What's your name?" the judge asked the first prisoner.

"My name is Chang the Eldest."

"For what offense were you punished with death?"

"I was guilty of no offense, Your Honor," the prisoner protested.

"Why are you here then?"

"Ask them," Chang pointed at the fiends angrily. "They dragged me here for no reason."

"Your Honor," the horse-headed fiend answered, "the prisoner was fond of drinking. Three years ago, at his fiftieth birthday, I saw him totally drunk and collapsed on the floor, but he was still demanding more wine. So I choked him and brought him here."

"Is that right, Chang the Eldest?" the judge asked.

"Yes," the man answered. "I begged the ugly creature to at least let me finish the drink, but he was rude and impatient."

"Stand aside," the judge ordered. He then turned to the second prisoner. "What was your offense?"

"My name is Ling the Handsome," the second prisoner answered. "I committed no offense."

The judge turned to the fiends. The buffalo-headed fiend stepped forward.

"This young prisoner liked to indulge himself in the local brothel," the fiend began. "Three years ago, after he finished with one prostitute, he started with a second one called 'the Powdered Bosom.' So I kicked him in the loins and dragged him here."

"You evil creature," the young prisoner cursed at the fiend. "You made me crush onto the most delicate sister in the brothel, crushing I don't know how many delicate ribs of hers."

"Stand aside," the judge ordered the young man and turned to the last male prisoner.

"My name is Wang the Monkey," the prisoner volunteered. "I was guilty of an offense."

"What was that?" the judge asked.

"I practiced sodomy."

"Your Honor, even in his dark prison cell, he's been ogling Ling the Handsome all the time," the chief clerk added.

"Let the prisoners hear the verdict," the judge stared at the prisoners for a few minutes and announced.

"Kneel," the chief clerk shouted at the three men.

They knelt.

"I found all of you guilty of behavior detrimental to the good order and morality of society."

The three men started to cry.

"Our officers were justified in terminating your lives as humans," he further announced.

The crying became louder and angrier.

"I sentence you to be reborn as flying creatures," the judge pronounced.

"Oh, no, we want to be humans, not flying creatures." The three naked men started to run amok in the courtroom, yelling and cursing, until they were subdued by the fiends.

Ignoring the prisoners, the judge continued his sentence. "Since Chang the Eldest likes to drink, he shall be an oriole. Since Ling the Handsome spent his money on prostitutes, he shall be a butterfly..."

Wang the Monkey, kowtowing, begged the judge, "Let me be a butterfly too, so I can be with Ling the Handsome."

"You are the sodomite," the judge answered. "You should be a bee and have a sting in your backside."

"Oh, my dear, what can I do with a sting?" Wang the Monkey wailed.

"Thank His Honor, and off with you now," the chief clerk yelled.

"Please, Your Honor, let me become a butterfly," Wang the Monkey pleaded. "If you make me into a bee, I'll come back here and sting your big and bony head."

"That's enough. Off with you all. Fly away, quick!" The judge banged his gavel three times.

The prisoners instantly froze and metamorphosed one by one into an oriole, a butterfly, and a bee. They circled the courtroom several time and finally flew away into a dark crevice.

"What is the female prisoner charged with?" the judge asked the chief clerk after the flying creatures were all gone.

"She is charged with free love."

"Call the female prisoner," the judge ordered.

Liniang came into the court. One hand covering her breasts and the other hand covering her lower belly, she looked mortified. But at the same time, she was happy that she had gone through the yellow gate and finally had a chance at reclaiming her human life.

"Oh, my heaven, what an unearthly beauty," the judge grabbed the candle on his table and shone it on Liniang. His eyes transfixed on her.

Embarrassed, Liniang lowered her head, "Your Honor, please."

"I am sorry, your prettiness. I couldn't help myself," he apologized to Liniang.

The chief clerk, seeing his boss's interest, whispered in his ear. "If you like her, sir, why don't you keep her as your concubine?"

"Be my matchmaker," the judge told the chief clerk, his eyes still on Liniang.

The clerk drew Liniang aside and whispered, "Congratulations, young lady. The judge wants you to be his concubine."

Liniang lowered her head, "I'm flattered, but I can't."

"You refuse to accept his proposal?" the chief clerk was surprised. He could not imagine why a prisoner whose fate depended on the good will of the judge would flatly refuse such an opportunity.

"Yes, sir. I'm sorry."

"Don't be stupid, young lady," the clerk admonished Liniang. Then he lowered his voice further. "If I were you, I would live with the old man for a few years. When he got bored with me, I would then ask the old man to give back my human life. I'm giving you this advice because I like you, young lady."

"Thank you very much, sir, but I can't."

"You can't refuse him," the clerk was annoyed by Liniang's stubbornness. "He can burn you, he can slice you, he can hammer you, he can grind you, or he can turn you into the lowest life form."

"Please don't do it to me," Liniang begged.

"Then be his concubine."

"I can't," Liniang again shook her head.

The chief clerk turned to the judge, "Sir, maybe I should take the young lady on a tour of the red cave."

"Why can't you be my concubine, my prettiness?" the judge asked Liniang. He looked deeply hurt. "Am I too old?"

The judge's hair was completely white, his face was deeply wrinkled, and his head shook sideways as he spoke. To Liniang, he looked at least in his eighties. But Liniang was too clever to speak her mind. "No, you look young to me."

"Am I too ugly?"

"No, Your Honor. You are very attractive."

"Then why can't you accept my proposal?"

"I am in love, Your Honor."

"In love? With whom?"

"With a man I met in my back garden. He was very affectionate and loving."

"Did your parents approve of him?"

"My parents did not know of it."

"You had a liaison with a man before the holy ceremony of marriage and without the consent of your parents—this is free love, a very serious offense, my prettiness," the judge said sternly.

"Your Honor, all that happened in a dream," Liniang pleaded.

"In a dream?" The judge turned to his chief clerk. "Don't tell me our officers are snatching up pretty young girls just because they had an amorous dream?"

"What was your justification?" the clerk turned to the horse-headed fiend that was standing beside him.

"Your Honor," the fiend answered, "this young lady had a dream in the garden, which was morally repugnant but not a criminal offense. However, after the dream, she pined away, visiting the garden everyday, rain or shine. That surely was a flagrant disregard of maidenly virtues."

The judge nodded his head. "Although you are not guilty of free love as charged," he told Liniang, "you are guilty of self-indulgence. Accept my proposal, or I'll have to turn you into a flying creature."

"Please give back my life," Liniang pleaded with the judge, "and let me wait for him in my garden."

"Wait for him in your garden?" the judge laughed hilariously. "What makes you think that the man you dreamed of in your garden dream will reappear in your garden?"

"He asked me to wait, and I believe him."

"You are crazy, my prettiness," the judge told Liniang.

"Crazy or not, please give me a chance," Liniang begged the judge with tears in her eyes.

The judge hesitated. He knew it was a ridiculous idea, but he hated to disappoint a pretty and earnest girl who had just told him that he looked young and attractive.

"Please give back my life."

"May I remind Your Honor of a tradition here?" Irked at the female prisoner's disregard for his advice, the clerk whispered to the judge. "Anyone who is guilty of self-indulgence, no matter how minor it is, cannot get his former life back. He has to be reincarnated into a lower life form."

"Shut up," the judge pushed his chief clerk away from him. "I am the judge and I decide as I see fit."

"Of course, Your Honor," the chief clerk retreated, his face red with embarrassment.

"Well, my beauty, I shall give you a chance on one condition," the judge told Liniang.

"What is it, Your Honor?"

"Your spirit will have one year to roam freely in your former residence and the attached garden. If, during the time period, you meet the man of your dream and you two unite in holy matrimony, I shall let your spirit return to your body. If not, you have to willingly and happily become my concubine."

Liniang wavered. She was not sure whether the man in her dream would ever appear again, but the judge's offer seemed to be her only opportunity.

"What do you say?" the judge urged her.

"I accept your proposal," Liniang told the judge.

"Very good."

"Kneel," the clerk yelled at Liniang, sore that she got a better deal than the one he had brokered.

Liniang knelt and thanked the judge for his generosity.

"Get up, young beauty. I like it better when you are standing." As if it were only an afterthought, the judge added, "By the way, every morning when roosters crow, you must come here to report to this court on your progress."

"Can I put on something when I come to report?" Liniang asked bashfully.

"A spirit has no worldly possession, at least not in this court," Judge Hu gazed at Liniang for a few seconds and burst into a hearty laughter.

"Treat this wandering spirit well and make sure that her body remains intact and fresh in the grave," the judge ordered his chief clerk. "Remember she will be my favorite concubine in one year."

After Liniang agreed to his condition, Judge Hu allowed her to wait in a guest cave adjacent to his court for the nightfall.

The guest cave was as dark and damp as her prison cell, but there at least she could stand up and pace the floor, something she could never do in her little prison cave. Besides, it was a quiet place. She heard no terrified wailing of pain from tortured inmates.

But time ticked by very slowly, more slowly than in her prison cell. From time to time, she asked a thin and tall guard in a bright red uniform, who squatted by the door because the roof was not high enough for him, what time it was. The guard would shake his head, without an answer or a word of explanation.

After a long time, she heard a bugle blowing, one, two, three, four, five times. Suddenly, the court was filled with noise. Grotesque creatures of all shapes and sizes appeared from nooks and crannies she had not known existed. They greeted one another, bickered over work assignments, and laughed over jokes Liniang did not understand.

"What disgusting creatures," Liniang couldn't help but exclaim.

"Shh, young lady," the guard, who had not spoken for the whole day, unexpectedly told Liniang. "Unfavorable descriptions of officers on duty are a misdemeanor punishable with thirty days in jail."

Liniang had enough of the jail in the underworld. She didn't want any more of it. "When I say *disgusting*, I actually meant *lovely*," she corrected herself hastily.

"Flattering officers is also a misdemeanor," the guard told her curtly.

"I am sorry. I'll just shut up," Liniang apologized.

"All day long, you wanted to leave. Now that it is time for you to leave, you want to talk. Do you know I have a wife and two kids who are waiting for me at the dinner table?" the guard grumbled.

"I am sorry. I didn't mean to delay you."

The guard impatiently brushed off her apologies. "Here is your passport. Remember to come back after the first cockcrow." Quickly taking off his bright red uniform, he rushed off into one of the numerous tunnels that connected the courtroom with other parts of the underworld.

Liniang looked at her passport and suddenly wondered how she was supposed to leave the underworld and get back to her house. Holding her passport tightly, she walked out of the guest cave nervously. There was no one to ask except the ugly-looking fiends.

"Excuse me, officers," she asked nervously.

The creatures ignored her. They carried on their conversations as if they had not seen her or heard her.

Liniang rushed along the edges of the cave that housed the courthouse. There were at least a dozen tunnels. None of them was marked, and all of them were dark and unfathomable.

Liniang was desperate. She wanted to get out of the underworld immediately and did not want to wait for the judge until tomorrow.

Then she saw the fiends lining up at one of the larger tunnels and crawling into it one by one. She waited patiently until all of them were out of the courthouse. Then she followed them.

The tunnel was narrow and dark. But the fiends seemed to be very familiar with the terrain, and Liniang soon lost track of them. Without their noise to lead the way, Liniang had to pick her way very carefully with her hands.

Finally, Liniang saw a dim light coming into the tunnel. As she crawled closer to the light, she saw a dark blue night sky studded with stars. The tunnel ended in the middle of a vertical cliff. Holding tightly onto a rock, Liniang looked down into the valley beneath the cliff. Everything was cloaked in darkness and silence. Only ominous shadows of bats seemed to exist in this valley. Liniang almost fainted.

"How can I get out of here?" Liniang sat down at the edge of the opening, frustrated.

Suddenly, a strong wind blew up from inside the tunnel. The current rushed out toward the night sky, blowing dirt and pebbles with it. Liniang held tightly to the rock. But the wind grew stronger, and Liniang felt that she was losing grip of the rock. Finally, a violent gust wrestled Liniang out of the tunnel and into the air.

"Help!" Liniang yelled.

The current seemed to have come out of the tunnel with her. As she tumbled down through the thin air, she suddenly hit the soft cushions of the gust. It surged below her and buoyed her up. She started to fly effortlessly toward the direction where the moon was.

The journey did not take long. Before Liniang had time to figure out what was happening, she saw the city of Nan'an, the hill, the river, the estate house, and the back garden.

"I'm home," she cried happily.

Soon, she found herself hovering over the clearing amid the plum trees in the back garden where the willow man had taken her. Before she died, she had asked her mother to bury her here. Now she could see a marble tombstone shining in the moonlight.

It was a night with a bright moon and a gentle breeze. A sweet scent of incense drifted up from her grave and two human forms were praying in front of it amid candles of light and among overgrown grass and bushes.

"They must be my mother and Fragrance, my maid," Liniang told herself.

Hovering closer, however, Liniang recognized the older woman as her mother's friend, Sister Stone, who had come to the estate on the day of her death to burn a pyramid of willow trees. Beside Sister Stone was a young and slender woman, who was also in a Taoist garb, but Liniang could not recognize who she was.

Liniang was disappointed that the two women were not her mother and Fragrance, but she was nonetheless grateful to Sister Stone and her companion.

"Hello, sisters," Liniang alighted on her tombstone and greeted them.

The two women did not seem to see her or hear her; they continued to pray.

"I'm a spirit, and I'm invisible to mortal eyes," Liniang suddenly realized.

Liniang flew to the pavilion. Its floor was covered with layers of leaves and one side of its roof had collapsed, but the peony shrubs that surrounded the pavilion were growing as healthily as ever. She picked several leaves and flew back to her grave. There she scattered a few leaves onto the two kneeling women.

The descending leaves surprised the nuns. Looking up and around, the young woman asked Sister Stone, "How did the peony leaves come here in a gentle breeze?"

"I don't know, Sister Shy," Sister Stone answered in bewilderment. "I have been taking care of the grave since Madam Du left for Yangzhou, but I have never seen this happen."

Liniang now knew why her mother was not at her grave. "Thank you, sisters," she threw the rest of the leaves onto the nuns.

The two women were silent for a moment. Then the young nun said, "Liniang's spirit must be present today and she must be showing her appreciation."

"Yes," Liniang answered, and she flew to the pavilion again, picked a few more leaves, and dropped them over the two nuns.

As the third wave of leaves fluttered down, the two women looked up in wonder, their faces pious and devout.

Liniang was happy that on her first night out of the underworld, she was able to witness such respect for her. She was also happy that she was able to communicate her presence to the two good nuns.

"I need to get my self-portrait," she suddenly remembered.

Flying to the main house, she saw the oak door padlocked and all the windows closed.

"I am a spirit now," Liniang told herself. "I must be able to walk into the house even if it is locked."

Anyway, was that what all the ghost stories she had heard said? A ghost should be able to walk into any house. Assuring herself, Liniang took a few steps back, eyed the door intently and rushed at it.

Uncertain of the truthfulness of the ghost stories, Liniang expected a painful collision. But there was no collision. Instead, she flew through the door as painlessly and effortlessly as she flew through the air. Besides, although the center hall was pitch dark, she could see everything clearly as if she had an owl's vision.

Liniang hurried into her own apartment. She went through all the rooms. They were all dark and empty, void of any human presence. All she smelled was the stale smells of past years. There were no more scents of shrubs, flowers, and herbs that Fragrance had been so fond of.

She opened the chest of drawers in her bedroom. In the top drawer, she saw the rosewood box. Opening the box and unrolling the scroll, she saw her self-portrait smiling at her. Liniang wiped a tear off her face and smiled back at the portrait.

Chapter Eight

AFTER HE fell into the icy water in front of Du's estate in the depth of winter, Liu Mengmei caught a bad cold. But he had a strong constitution, and Sister Stone took good care of him. She fed him rice, vegetables, and salted fish. He soon recovered.

"Thank you for your hospitality," Liu thanked Sister Stone. "I must leave for Hangzhou now."

"Wait until spring," Sister Stone told the young man. "You don't want to meet with the wolves again. They are getting hungrier by the day."

Liu Mengmei hesitated. He had been leery of Sister Stone's intentions at first. She had stared at him for too long and had made comments too off color for a nun. But as time went by, his suspicion dissipated, and he started to like the nun as well.

"I need to go to Hangzhou early to prepare for the exam," Liu explained.

"There is a large library in the west house."

Liu followed Sister Stone as she unlocked the door to the library. Surprised by the large collection of books in the library, Liu smiled and agreed to stay on.

Liu spent days and nights in the library, going through the classics Du Bao had left behind. He had always loved books. He had even loved the school where everyone made fun of him because of his torn clothes and his sweaty smell.

Time passed quickly, and spring soon arrived. Winds mellowed, snow melted, and colors came back to earth. Visitors started to come to the estate. Chen the Most Virtuous paid a visit. The head farmer came to see Sister Stone as well. Both of them said hello to Liu Mengmei and chatted with him amicably.

When they were alone with Sister Stone, they winked in the direction of the west house and shook their heads.

"You are a nun," Chen the Most Virtuous told her.

"Don't have any dirty thoughts," Sister Stone replied. "He's just a scholar preparing for the big exam, and he has nowhere to go."

A few days after Chen's visit, a traveling nun from West China came to stay at the estate for several days. Her name was Sister Shy. She was a diminutive woman, young and attractive.

The first night of her arrival, she went with Sister Stone to the back garden to pay respects to Liniang's grave and witnessed the showering of peony leaves. She was awed.

As soon as he saw the young nun, Liu Mengmei lost his interest in the books. He became listless and enervated. The young nun seemed to have stirred up an indescribable yearning in him.

"I felt strangely restless," he confided to Sister Stone one evening after dinner when the young nun had gone back to her bedroom.

Sister Stone smiled with a hint of jealousy. She knew what was torturing the young man. "It's time you were on your way," the sister replied.

For some reason, Liu Mengmei did not want to leave although the roads were clear for travel after the winter. Subconsciously, he felt that there was something he was destined to do but had not done yet.

"The exam is still more than a month away, and I have a few more books to finish here," he told Sister Stone.

"When I see you sigh and stretch a thousand times a day," Sister Stone continued, "I know you shouldn't be staying here anymore."

"I think I must be reading too much in the library. I will take a walk now."

Sister Stone really did not mind the young man staying a few more days. She wouldn't mind even if he decided to stay for another year. She would get him to work around the house and in the garden.

"Don't be long. It's getting dark."

Liu had walked in the garden many times in daytime, but it was his first time to visit the garden after dusk.

Liu was familiar with the pond, the woods, and the hill, but the moonlight gave these familiar scenes a not-so-familiar face. Shrouded in a mist of darkness, they became mysterious and ancient. Liu felt strangely exhilarated.

Liu first went to the grave in the plum woods. It was a lonely sight at night. Sister Stone had told him that Madam Du had invited her to the estate to take care of her daughter's grave. Sister Stone, however, had never told him how Liniang had died. Liu felt sad and said a few prayers for the young girl's soul.

Liu then walked around the pond. Some parts of the pebble path were overgrown with shrubs and brambles, and the pond was filled with dead leaves.

"I will come here tomorrow to clear the path," Liu told himself.

Then, in the moonlight, he noticed a shiny rectangular-shaped object on the marble table in the center of the pavilion.

Curious, he walked to the pavilion. The rectangular shape turned out to be a rosewood box, carved with intricate patterns.

"Who has left this precious thing here?" he looked around.

There was no one around.

He opened the rosewood box. Inside the box, there was a rolled-up scroll. Carefully, he rolled it open. When he saw what was on the scroll, his heart almost missed a beat: a beautiful girl was looking at him from the scroll, smiling. Liu looked closely at the scroll in the moonlight. No, he was not dreaming. Her lips were moving as if she wanted to murmur something to him, and her eyes were moving as well, shyly, but full of tenderness.

On the margin of the scroll, there were three simple words, "To My Love."

"Who is this girl? Who is her love? Who has left the portrait here? Why?" Liu wondered.

Liu looked around him again. There was no one. He circled around the pond. There was no one. He looked into the dark plum and willow groves. There was no one.

He came back to the pavilion and gazed at the girl on the scroll again. He knew the right thing to do was to leave the box where it was, but he did not want to do the right thing. Instead, he put the scroll back into the rosewood box, hid the box inside his robe, and hurried back toward the estate.

It was already very late, and there was no light in the kitchen. Not wanting to wake up Sister Stone or Sister Shy, Liu scurried directly to his room in the west house.

Sister Stone, however, was not asleep. Hearing his steps, she opened her door with a lantern in her hand. "What happened? Why did you come back so late?" she asked in a worried voice.

"I was enjoying the view in the moonlight," Liu muttered. He did not want Sister Stone to know what he had discovered in the pavilion.

Sister Stone was suspicious. Walking across the courtyard, she shone the lantern on him.

Hurriedly, Liu opened the door and stepped into the west house. "Good night, Sister Stone."

"What is it that is bulging inside your robe?" Sister Stone asked.

"Don't joke, sister," Liu laughed nervously. "I don't have a bulge anywhere inside my robe." Then he said good night and closed the door.

It was the fifth night Liniang spent at the pavilion.

The first night she was out of the underworld, Liniang had swept clean the pavilion floor and placed the rosewood box on the marble table. Then she waited.

Sometimes, bats flew into the open rafters and took a break. Other times, mice scampered by quickly in their search for food. In the pond, frogs crackled for mates. In the grass, light bugs congregated. It was lonely to spend the nights with only the animals.

No one came to the pavilion during Liniang's vigil. Likewise, no one seemed to have come to the pavilion during the daytime. Every night, when Liniang came to the pavilion from the underworld, the rosewood box remained untouched and unclaimed.

Perhaps, as the judge had told her, she was silly. It was only a dream. Could a dream be true? Would her love come after three years? Or had he already come and left during her imprisonment in the underworld?

Maybe she should go back to Judge Hu and tell him to turn her into an oriole. An oriole at least could date and love. But she knew she couldn't change her mind now since she had already agreed to be the judge's concubine if her love did not come to the garden.

On her fifth night, Liniang felt dispirited and tired. Perching on a rafter, she soon closed her eyes and fell asleep. She didn't know for how long she slept. When she woke up, she suddenly noticed that the box was no longer on the table. Who could have taken it? Liniang looked around in the darkness.

Could it be the willow man she had been waiting for? Liniang's heart pounded. Expectantly, she flew over to the willow woods, combed through it several times, but there was not a shadow of a man there.

It must be Sister Stone, Liniang realized with some disappointment. Several nights ago, Liniang had seen her and her companion praying at her tomb. She could have come again earlier tonight. After praying at the grave, she might have taken a walk along the pond, and passing the pavilion and seeing the rosewood box, she might have taken it back to her room.

Liniang flew to the estate house immediately. She wanted to get her box back and return it to the pavilion. She did not know where Sister Stone slept, but of all the rooms, only the one in the west house had a flicker of a candle light reflected on its window screens.

Liniang could fly into the room, but she wanted to make sure that the portrait was there before she took any action, so she poked a hole in the paper screen and peeped.

Her portrait hung on a wall, and the opened box lay on the bedside table. Sister Stone was already asleep, a large blanket covering her head and toes, but the candle had not been put out, its light shining on the portrait.

Liniang knew Sister Stone would be very alarmed when she saw the scroll gone tomorrow morning, but Liniang had to retrieve the scroll and bring it back to the pavilion. "Sorry, Sister," Liniang said apologetically and was ready to fly into the room.

Sister Stone tossed in her bed and turned her face toward the window. The blanket slipped off the bed.

To Liniang's great surprise, the face she saw did not belong to Sister Stone, but to a man, a young man with a stubble of a beard and a mop of rumpled hair. Liniang almost fell off the window.

Liniang's face reddened. She had no business peeping at a man in his sleep, one voice told her. But another voice countered. This was her house, her portrait, and she had all the right to investigate.

The second voice won. Liniang peeped through the hole again. The young man tossed again in his bed and started to talk. The voice was indistinct at first. Then it became clearer. "My young lady, my young lady, please come and join me." He opened his eyes and gazed at her portrait on the wall as if mesmerized.

"He is calling for me," Liniang's heart pounded faster. "Is he the man I have been waiting for in the past three years?" She prayed that he were.

Liniang hurried to the main house, flew into her bedroom, and chose a silk embroidered dress from her wardrobe. Taking on her physical form and standing before a mirror, she combed her shiny black hair into a pigtail. She was happy to see that she was as pretty and as fresh as three years ago.

She flew back to the west house and gently tapped the window and peeped through the hole.

The young man was surprised by the knocks. He jumped out of the bed, hurriedly put the portrait back into the box and hid the box under his bed.

"Is it someone out there?" he asked.

"Someone is out here," Liniang answered, her face reddening.

"Is it Sister Stone?"

"No, I'm not Sister Stone."

"Is it Sister Shy?"

"No, I'm not Sister Shy either."

"Who are you then?" Liu sounded perplexed.

"Open the window. Then you will see who I am."

Liu opened the window. As soon as he saw Liniang, he was dumbfounded. He had never seen a girl as beautiful before, and he had never expected a girl to appear at his window, uninvited, in the middle of the night.

"Who are you?" Liu stuttered.

"You must guess, young sir," the young lady answered in a playful and flirtatious voice.

"Can you be a goddess having some fun on earth?"

"No," she shook her head, smiling.

"Are you a young maiden mistaking me for some hero of romance?"

"No," she shook her head again. "Are you going to invite me in, young sir?"

Liu's heart raced, and sweat broke out on his forehead.

Without waiting for an answer, Liniang lithely jumped over the window into the room. Folding her hands and bowing, Liniang greeted Liu, "Blessing on you, young sir."

Liniang's effortless vault into the room and her unearthly beauty in the candlelight surprised Liu even more. He was speechless for a long time. Liniang smiled shyly, but she did not say anything.

Finally, Liu composed himself and managed to ask stiffly, "May I ask where you come from and what cause brings you here in the middle of night?"

"Sir, I never saw you before in this house. Can I ask you some questions first?"

"Sure," Liu answered.

"Who are you? Where are you from? Why are you here?"

"My family name is Liu."

"Liu meaning *Willow*?" Liniang asked eagerly.

"Yes, my young lady." Liu continued, "My first name is Mengmei."

"Mengmei meaning *Dream* and *Plum*?"

"Correct."

"Willow, dream, and plum," Liniang went over the three words slowly and tenderly, and her eyes filled up with tears.

"Are you okay, young lady?" Liu was surprised that his name was able to inspire so much emotion in a total stranger.

"Yes, I'm just feeling very happy," Liniang gazed at the young man, wiped the tears from her eyes, and smiled joyfully.

Just a few moments ago, she had doubted whether she had placed too much faith in her dream. Now, standing before her very eyes was the man she had dreamed. He was tall, he was strong, and he was handsome. The only difference was that he was not dressed in willows, but he did have "willow" as his last name.

"You must be the man I have been waiting for."

"You must be the man I have been waiting for."

"Why have you been waiting for me, young lady?" Liu was puzzled.

"It is a long story, young sir. I beg you to finish your story first."

"I am from Guangzhou, and I was a student of the local academy."

"You are a scholar as well," Liniang was impressed.

"Last winter, I was on my way to the capital for the national examination. Unfortunately, I fell into the river in front of this estate and became ill. Sister Stone saved me and restored me to health. I should have been on my way days ago now that I am recovered and the roads are fit for travel. However, I feel there is something I need to do here before I can leave."

"What is it you need to do?"

"I don't know," the young man pondered for a while. "It is just a mysterious feeling."

"Can it be meeting me?" Liniang beamed, sure that it was.

Liu's mind wandered. He thought about his dead parents, his life on his uncle's farm, Inspector Miao, and his journey to Hangzhou. All of a sudden, he remembered his dream under the willow tree. He had started the trip because he had met a girl in the dream and had wanted to find her. Could the girl in front of him be the girl he had dreamed of?

"Young lady," Liu's voice trembled and his heart pounded, "I had a dream three years ago. Did you have a dream as well?"

"Yes, I did," Liniang's voice quivered.

"Did you ... make love to a man under plum trees?"

"Under the plum trees in the back garden," Liniang blushed deeply.

"You are the girl I dreamed of!" Overcome with emotion, Liu impulsively grabbed Liniang into his arms and embraced her tightly.

"I have been waiting for you for three years," Liniang sobbed in Liu's arms.

Liu looked into Liniang's eyes. They were full of mystery, passion, and happiness.

"I love you," Liu tenderly whispered to Liniang.

"I love you too, young sir."

They kissed and embraced. The candlelight went off.

Sister Stone woke up in the middle of the night. As was her custom, she got out her bed, knelt on the floor, bid good-bye to the departing old day and welcomed the arriving new day. She was about to go back to her bed when she noticed that Liu's window in the west house was wide open.

Sister Stone lived in a room in the east house, next to the kitchen. She had put Liu Mengmei up in an apartment in the west house across the courtyard.

It's strange, Sister Stone thought. Liu never slept with his window open at night.

Sister Stone opened her door and walked across the courtyard. She wanted to close the window for him. It was not safe to leave the window open.

To her surprise, a female voice came out of Liu's room, a young and happy voice mingled with Liu's low and masculine southern accent. The girl must have climbed over the window into Liu's room and have forgotten to close it. Indignant and dumbfounded, she stood in the middle of the courtyard for a few minutes, not knowing what to do.

Sister Stone finally went back to her own room and sat down at her window. She wanted to see who it was when the woman came out. She waited for a long time and fell asleep before she saw anyone.

When she woke up in the morning, Sister Stone went to the kitchen, waiting for Sister Shy. She wanted to tell Sister Shy what had happened last night. Liu always slept late, but Sister

Shy got up as early as Sister Stone did since she came to the estate and the two of them always had breakfast together.

Sister Stone waited for a long time, but the young woman did not appear. Mystified, she went to the nun's room, which was in a corner in the east house facing the hedges and the fields. The door was closed. Sister Stone peeped through a crack in the door.

The young nun was awake, sitting in a chair. With her eyes staring at the ceiling, she looked enervated and possessed.

"What's wrong with her?" Sister Stone was worried.

Then she heard the young nun sing to herself:

> *I am pretty,*
> *I am fair,*
> *But I am passionless.*
> *Others yearn for man,*
> *While I search for eternal Essence,*
> *Free of canal desires and urges.*

Sister Stone became suspicious. Could it be Sister Shy who had visited Liu Mengmei in the middle of the night? She was young, she was attractive, and she had been acting a little too friendly toward the young man.

"I have to throw her out," Sister Stone decided. She was jealous, the nun admitted. But more importantly, she believed that it was wrong for a nun to violate her vow of celibacy and to have any relationship with a man.

Sister Stone knocked on the door. She wanted to confront the young nun and ask her to leave without making a big scene before Liu Mengmei got up.

Sister Shy opened the door. "Is it time for breakfast already, Sister Stone?" She looked as if she had just woken up from a dream.

"A good song, Sister Shy," Sister Stone greeted the young nun sarcastically, "but it seems that your pious search took you last night into the room occupied by Scholar Liu. Did you find essence or canal satisfaction?"

"Sister Stone, what are you talking about?" shocked by the accusation, the young nun stuttered.

"Don't pretend to be innocent," Sister Stone answered. "I heard your voice coming out of Scholar Liu's room last night."

Sister Shy's face reddened out of anger, but she controlled herself. "I am afraid you are wrong. I was sleeping in my room all night."

"Confess and desist."

"I have nothing to confess," Sister Shy lost her temper and fought back. "Yes, I am younger than you are; yes, I am prettier than you are, but I also have better control of myself."

"Now you turn around and slander me!" Sister Stone grew angry.

"Who brought him to this estate in the first place? Who allows him to stay here month after month?" Sister Shy had learned the story from Sister Stone, now she was using it as her weapon.

"Now are you accusing me of an affair with him?" Sister Stone stared at Sister Shy, irate and menacing. "Before you came, the young man spent the day on some silly classics and slept away the night without a sound. Now he came back from the garden in the dead of the night and had a noisy liaison after that. Who was he entertaining last night, if not you? I am hauling you off to the senior sister."

"You picked up some wandering vagabond, called him a scholar, and put him in the guest room for your pleasure. Now you dare to go to your senior sister."

Sister Stone rushed at Sister Shy, and the two women started to grapple with each other.

Just at that point, the two women heard a hearty laughter. Stopping the fight, they saw Chen the Most Virtuous at the door.

He was banging his head on the wall and laughing his head off. "What's this, two pious nuns competing for the favor of a young scholar?"

"Professor Chen, you don't understand," Sister Stone complained. "I saw Scholar Liu's window open in the middle of the night, and heard a noise between him and a female. In all good faith, I asked the young sister here why she was in Scholar Liu's room, but she started accusing me of keeping the young man in the guesthouse. I want her before the senior sister and want the affair investigated."

"I want the senior sister to clear my name and punish Sister Stone for keeping the young man in the name of charity," Sister Shy countered.

"You two nuns had better calm down," Chen the Most Virtuous stopped laughing. "If you go to the senior sister, you are going to ruin the reputation of this estate. Let's keep it in-house and I will see who between the two of you indulged your flesh last night."

The two women thought about it and agreed.

Chen the Most Virtuous started, "Sister Stone, how are you going to defend yourself?"

"My body is intact."

"How?" the man was curious. "Hadn't you been married before you became a nun?"

"Yes, but," Sister Stone hesitated.

"But what?"

"It's a long story," Sister Stone answered reluctantly.

"I always love a story," Chen urged Sister Stone enthusiastically. He sat down on a chair and motioned the two nuns to sit down as well.

Twenty-two years ago when Sister Stone was eighteen, her name was Blue Orchid, and she was a much sought-after maiden in a village just south of Madam Du's farm. She wasn't a beauty, but she was by no means ugly. The main reason why she was so popular in the village was her strength and farming skills. Many a farmer told their sons that if they married her, they would not only gain a wife, but also an able farmhand who did not need to be paid. Moreover, such a strong wife would definitely produce big and strong boys, raising the quality of the family line.

After much comparison, Blue Orchid's father accepted the marriage proposal of a young man next door. At their wedding banquet Blue Orchid's husband got drunk and could hardly stand on his legs. But he had not forgotten there was some important business to be done. Amid the cheers of his family and his friends, he hugged Blue Orchid and carried her into the marriage chamber.

"Wait," Blue Orchid told her husband.

"I can't wait anymore, my bride." Her husband threw her on the bed and took off everything he wore. He then started to rip at her dress.

"Wait," Blue Orchid pushed her husband away and pointed at the door.

The door was still open, and a crowd of young men had gathered at the door, watching and cheering.

Her husband pushed away the spectators and bolted the door.

Blue Orchid blew off the candlelight, and her husband started working. However, after a long time, he still couldn't have his way.

Wondering what was wrong, he lit the lantern, went down to look, and poked with his fingers. "My bride, the thing you've got here is hard," he exclaimed.

"My bridegroom," Blue Orchid told him, "the thing I've got there is chastity. It's all preserved for you, but don't think you can have it without hard work."

"You are right, my bride," he said. So he started working again. After a few more moments, he was panting away, but he just couldn't get through. In frustration, he left the marriage chamber for more drinks.

It was past midnight. Older folks of the village had already retired, but the young men were still at their tables in the dining hall, carousing and singing.

"Did you enjoy your wife?"

From the half-opened door, Blue Orchid could hear the young men drunkenly and lasciviously ask her husband.

Her husband did not answer.

"Did you not?" the young men clamored, more curious than before.

"She is hard down there," Blue Orchard heard her husband's disconsolate voice.

There was a long silence. The crowd seemed to be taking some time to digest the news. Then a man said in a low voice, "Perhaps we should go home now." The crowd quickly dispersed.

Her husband came into the marriage chamber again, sobbed a little, and fell into a drunken sleep.

Blue Orchid felt ashamed. Why should she expect her husband to keep an impenetrable bride? After all, people got married to have fun and babies. For a moment, she wondered if her husband's tool was good enough, but she quickly dismissed the thought and blamed it all on herself.

While her husband was snoring, Blue Orchid packed her clothing in a bag, slipped out of the chamber, and left the house. She did not go back to her parents' house next door because she did not want to humiliate them. Instead, she went to the Purple Light Convent in the Western Mountains.

The senior sister of the convent was surprised to see a new bride at her door early in the morning. After hearing her story, the sister agreed to take her in and renamed her as Sister Stone.

❀❀

"'Sister Stone,' what an appropriate name!" Chen the Most Virtuous burst out laughing. Sister Shy could not help laughing as well.

"Stop it!" Sister Stone yelled at him. "Now ask her."

Chen suppressed his laughter and turned to the younger nun. "Sister Shy, what do you say in your defense?"

The traveling nun blushed deeply. "I don't have any such story to tell."

Chen looked disappointed.

"But my body is intact."

Chen the Most Virtuous was amused. "Sisters, I think you two can check each other out." He winked at the two nuns. "It is really not my specialty unless you insist."

"You lascivious old man," the two women turned on him in unison.

Laughing wildly, the old man had to run for his life toward the stone gate.

Sister Shy sat by the window in the darkness. She couldn't fall asleep.

The crescent moon, bright and serene, was high in the sky. A cool and gentle breeze blew in through the window. But Sister Shy was still angry with Sister Stone for falsely accusing her of having a liaison with Scholar Liu.

Sure, she liked him. After all, he was handsome and very personable. He must be bored and lonely, spending many hours in the library. That was why she lingered here at Madam Du's estate longer than she had planned. She wanted to keep him company for as long as possible. But for Sister Stone to suggest that she would abandon her faith for a man, no matter how attractive he was, was an insult that deeply offended her.

The night wore on. The young nun closed the window and went to her bed. She still couldn't sleep, so she tossed and turned.

Then Sister Shy heard steps outside her room. Surprised, she sat up on her bed and listened intently. She heard a light tap on her door. Then another.

"Could it be Scholar Liu at the door?" the young nun suddenly wondered, and the thought startled her. She started to sweat. "Could it be that I visited Scholar Liu last night without my knowing it?" She had heard stories about people who wandered about in their dreams at night and who were unable to remember the outings the next morning. "Could it be that he is returning my visit tonight?" Her heart started to pound.

There came another tap. "What should I do?" Sister Shy got out of her bed.

"Well, I could definitely tell him whatever I did last night was not right and ask him to break it off. But what if he refuses and forces himself on me? Well, I guess I will not be sinning if I am forced into it." With that thought, Sister Shy tidied her crumpled sleeping gown, arranged her hair, and opened the door.

A dark figure pushed into her room and closed the door behind it.

"Please don't, I am a nun," Sister Shy pleaded, her voice trembling.

"I am Sister Stone," the dark figure whispered.

A wave of strong feelings swept over the young nun. First it was disappointment, then relief, then disgust with herself for fantasizing about Liu, and finally anger with Sister Stone for pursuing her so relentlessly.

"Why do you barge into my room in the middle of the night?" Sister Shy protested. "I don't have any man in my room."

"Quiet," Sister Stone put a hand over Sister Shy's mouth. "There is a girl in Scholar Liu's room now," she whispered to the young nun.

"It can't be me since I am here in my room," Sister Shy responded sarcastically.

"I'm sorry I wrongly accused you this morning," Sister Stone apologized to the young nun. "Now let's go and see who Scholar Liu is entertaining."

Sister Shy refused.

"Let's go," Sister Stone urged her.

"Why don't you go yourself? I am not interested."

"I can't go to a man's room alone. That's what the Book says. Please."

"All right," Sister Shy agreed reluctantly.

The two women tiptoed across the courtyard and to Liu's window. The room was dark, and the window was closed.

"Listen," Sister Stone whispered to Sister Shy.

Sister Shy affixed her ear on the window.

"What do you hear?"

"I do not hear any conversation, but I do hear moans and groans."

"Stay here," Sister Stone told Sister Shy. "Don't let anyone jump out of the window." Then she walked around to the door and knocked.

"Who's there?" Liu asked, his voice full of alarm.

"Sister Stone, bringing tea for you."

"In the middle of the night? My dear sister, I am already asleep."

"My young sir, are you sleeping with a guest?" Sister Stone asked.

"I don't have a guest," Liu protested.

"Young sir," Sister Shy joined in from the window, "we just want to meet your girl friend."

"I don't have a girl friend."

"Open the door then," Sister Stone became impatient.

There was some fumbling noise in the room. Then Liu opened the door slowly.

"Light the candle."

Liu lit the candle reluctantly.

With the window in her view, Sister Stone shouted to the young nun, "Now you come to the door as well."

Sister Shy ran over to the door, and the two nuns barged into the room, looking everywhere, under his bed, behind his screen, and inside his wardrobe. It was a small apartment, but there was no trace of any woman.

"This is strange. I did hear a female voice coming out from your room," Sister Stone told Liu, her face covered with doubts.

"You must be mistaken," the young man answered, his voice calm and his face relaxed now.

"I heard it as well," Sister Shy said.

"You must be mistaken as well, my young sister."

"This place must be haunted," the young nun turned to Sister Stone. "I'm leaving tomorrow morning."

Chapter Nine

A HEAVY rain was pouring down. Liu Mengmei, pacing in his room anxiously, peeked out of his window into the dark and ominous sky from time to time.

He knew his love would not come tonight. The weather was too bad, and the two nuns who had barged into his room last night must have frightened her. Still, deep in his heart, against all rational thoughts, Liu hoped that his love would come to visit him again.

At around midnight, as suddenly as it started, the rain stopped.

Liu Mengmei opened his door and stepped into the courtyard. Closing the door behind him, he walked across the courtyard toward Sister Stone's room. There was no light from the room, and the only noise he could hear was the occasional snoring.

After the heavy rain, the stifling heat had been swept away, and the air was fresh and invigorating. Liu breathed deeply, stretched, and gazed at the sky. The moon was shining amid thousands of stars. How fast the clouds had disappeared, Liu wondered, as fast as his love had disappeared last night when the two nuns rudely knocked on his door.

Liu went to the stone gate. He opened the creaking gate slowly and peeked out. The water in the river had risen almost to the banks, and it was rushing furiously toward the east. Frogs were calling to each other loudly, but otherwise the world was eerily quiet. As far as his eyes could see, there was not a single light from the farmhouses and not a single soul on the road from the city.

He closed the gate and went back to his room.

"Surprise," a female voice came from his wardrobe.

Liu Mengmei jumped up. Then he knew immediately it was the voice of his love. He quickly walked over to the wardrobe and pulled its door open. In the candlelight, he saw Liniang grinning at him.

Liu embraced her tightly, his hands caressing the delicate curvature of her slender waist.

"Let's close the window. I don't want Sister Stone and Sister Shy to hear us again," Liniang giggled.

"My love, I don't want you to be further distressed like last night."

"Are you going to kick out the two nuns?" Liniang joked.

"Sister Shy left in a hurry in the morning. But I can't kick Sister Stone out. She let me stay here in the first place," Liu explained earnestly.

"Sister Stone is an old friend of mine as well."

"I want to marry you so that we can love each other openly," Liu proposed.

"Thank you, young sir," Liniang's face beamed. She looked into Liu's eyes tenderly for a long while. Then she asked, "Don't you think you should get to know me better before making such a big decision?"

"You are right, my darling. Love has befuddled my mind. May I ask whose daughter you are?"

Liniang thought for a while. "Young sir, did you see me leave the room when the two nuns knocked last night?"

Liu shook his head. He recalled his panic when Sister Stone knocked on his door and his bewilderment when Liniang, after saying "See you tomorrow," inexplicably disappeared from the room.

"I am as light as a spirit, soundless and shadowless," Liniang explained. Though her tone was still playful, her face took on a more serious expression.

Blinded by love, Liu ignored the obvious hint. "I didn't know my darling is so airily spirited," he answered jokingly.

Amused by Liu's infatuation, Liniang kissed Liu on his lips. "I dare say this is not the only thing you don't know about me, young sir," she hinted again.

"I'm sure I'll get to know you better after our marriage."

"But I want you to know me better before you propose," Liniang insisted.

"All right, tell me about yourself."

"Where is the portrait from the pavilion, young sir?"

"The portrait?" Liu was a little embarrassed. He didn't want anyone to know that he had taken the portrait.

"I want you to take another look at the portrait."

Sheepishly, Liu fetched the rosewood box from under his bed.

Liniang opened the rosewood box, took out the portrait, and held it in front of her.

"Am I as pretty?"

Liu looked at the portrait, and then looked at Liniang. He was surprised. "Why, it is the very image of you."

"Yes, I am the girl in the portrait."

"Tell me your name, my darling."

"My name is Du Liniang."

"You mischievous girl," Liu laughed. "You are never serious. Du Liniang died three years ago."

"You're right. I died three years ago, and I am a spirit now."

"A spirit?" Liu repeated incredulously.

"Yes," Liniang answered calmly. "Do you want to know how I could leave the house freely when the two nuns came last night?"

"Sure," Liu nodded his head.

"Let me show you." Without any movement or any noise, Liniang suddenly disappeared from the room.

Liu was stunned, his eyes wide open and his mouth agape. With bewilderment, he looked around the room. There was not a trace of the girl he loved.

Then Liniang reappeared in the room. "Here I am," she greeted Liu almost playfully.

"You *are* a spirit," Liu backed toward the door, alarmed. Now many things made sense to him: her unearthly beauty, her appearance late at night out of nowhere and her apparent ease of entry and departure.

"Don't be alarmed, young sir," Liniang sat down on Liu's bed and motioned Liu to sit down on the chair.

Liu sat down on the edge of the chair, his eyes uncertain and fearful.

"Here is my story," Liniang started, her expression now serious. "Three springs ago, I met you in a dream at the pavilion and I fell in love with you."

"How did you die?"

"I waited for you day and night. I pined and wasted away. Then fiends took away my life for loving you without the knowledge and the consent of my parents."

"My poor girl," Liu stood up, hurried over to his bed, and held Liniang tightly in his arms.

"Judge Hu of the underworld took pity on me. He allowed my spirit to wait for you here, and you, as you promised three springs ago, finally came." Tears streaked down Liniang's cheeks as she looked up at Liu gratefully.

Liu tenderly licked the tears off Liniang's face. He was deeply moved. "My love," he answered, "I don't care whether you are a mortal or a spirit. From now on, we will live together forever."

Liniang cried joyfully and inconsolably in Liu's arms. After a long while, she raised her head and looked into Liu's eyes. "Are you sure you love me even though I'm a ghost?"

"My darling, ghost or not, you are the sweetest girl I have ever met. Do not doubt any more. I'll light some incense and I will give you my marital vows here and now."

Liu opened the door and went into the storage room across the courtyard in the east house. After a few moments, he came back with a small copper container with some dried, cut-up grass in it.

Liniang immediately recognized it as the apparatus her mother had used to keep away mosquitoes. Amused, she said, "Young sir, this grass is burned to keep away the mosquitoes, not to witness holy vows."

"I didn't want to wake up Sister Stone looking for the right incense. Besides, we do have a few mosquitoes in this room." As he said this, he swatted his hands against the insects buzzing around them.

Liniang laughed. Picking a stem of the grass, she lighted it on the candle.

Seating Liniang on the chair, Liu knelt on the floor and recited his vows:

> *Heaven and earth,*
> *Witness this union,*
> *Liu Mengmei, Liu Mengmei,*
> *Scholar from Guangzhou,*
> *Loves this maiden Du Liniang*
> *Who dies three years ago for love,*
> *And faithfully takes her for his wife.*
> *In life one room,*
> *In death one tomb;*
> *Should his heart betrays,*
> *Death burns him to ashes*
> *Just as it burns this incense.*

Liniang raised Liu from the floor and kissed him passion-ately. Then she said, "Judge Hu promised to give back my mortal life when we unite in matrimony. Now I can feel my cold bones in the grave warm up and take on a fleshly shape."

"You do?" Liu asked excitedly.

"Yes, my love. I can feel it, I can feel it," she repeated with increasing conviction and urgency.

"My love, I am going to the grave immediately. I will move the earth, open the coffin, and bring you back to life."

"Thank you, my love," Liniang embraced Liu fervently. "I am waiting for you in the grave." Then she disappeared in a wisp of air.

Liu Mengmei put on his robe and shoes. He opened his door and walked into the courtyard.

At that time, Sister Stone's door creaked open, and the nun appeared in the doorway, still in her sleeping gown.

"I hope you slept well, Sister Stone?" Liu hurriedly greeted her.

"How could I sleep well when you, my guest, entertained a lady friend in your room without my permission?" Sister Stone replied in an annoyed voice. "Tell me who was in your room."

Liu thought for a while. Then he told Sister Stone, "Come to my room. I want to show you something."

"You know I can't go into your room alone."

"Wait at my door then," Liu told Sister Stone and went into the room. He came out with Liniang's portrait.

"Liniang's portrait? Where did you get it?" Sister Stone asked suspiciously.

"Sister Stone, Liniang and I have spent a few nights together."

"Nonsense, Liniang died three years ago. I was at her bedside when she died, and I sang her memorial service when her body was buried in the back garden."

"To be more precise," Liu tried to explain, "it was her spirit I have been with."

"Her spirit?" The unusual occurrences in the past several days started to come together. Peony leaves fluttering down on her and Sister Shy, Liu's nocturnal outing in the back garden, the noise from Liu's room, and the uncanny disappearance of the girl when she and Sister Shy forced themselves into the room.

"Yes. Her spirit is more lovely and more loving than any girl I have seen in my life." Liu gazed at the portrait tenderly.

Following his gaze, Sister Stone saw Liniang smiling at her sweetly from the scroll. She smiled back at the portrait and said a prayer for her soul. Then she suddenly remembered that Liniang had dreamed of a willow man before her death.

As if he could read Sister Stone's mind, Liu told her, "I am the willow man in her dream."

"What uncanny coincidence!" Sister Stone exclaimed. The young man did have a last name that meant "willow."

"Sister Stone, Liniang is coming back to life," Liu announced.

Sister Stone gazed at him intently, as if searching for signs of madness. The young man looked haunted, his expression dogged and his eyes fervent.

"Liniang is coming back to life," Liu repeated, returning her gaze.

Grabbing Liu by the shoulders, Sister Stone shook him. "A dead person does not come back to life," she told him loudly.

"Liniang is coming back to life," Liu insisted, his eyes staring at the portrait.

"You are possessed by her spirit," Sister Stone concluded. She said a new prayer. "I have to burn the portrait to save you."

"No!" As if suddenly threatened with a catastrophe, Liu abruptly turned and walked into his room. He kissed the portrait on the lips, rolled it up, and put it back into the rosewood box. He placed the box inside the chest of his robe.

"I'm going to open up her grave," he told Sister Stone.

Sister Stone jumped up in disbelief. "Are you crazy? I won't let you do it."

Liu quickly walked toward the garden, ignoring Sister Stone.

Running after Liu, Sister Stone was desperate. "You are a scholar. You know the law prescribes death for anyone who opens a grave without good cause."

Turning back toward Sister Stone, Liu shouted passionately. "Liniang is coming back to life. She is kicking and she is yelling in her grave. Is this good cause?"

"She is not kicking, she is not yelling, she is a pile of bones." Sister Stone shouted back.

"You say she is a pile of bones, and I say she is struggling to get out. How can you convince me or I convince you without opening the grave?"

Sister Stone considered Liu for a long while. He looked obstinate and determined. She couldn't stop him now, she realized. She should get some help.

"Get a shovel and a spade from the storage room," she told Liu. Watching him disappear with the tools, she thanked heaven that Sister Shy had left the previous morning.

Dawn broke. Roosters started crowing, and birds started singing.

Liu had been working with his shovel at the grave for some time now. His robe hung on a tree branch. His back was covered with beads of sweat. And he had removed much of the soil that covered the coffin.

Suddenly, a loud order came from behind his back.

"Stop digging, you bold grave robber! Kneel or you are dead!"

Liu dropped the shovel and knelt on his knees. Sister Stone must have called the local authorities. The ignorant nun.

The man pushed him to the ground. "You are under arrest for desecrating a grave and for disturbing the dead," he told him.

He froze cold. Now he couldn't continue, Liniang surely would suffocate in the dark confines of the coffin. "Please, officer," he cried into the soil he had dug up.

"Stop it, Scabby Turtle."

The voice of Sister Stone came from amid the plum trees and her hurried steps ran toward them.

"Don't scare the poor young man. He is already crazy enough."

Liu Mengmei turned around, and saw a man of short stature dressed in a shabby overall, his face scarred by fights and roughened by weather.

"This is Scabby Turtle, my cousin and a professional grave digger," Sister Stone introduced.

Humiliated by his fright, Liu jumped up to his feet and rushed at the short man. Scabby Turtle jumped out of his reach agilely.

"And this is Scholar Liu," Sister Stone stopped an irate Liu. She looked at the disheveled grave site disapprovingly. "Scabby Turtle knows how not to make a mess," she told Liu.

Scabby Turtle greeted Liu contemptuously. "You call your-self a scholar, but you seem to be more stupid than I am."

"Scholar Liu is in love," Sister Stone tried to explain.

"With a corpse? There are many pretty women in Nan'an who are looking for scholarly husbands," he sneered.

"Stop it," Sister Stone snapped. "Start digging and show scholar Liu that a dead person does not come back to life."

"I don't know why I have to show him that a dead body does not come back to life. If I had time, I would rather show him that a rooster does not lay eggs. Besides, if the authorities get wind of this, we will all be digging our own graves."

"Don't tell me this is your first time opening up a grave, Scabby," Sister Stone threatened.

"For heaven's sake, I have opened graves for jewelry in the past, but I have never opened a grave for such a stupid reason," Scabby retorted.

"If there is any jewelry in the grave, you will get a part of it. I promise, Scabby," Sister Stone tried to mollify him.

"If you promise," Scabby answered resignedly. He picked up the spade and started digging with Liu.

Scabby Turtle was truly a professional. He dug fast, and he dug noiselessly. Soon, they reached the coffin. They pried out the nails and inched the heavy mahogany coffin lid to one side. While the lid was being moved, they saw a white silk sheet covering Liniang's body. Remarkably, after three years underground, the sheet showed not a trace of decay. It was still pure white without any stain.

Impatiently, Scabby ripped the sheet off.

The three of them stared at what lay beneath the sheet, eyes wide open and mouths agape.

Lying on her back, Liniang was in her full dress. Her hair was neatly combed and held back in a bun. Her eyes were closed, but her face had a radiant color, and she was breathing gently.

"My mother," Scabby exclaimed, "we don't have a body here. We have a sleeping beauty."

"It is a miracle," Sister Stone murmured in awe.

Liu simply looked at Liniang, mesmerized and speechless.

"Fancy a pretty girl sleeping alone in this cold place," Scabby continued. "I should have come to dig months earlier."

Liu pushed Scabby away and gently called, "Liniang, Liniang, wake up."

Without opening her eyes, Liniang slowly turned her head to Liu's side and coughed. A lump of silver, which was used as charm at the burial, came tumbling out of her mouth.

"This must weigh twenty *taels*," Scabby Turtle reached into the coffin, grabbed the silver, and deposited it into his pocket. "Scholar Liu, you keep the girl, and I keep the silver."

"Her eyes are moving," Sister Stone whispered in amazement.

Liniang rose from the coffin. Her eyelids flickered. Then for a second she opened her eyes.

"Why is it so bright?" Liniang asked faintly and closed her eyes.

Looking up, Liu realized that it was almost noon. The grave was in a clearing amid the plum trees, and the light was too much for Liniang who had slept in total darkness for the past three years. He took his robe off the tree and covered Liniang's face with it. Then he stretched and pulled Liniang into his arms. Struggling up the soil they had dug out, he carried her to the trunk of a big plum tree and laid her down on the soft grass.

"Liniang, Liniang," he took the robe off her face and called gently.

Liniang opened her eyes and then closed them again. Finally she got used to the light and looked at the three people at her side in bewilderment.

"Young mistress," Sister Stone greeted Liniang, "your mother asked me to be guardian of your grave and the estate. I am happy to see you come back to life."

"Thank you, Sister Stone," Liniang answered, her voice still a whisper. "It's good to see you again."

"I am Scabby Turtle, Sister Stone's cousin."

"It is nice to meet you, sir," Liniang greeted him.

"I specialize in putting bodies into graves and getting the jewelry out of them later," Scabby Turtle added, grinning.

"It must be an interesting profession," Liniang smiled.

Liniang rose from the coffin.

"And I got your body out of the grave today."

"My gratitude, sir."

Liniang then turned to Liu. "Your face is familiar, young sir."

"I am Liu Mengmei," Liu introduced himself. "Liu for willow, Meng for dream, and Mei for plum. Do you remember me?"

With the help of Sister Stone, Liniang sat up against the plum tree, but her memories were still clouded.

"Wait." Liu rushed off toward the grove of willow trees. He broke off a branch and curved it into a crown. Putting the crown around his neck, he asked, "Remember me?"

Liniang shook her head apologetically.

Liu pointed at the plum trees overshadowing them.

Liniang shook her head again.

Liu then knelt in front of Liniang and slowly recited his marriage vows:

> *Heaven and earth,*
> *Witness this union,*
> *Liu Mengmei, Liu Mengmei,*
> *Scholar from Guangzhou,*
> *Love this maiden,*
> *Who died three years for love,*
> *And faithfully takes her for his wife.*
> *In life one room,*
> *In death one tomb;*
> *Should his heart betrays,*
> *Death burns him to ashes*
> *Just as it burns this incense.*

As Liu recited, Liniang's eyes brightened. Past events floated back, first as unconnected episodes, then all the pieces slowly fitting into three years of her young life.

"My love," Liniang's eyes welled up with tears and she fell into Liu's arms, overcome with emotions.

Liu Mengmei carried Liniang to the estate. When he reached the courtyard, he headed directly toward the west house.

"Wait a minute, young man," Sister Stone shouted after him. "Bring young mistress into my room."

"Sister Stone, we are already married," Liu explained, "and we have slept for a few nights already."

"Young man, young mistress' wandering spirit slept with you for a few nights and married you, but now she is a living person. Please follow the tradition and ask her parents for permission first."

"But her parents are in Yangzhou," Liu protested.

"So what? If you want to marry her, you should be willing to travel even to the farthest corner of the earth."

"What if Governor Du refuses to accept my proposal?"

Sister Stone faltered. It was very likely that Governor Du would reject Liu's proposal. After all, Liu had no property, and he had not even passed the provincial examination.

"Sister Stone, since my parents are far away and since you are here as my guardian, could he ask you for permission?" Liniang asked.

"I am only the guardian of your tomb and the estate," Sister Stone hesitated.

"Please help us, Sister Stone. We love each other."

Sister Stone knew the two young people loved each other, but in the eyes of parents, love counted for very little. Governor Du had always insisted on his right to select a husband for her daughter according to the tradition, and he would take it as a great insult and a great loss of face if they married without at least his consent.

But sending Liu Mengmei to Yangzhou in all probability would be a futile attempt. Moreover, Sister Stone realized, Governor Du would never accept the story of Liniang's resurrection. He was too versed in the classical tradition of learning to consider it remotely possible. In fact, Sister Stone conceded, she herself would not have considered it possible if she had not witnessed the whole event.

"Please, Sister Stone," Liniang pleaded.

"All right," Sister Stone gave in.

The three of them walked into the reception hall in the west house. Sister Stone and Liniang sat down at the large table.

"Let's start," Liniang told Liu Mengmei.

Liu Mengmei knelt before Sister Stone.

"No," Liniang stopped him with a mischievous grin. "You start with me first."

"Of course, my love." Liu stood up, bowed to Liniang, and proposed. "My young lady, please marry me."

"Young sir, you are embarrassing me," Liniang answered, imitating in a singing voice a famous scene in a classic opera. "Ask my guardian. If she says yes, I'm all yours."

Liu knelt before Sister Stone, "Madam Guardian, please accept my marriage proposal."

"What do your parents do?" Sister Stone asked in an earnest voice.

"They are dead."

"Do you have property?"

"No."

"This is not good," Sister Stone blurted out.

"But I told Liniang that, and she said it did not matter," Liu protested.

"Listen, young man," Sister Stone reminded him sternly, "Young mistress does not decide; I decide. Have you passed the royal examination?"

"Not yet."

Sister Stone's face clouded. "Young mistress comes from a respectable family. She is not allowed to marry someone without a royal degree."

"What are you talking about, Sister Stone?" Liu was again exasperated.

"Madam Guardian, please," Liniang pleaded, kneeling in front of Sister Stone, "I love this young man. If you don't allow me to marry him, I'm going to kill myself."

"Oh, no, young mistress, what you say is not pious."

"I don't care," Liniang answered fervently. "I want to marry this young man, here and now."

"But he has no property, nor does he have a royal degree."

"I love him. Do you understand, Madam Guardian?"

"Love? Are you sure that's what you want?"

"Yes. I'm absolutely sure."

Turning to Liu, Sister Stone said, "You are a lucky man. Young mistress thinks love is more important than anything else. I think she is silly, but it so happens that I have a tender heart and I don't want to disappoint her. You can marry her."

"Thank you, my love. Thank you, Sister Stone." Liu stood up and happily took Liniang into his arms.

Chapter Ten

IT WAS morning. The narrow street was filled with venders and shoppers who bargained and bartered.

Chen the Most Virtuous sat at the high counter in his drug store, surveying the street scene. He looked well fed and contented.

A few kids and dogs came into his view. They romped about, making a great deal of noise.

"Look at the fat dogs," Chen shouted to his assistant in the back room. "No one bothers to trap them for meat."

"Time is good, sir," his assistant answered.

The assistant was a quiet, shy young man in his twenties. He sat on a wooden stool cutting dried herbs. He mixed them in a large porcelain bowl, measured them and wrapped them in small paper bags.

"Absolutely," Chen looked around his drug store and nodded his head in total agreement.

The walls of his store were freshly painted. So was his counter. A golden placard with the words "Learned Doctor" hung prominently in the center of the wall facing the street.

Chen the Most Virtuous had good reasons to be content. Since Liniang died three years ago, he had been Madam Du's bookkeeper for the estate. He authorized expenses, audited the sale of farm products, and collected rents from the head farmer. Chen spent a small part of the money from the farm on the maintenance of the governor's estate, putting the rest in safe keeping for Madam Du. He drew a good salary for his work.

Through his wise advertisement of his association with the former governor, Chen's drug store was prospering. He hired an assistant. Everyday, his assistant prepared medicines in the back room while he sat at the front counter, taking care of his clients.

As Chen sat at his high counter, pleased with the happy turn his life had taken, he saw a woman come into the street. She carried a bamboo pole on her shoulder, two bamboo baskets hanging from both ends of the pole.

Although the woman was not wearing her black Taoist robe, Chen immediately recognized her as Sister Stone.

"What can I do for you?" Chen greeted her.

"Do you have any tonic to improve a person's general well being?"

Chen scrutinized Sister Stone. He was not sure whether she was serious.

"I need a tonic," Sister Stone told him again.

Seeing that the nun was serious, Chen became animated. "Of course, I do. I have secret prescriptions handed down from my grandfather." Chen loved to tell anyone who was willing to listen about the efficacy and the potency of his family prescriptions. "Is it for you, sister?" he asked.

Sister Stone hesitated. She wanted the tonic for Liniang, but did not want to tell Chen the long story about Liniang's resurrection. Chen would never believe her. Worse, he might go to the authorities. She knew very well that if he went to the authorities, she, Liniang, and Liu Mengmei would all be burned at the stakes for witchery.

"So it's for that young man Liu Mengmei," Chen the Most Virtuous chuckled.

"No. It's not for him."

"Your secret is safe with me," Chen told Sister Stone in a conspiratorial voice. He wanted Sister Stone to know that she had committed indiscretions and that he could use them against her.

"I tell you it is not for him."

Ignoring Sister Stone's protestation, Chen pointed at two clods of earth inside a wooden bowl displayed on a shelf, "They come from beneath the bed of a widow of certain age and certain lineage. Mixed with my special wine, they cure a man's flaccidity problems if he has the problem and increases his vigor if he does not have the problem."

Sister Stone tried to turn the table on Chen the Most Virtuous. Looking at Chen's crotch critically, she said, "Yours does not look any better than any old man's."

Chen was ready for the taunt. "You really shouldn't underestimate it. It can drill through stone easily." Chen laughed loudly.

"Shut up," Sister Stone's face reddened in embarrassment. She raised the carrying pole threateningly at Chen.

"All right," Chen stopped laughing. "I shut up. Just put down your bamboo pole."

Sister Stone put down the pole. "I want a prescription for a woman," Sister Stone told Chen, still red-faced.

"So it's you who are weakened and need a boost," Chen burst out laughing again.

"Do you have it or not?" Sister Stone was getting angry.

Pointing to a pair of dirty pants hanging from a hook on the wall, Chen said proudly, "That came from a particularly virile man. Burned into ashes and soaked in my special wine, it is a tonic for women."

"Are you sure?" Sister Stone inspected the soiled pants doubtfully.

"It works like magic, guaranteed," Chen assured Sister Stone. "Do you want some, sister?"

Sister Stone nodded her head.

"Prepare some tonic for Sister Stone," Chen told his assistant.

The assistant came out from the back room with a pair of scissors in his hand and a dirty-looking earthen jug.

"Cut the best part for our sister," Chen instructed his assistant.

The assistant cut a few small pieces from the seat of the pants and went back to his workroom. A burning smell soon filled the air.

In a few minutes, the young man came out with a small bowl of black ash. He poured it into the jug, stirred it with a pair of long chopsticks, and sealed the jug with a piece of oily paper.

"Just don't tell me again you heard Sister Shy in Scholar Liu's room," Chen smirked.

"Sister Shy has left and I am sorry I wrongly accused her, but it is not what you think," Sister Stone was tempted to explain, thought better of it, and then gave up.

"You owe me sixty *taels*," Chen wiped the jug clean with a cloth.

Sister Stone placed the jug into one of her baskets. "Send your assistant to my house," she told Chen. "He can have five pounds of dirt under my bed."

"Sister Stone, I am not sure whether you are much of a widow," Chen was not happy with the proposed barter.

"Then write it in your book. I will pay you when you have some money to pay me for the upkeep of the house." Sister Stone tied the baskets to her pole. "Good-bye, old man."

"Wait a minute," Chen grabbed Sister Stone's carrying pole.

"What do you want?"

Opening the cover of one basket, Chen poked inside at the meat, the fish, and the wine Sister Stone had bought. "My dear sister, you seem to be living a good life."

"This is the first time I came to shop in a year," Sister Stone defended herself. She was telling the truth.

"Well, I don't care whether it is the first time or second time," Chen paused and put on a sanctimonious air. "I just want you to remember that your good life depends on the continuing favor of the Du family."

"What are you trying to say?" Sister Stone was getting impatient.

"According to my calendar, tomorrow is an auspicious day for visiting the departed," Chen explained. "I'm planning to pay a visit to my student's grave tomorrow morning. I hope you and Scholar Liu can join me."

Sister Stone's face blanched, the baskets slipping off her shoulder.

"Are you all right?" Chen asked.

Sister Stone nodded her head, picked up the baskets, and left the store in a hurry.

Chen the Most Virtuous woke up early the next morning. He hired a young boy with a healthy-looking donkey and soon reached the governor's estate. To his surprise, Chen found the stone gate padlocked.

He knocked and shouted, but no one answered.

"There can't be anyone inside, sir," the donkey boy told him.

"Where have they gone?" Chen the Most Virtuous was irked.

"Maybe they have gone to the city to buy offerings," the boy suggested.

Chen and the boy sat down at the stone gate and waited. Chen soon fell into a sleep. When the boy woke him up, the sun was in the middle of the sky, but the gate was still locked and no one appeared on the road.

"I can't wait here any more, sir," the donkey boy told him. "I have to get more business."

"I'll pay you double," Chen answered impatiently.

Chen waited some more time. He was getting both hungry and angry. He had told Sister Stone yesterday that he planned to come over, but she had apparently decided to lock him out. "What an ungrateful woman."

Chen walked around to the side of the estate and found a small hole in the hedges. He managed to squeeze through, but his new silk robe caught on the hedges and was torn in several places.

Indignantly, Chen hurried to the back garden, carrying incense and paper offerings in a cloth bag. Grass and shrubbery had grown over the pebble path, and he had to pick his way carefully.

When he saw the grave, the old man was stunned. The marble tombstone was on its side, the soil that covered the coffin was removed, and the coffin itself was pried open. Inside the coffin, there were no bones, nor any burial jewelry. A shovel was in the upturned soil, and a torn white silk sheet, caught in a branch, flapped forlornly in the wind.

"Grave robbers," he cried.

The old man ran back toward the house. He fell several times, but he picked himself up and continued running. When he reached the courtyard, he shouted, panting, "Sister Stone, Scholar Liu, grave robbers have desecrated the grave."

The whole estate was cloaked in silence. No one answered him. Gazing at the padlock on the kitchen door, and remembering Sister Stone's sudden loss of composure yesterday, Chen the Most Virtuous grew suspicious.

Picking up a brick, Chen hit the padlock several times. It broke, and he pushed the door open. A faint smell of raw meat and fish greeted him. As he searched for the source of the smell, he saw in a corner of the kitchen the two baskets Sister Stone had carried the previous day.

The jug of tonic his assistant had prepared for Sister Stone stood on the table, unopened and untouched.

Chen then pushed open the connecting door to Sister Stone's room. It was in total chaos. The wardrobe was open, and discarded clothing was strewn all over the floor.

Chen sat down on Sister Stone's chair. He tried to figure out what had happened.

Suddenly, he knew. Sister Stone had suspected that he knew the liaison between her and Scholar Liu, especially after she came to buy the tonic he had concocted from cheap rice wine and dirty old clothes. Fearing shame and punishment, Sister

Stone and Liu Mengmei had robbed the grave and escaped over-night.

"What treachery," Chen fumed. He must report the crime to the local authorities immediately. He must also report the crime to Governor Du and Madam Du in person. After all, it was they who gave him a good life. Loyalty demanded no less than a special trip to Yangzhou.

But before that, he had to find the bones and rebury them. He couldn't possibly leave Liniang's bones scattered in the garden and exposed to the weather.

The old man picked himself up from the chair and hurried back to the garden. He searched through all the areas near the grave, wading into the pond, and crawling into brambles, but he saw no trace of them. "What rascals!" Du cursed angrily and gave up the search.

When Sister Stone had hurried back from the city the previous noon, she was sweating profusely and in a very bad mood.

Chen the Most Virtuous would surely go to the authorities when he saw the grave, she told Liniang and Liu Mengmei in a gloomy voice. The authorities would arrest all of them and burn them at stakes.

Sister Stone could almost image how the official history would record the event. Two secret practitioners of witchcraft, Sister Stone and Liu Mengmei, were able to disturb the dead, recall the spirit from the underworld, and turn it into an illusory living form. Such practice seriously threatened the natural order of life and death, so the local authorities burned the three at the city gate, an event witnessed by thousands of cheering citizens.

"Calm down, Sister Stone," Liniang gave the nun a towel and a glass of cold water. "I can explain to him what has happened, the whole story, from the very beginning."

"No one will ever believe your story," Sister Stone pronounced pessimistically. "I wouldn't if I didn't see you coming back to life with my eyes."

"Let's go to Hangzhou, my love," Liu proposed. "We can avoid the trouble here. I can also take the royal examination."

"A very good idea," Liniang agreed. "Can you go to the city and hire us a boat while Sister Stone and I prepare for the journey?"

When darkness fell, Liniang, Liu, and Sister Stone boarded a hired boat. They stood on the deck, silently watching their house and the city of Nan'an disappear in the night.

"A new life," Liniang prayed solemnly.

"A happy new life," Liu joined her.

Early in the spring, Inspector Miao came to Hangzhou, the capital of the southern court. As he had been doing for the past years, he presented his collection of jewels to the emperor and his harem. The emperor, as usual, was drunk, but his lack of sobriety did not seem in any way to hinder his appreciation of the jewelry. In fact, Miao believed, it enhanced it. Examining the jewels and passing them on to his many women, the emperor was pleased.

"How long have you been working for me as an inspector of jewelry?" the emperor asked.

"For over eleven years now, Your Majesty."

"I think you deserve a promotion," the emperor said kindly.

Miao believed he did as well, but he was not sure whether the emperor meant it seriously or simply said it out of drunkenness. In the past, the emperor had said the same thing before dismissing Miao, and he had never followed up on his comment.

"I am not too happy with the candidates we selected through royal examinations in the past years. They gave me a mouthful of classical quotes, but they had no clues how to fight off the

"A new happy life."

northern barbarians. This year I'm appointing you Commissioner for Royal Examinations. Help me select scholars who are strategists, not pedants."

Miao was happy and worried at the same time. It was time for a change, he thought. He was bored with Guangzhou, especially with its humid climate and culinary tastes. He wanted to come back to Hangzhou, his hometown.

On the other hand, he came from a family of jewelers, had no training in the classics, and had never passed any examination, provincial or national, himself. He did not know whether he would be able to do the work the emperor was expecting him to do.

The emperor seemed to read his mind. "You know how to pick extraordinary jewels from the common. The same principle applies in picking the best qualified candidates."

Miao was not sure whether it did, but even if it did, Miao did not know how long it would take him to finish reading the one thousand or so essays expected in every royal examination. In the past eleven years, Miao's reading was limited to official communications and family correspondence. He had never touched a classical book or a new political treatise.

Miao, however, was not a person to contradict the emperor. Moreover, he could not very well refuse a handsome promotion and a transfer to the capital. That would be plain stupidity. There must be a way to handle all the papers, Miao reassured himself. So he told the emperor, "I will do my best to select the candidates who are able to serve the needs of your majesty."

Miao was quite happy with the examination question he came up with. It asked which policy, appeasement, attack, or defense, was the most appropriate policy to deal with the barbarians from the north. He thought he was quite clever.

Now the essays were here for him to read. He looked at the thick piles of papers on his desk, frowned, and felt every blood vessel in his head pulsating. "There is a way to every problem," he closed his eyes and repeated the maxim to calm himself. Sure enough, an idea came to him.

"Sort these essays into three piles, one for appeasement, one for defense, and one for attack," he ordered his examiners.

Then he picked three senior examiners, ordered them to each take a pile and rank the essays according to their merits. "Remember, this time we are selecting strategists, not pedants. Be conscientious. I will go over the ranking after you finish, and your future employment will depend on your performance," he told them.

It took the examiners three days. When they left the three ranked piles on his table on the morning of the fourth day, he ordered, "Close the door and leave me alone. Do not enter unless I call you."

The examiners left his office quietly.

The first step was to pick the passing essays. In the past, roughly one hundred people passed the examination every time. Miao believed that this time he should be stricter to show the emperor that he was a tougher examiner who was willing to fail the essays that had more pedantry than strategy. He looked at the three piles and decided to choose twenty from each pile. That would make a total of sixty, a welcome reduction from the past.

He quickly marked the first twenty essays from each pile as passing without bothering to read any one of them.

The second step was to select three essays for the first prize, second prize, and the third prize. This task was not as simple as the first one. He had to read the three essays and rank them carefully because the emperor, as a deputy told him, always read the top three essays.

He picked up the top essay from the pile favoring appeasement and started reading. "Your servant believes that the court's appeasement of bandits may be compared with a husband complying with the whims of his favorite concubine."

He then picked up the first essay from the pile that favored defense. "Your servant believes that his majesty's defense of his realm may be compared with a maiden's defense of her virginity."

Lastly he picked up the top essay from the pile favoring attack. "Your servant believes that the policy of attacking may be compared to a Yang penetrating a Yin."

"None of them is making too much sense to me," Miao told himself. "But the emperor seems to be favoring an attack policy while disdaining an appeasement one. I will pick the last one for the first prize, the second one for the second prize, and the first one for the third prize."

Having selected the sixty passing papers and the first three prize winners, Miao relaxed. All the worries in the past month seemed to melt away. He stretched and extended. After all, life wasn't so difficult for him.

Liniang and Liu's trip to Hangzhou had started without a hitch. They spent a night on the river that came down from the Western Mountains and wound its way to the Yangtze River. Then they spent two days on the great river. By dusk, they had reached the mouth of the Grand Canal, which connected the Yangtze River to the capital city.

"Three more days," the boatman told Liniang and Liu after he anchored the boat for the night, "then you'll be in Hangzhou."

When they woke up the next morning, however, they saw a long convoy of boats carrying troops and supplies spilling out of the canal and heading north.

"The canal is closed to civilian traffic," a soldier on a patrol boat told them as they approached the canal.

"For how long?" Liu asked.

"Two days," the soldier answered.

They waited for two days, but the boats carrying troops and supplies were still coming out the canal.

"Two more days," the soldier told them after they asked again.

"I'm going to miss my exam," Liu paced the deck anxiously.

"You can explain to the examiner why we got delayed," Liniang tried to comfort her husband.

After waiting for twelve days, the canal was finally reopened for civilian traffic.

Unlike the two rivers they had traveled, there was no current to carry the boat in the canal. In his eagerness to reach Hangzhou, Liu took turns with the boatman and his son in pulling the boat along the bank with a thick rope. After two days and two nights on the canal, they finally reached the shantytown outside the North Gate of the imperial city.

Liu and Liniang started to look for a rental house. They found one on Main Street, which was a thoroughfare teeming with stores, people and donkeys, mules, and horses carrying rice, vegetables, and other commodities.

To the south, a huge stone wall stood, separating the town from the city. The gate was five stories tall. On the gate, colorful pennants flapped in the summer breeze. To the north and to the west, green hills formed a protective circle around the town. To the east, a huge river shed thousands of tons of water into the sea.

Liu Mengmei rushed into the city, without even changing his sweat-soaked robe.

"The exam closed four days ago," the guard at the Royal Examinations Office told him.

"I know, but I have a letter from Inspector Miao of Guangzhou for the commissioner."

"Inspector Miao is the Royal Commissioner now," the guard told him.

Liu couldn't believe his good luck. He showed the guard the letter.

The guard took Liu to Miao's office and knocked on the door. It took Miao a few minutes to wake up from his nap and to open the door. "What is it?" he asked the guard, annoyed.

"Commissioner Miao," Liu knelt on the steps, "do you recognize me, a student from Guangzhou?"

Miao immediately recognized him. "Why did it take so long for you to get here? I thought you took my money and disappeared."

"I was ill for a while. In addition, I married, and then my boat got stuck at the entrance to the Grand Canal for twelve days to make way for military convoys," Liu explained.

"That was our reinforcements for Yangzhou," Miao told him.

"My wife and I arrived here this morning. Without any delay, I rushed here to beg for admittance."

Miao looked at Liu's dirty clothes, sweaty face, and bloodshot eyes. He was satisfied that Liu was telling him the truth. More importantly, Miao knew fully well that passing someone from Guangzhou, if he was at all good, would help to build a network of high government officials whom he could rely on as political allies later on.

"Considering your special situation, I will admit you for examination," he told Liu Mengmei.

Liu knelt again, "Thank you for your understanding, sir."

Miao read the topic to Liu Mengmei. "Now that the troops of the northern barbarians threaten the frontiers, which is the most appropriate of the three possible policies: attack, defense, or appeasement?"

Turning to the guard, he ordered, "Take this young man to the examination hall."

"Excuse me, sir," Liu asked sheepishly, "can I have something to eat first? I haven't had breakfast yet."

"Take him to a restaurant first," Miao told the guard.

At the restaurant, Liu ate a bowl of noodles with two fried eggs. Then he ordered a strong pot of jasmine tea. Over tea, he mulled over the essay question and pondered the advantages and disadvantages of each strategy. When he was ready to write, he paid the bill and went back to the examination hall.

"Which policy did you argue for in your essay?" Liniang asked her husband when he came back from the city and told her and Sister Stone about the exam.

"I advocated a combination of the three. A wise doctor uses different drugs together, one drug to attack the outer symptoms, another drug to strengthen body defense, and the third drug to appease the underlying causes of the illness."

Liniang was impressed. "I didn't know you are such a strategist, my husband."

"I don't think I'm going to make the list though," Liu answered.

"Why not?"

"I used only four quotes from the classics. My schoolmaster had advised me to use as many quotes as possible."

"Why didn't you?" Liniang asked. She had also heard from her father that the examiners often considered a large number of quotes a benchmark of erudition.

"They did not seem to be relevant to the issue."

"Don't worry about it," Liniang comforted her husband. "Commissioner Miao might be totally different from the previous commissioners."

"I hope so."

Liniang woke up in the middle of the night. In the darkness, she seemed to hear a creaky noise outside the door. Alarmed, she searched for the source of the noise. The window was closed and the curtains were drawn. She got out of her bed and tiptoed into the hall. The door was also locked. However, in the small rectangular ventilation opening above the door, she saw a dark face peeking at her. His hand was inside the opening with a long stick. Liniang screamed.

"What is it?" Liu jumped out of the bed and raced into the hallway.

"Someone tried to break in," Liniang shouted, pointing at the long stick that had fallen on the floor.

Heavy footsteps scurried away. Liu, Liniang, and Sister Stone worked together to push a heavy long table against the door. Liu then grabbed a pillow from his bed and jumped onto the table to sleep.

Liniang was woken up again, this time by the noise from the street. The sunlight streamed into the hall through the rectangular opening above the door. Her husband, still on the table, was already awake and was looking at her tenderly. They moved the table back to its original place and opened the door. Outside the door, an old broken chair stood in their way, witness to the attempted midnight intrusion.

Chapter Eleven

LI THE Bandit was a happy man. Back from a trip to the barbarians in the North, he was at the head of a large column of caravans of military supplies. Li the Bandit was a big man, barrel-chested with strong muscles. He rode a shiny black horse, his shirt open, showing off a chest full of thick hair. His big head, however, was shaved totally bald, which, together with his chiseled face and stern expression, gave him a fierce look.

After five days of journey on rugged roads, he had finally reached his stronghold in East China. His camp, a cluster of tents and sheds, stood at the foot of a steep mountain in the distance. Smoke slowly rose into the sky in the gathering dusk.

The column of caravans was moving slowly, and Li was getting impatient. He raced forward alone, then waited for the column to arrive, and then raced forward again. He wanted to tell his followers in the camp the big news, and he missed his dear little wife. Finally, tired of waiting for the caravans, he kicked his horse hard on its flanks and galloped all the way toward the camp, leaving the caravans behind him.

Li the Bandit rode into his camp triumphantly. Letting his horse carry him crisscrossing the camp, he shouted loudly, "I am back, I am back." Immediately, his soldiers came out from various tents and ran after him as he trotted through the whole camp. Li the Bandit finally stopped before his own camp. Waving a piece of paper in front of him, he shouted excitedly to his followers who had gathered, "Look at this paper, look at this paper."

"What is it, Great Chief?" His followers jumped around his panting horse and asked curiously and repeatedly.

Li the Bandit, seeing one of his top aids nicknamed "the Scholar" in the crowd, motioned him to squeeze closer to the horse and handed him the paper. "Read it aloud," he ordered.

The Scholar looked at the paper eagerly, but the paper was written in the Tartar language, which he did not understand. Embarrassed, he gave the paper back to Li the Bandit, mumbling, "I am a scholar; I don't read barbarian languages."

Li's followers booed and jeered. They seized the poor man, raised him over their heads, transported him in this manner to the edge of the ring surrounding Li the Bandit, and threw him into a thick bush.

Li the Bandit laughed at the feat of his followers. Then he turned to look at his own tent and bellowed, "Where is my wife? Summon Dame Li."

"Summon Dame Li," his followers shouted in unison.

Dame Li, a small attractive woman in her thirties, dressed in a flimsy red dress, came running toward her husband from her tent. "Welcome home, Great Chief," she cooed.

Li the Bandit bent down from his horse, grabbed his wife with one arm, and placed her in front of him on the horse. "Why are you so tardy, my old lecher?"

"I heard the noise outside and saw you arriving, but it took me a long time to find this dress."

It was a very attractive dress. Li the Bandit had selected the dress as a birthday gift for his wife after his followers had attacked a large estate and killed all the occupants a few days before he left for the barbarians in the north. But at the moment, he had little interest in the dress. Giving the letter to his wife, he said, "Read it to my soldiers."

"The emperor of the Tartars appoints our Great Chief the Prince of East China," reading the piece of paper, Dame Li announced loudly.

"The Prince of East China," the crowd echoed happily.

"From now on," Dame Li told the crowd, "no more *Great Chief.* You must call my husband *Great Prince.*"

"Great Prince," the crowd shouted.

"From now on," Li the Bandit announced, "no more *Dame Li,* you must call my old lecher *Great Princess.*"

"Great Princess," the crowd cheered.

"Now, my followers," Li the Bandit urged, "drink, eat, dance, and have a great party."

"Party, party, party," his followers chanted and moved happily toward the tents where food and alcohol were stored.

Dame Li turned around on the horse to face her husband, but she stopped her husband when he tried to embrace her. Waiting for the crowd to disperse, Dame Li waved the paper in her hand and asked, "Now my husband, is this useless piece of paper the only thing you got from the Tartars?"

"No, my old lecher," pointing to the north where the column of caravans was approaching slowly toward the camp in the descending darkness, Li answered happily, "I got plenty of gold, silver, weapons, and horses."

"What do you have to do for the Tartars in exchange for all these gifts?" Dame Li asked suspiciously.

"They wanted me to stir up East China, seize cities and villages, killing, burning, and raping. I told them no problem because that is what I like to do anyway."

"No raping for you, remember," Dame Li grabbed his loins. "If you ever forget, I will cut off your stick."

"My wife, you need to treat me with some respect, now that I am a prince of the Tartar Empire," Li the Bandit stared at his wife sternly.

"You were a henpecked bandit before; now you are a henpecked prince," his wife stared back.

"All right, all right, I am a henpecked prince," Li the Bandit conceded with an embarrassed chuckle. Li was a ferocious fighter and all his followers and his enemies feared him, but for some reason, he could never bring his wife under control, and he seemed to like this way.

Dame Li embraced her husband. "That is what I like, a henpecked prince. Let's get into the tent."

"My old lecher, can you wait for a while? I want to have a few drinks with my followers."

"I have been waiting for many days and nights. Let's finish our business first."

Li laughed heartily. Embracing his wife with one arm, he descended from his horse, and carried her toward his tent.

Everyday after the royal examination, Liu Mengmei went to the South Gate in front of the imperial palace where hundreds of candidates were waiting anxiously for the results of the examination. One evening, he came back from the South Gate gloomy-faced.

"Did you fail to make the list, my husband?" Liniang asked.

"The results have not been announced," Liu answered.

"Why do you look so gloomy then?"

Li the Bandit had launched a major military offensive in Yangzhou, Liu Mengmei told his wife. The emperor had decided that under the current situation, it was not appropriate to announce the exam results and to hold a celebration. "It has to wait until the military situation in Yangzhou stabilizes."

"Yangzhou is where my parents are," Liniang said anxiously.

"Yes, my darling," Liu confirmed. He wished that he could answer otherwise.

Liniang's heart was seized with apprehension. "My dear husband, since the results are not going to be published soon, let's go to Yangzhou immediately."

"No, darling, the roads are too dangerous."

"I haven't seen my parents for three years," Liniang pleaded.

"I'm afraid Scholar Liu is right, young mistress," Sister Stone, who had been listening to the conversation between the couple from the hallway, came into their room. "In a war, the roads are too dangerous even for men. Besides, it is very likely that your father will not believe your story and will treat you as an impostor."

Having lived in Hangzhou for more than ten days with her husband and Sister Stone, Liniang had almost forgotten about her death and resurrection. It had been so remote, almost like a nightmare that had occurred a long time ago. Now the painful fact came back to her and she agreed with Sister Stone that she would have trouble persuading her parents to accept her resurrection.

"What shall I do then, Sister Stone?" Liniang asked.

"When the situation in Yangzhou improves, write a letter to your parents, explaining everything. If they do not reject your story out of hand, you can then go and meet them. If they do, you have to wait. You should not force yourself on them."

"What if the situation does not improve?"

"May god help your father and the people of Yangzhou," Sister Stone prayed.

"My dear wife, why don't you write the letter now," Liu told Liniang. "I will leave for Yangzhou tomorrow morning to deliver the letter and to help your father defend the city."

"How can you help my father?" Liniang asked doubtfully.

"Remember you said I'm a good strategist several days ago?" Liu answered half-jokingly.

"You mustn't go either," Sister Stone told Liu Mengmei. "What are you going to say to Governor Du? That you brought young mistress back to life, that you married her, and that you have come to Yangzhou to help him? Governor Du is going to feed you to his dogs."

"Don't worry about me," Liu reassured Sister Stone. "I know how to handle it."

"Please let me go with you, my dear husband," Liniang pleaded.

Liu Mengmei kissed his wife. "Just write the letter. I will also bring with me your self-portrait."

Reluctantly, Liniang started to write her letter to her parents. As she wrote, emotions overcame her. Please believe me, she pleaded with her parents in the letter. I am your daughter, and I want to see you desperately.

While Liniang was working on the letter, Liu Mengmei left the rental house. After a while, he came back with a heavy iron bar and a pair of new padlocks. "Use them to lock the door at night," he told Sister Stone. Turning to his wife, who was still sobbing over the letter, he joked, "I am sure they can stop intruders, but I am not sure whether they can stop your spirit from wandering out."

Liniang wiped away her tears and grinned, "I promise you my soul as well as my body is staying with me inside this house and waiting for you."

Chapter Twelve

IT WAS midnight. The city of Yangzhou was deep in sleep. No one walked in the street, and no dog barked in the silence. Only the moon shone in the sky, looking down on a city tired from years of bloody fights with rebels and northern invaders.

The watchtower, the tallest building in the city, and Du Bao's military command center, was lit with light.

"Please stop, please," a piteous voice pleaded in the tower.

Du Bao sat at a desk in the watchtower, watching his soldiers beating a captured rebel officer with wooden sticks.

Du Bao had been Pacification Commissioner for three years now. When he first came to Yangzhou, he adopted many policies he had perfected in Nan'an. He set up food houses for the poor in every village and encouraged landowners and big farmers to contribute to them. He recruited poor but able-bodied young men to form local militias. Now most villages in the vicinity of the city had their own defense teams trained by his soldiers and supervised by village leaders. As a result of his policies, food riots and peasant uprisings in the region decreased. Support for Li the Bandit also dwindled.

Several days ago, however, the military situation began to worsen dramatically. Li the Bandit, strengthened by new troops and supplies from the North, started to launch midnight raids against villages in the region. In response, he had sent his troops to go to the aid of the villages, but once they were out of the city, they were ambushed and destroyed. He had lost a few thousand soldiers already.

Now he wanted to know what Li the Bandit's intention was.

"I don't know," the rebel officer stared at the ceiling blankly.

Du Bao made a hand motion to his soldiers. Four of them grabbed the rebel and held him tightly to the ground. Another of them took a red-hot iron bar from a burning stove and pointed at the man's face.

"Please no, no, no," the rebel wailed, shaking his head wildly.

"What is Li's plan?" Du Bao demanded.

The man stared at the hot iron bar in terror and started to talk. "He wants to weaken your army through nightly ambushes," the man stammered. "Then he plans a final assault on the city."

Suddenly, from outside the city, gongs and drums started to beat. Dogs barked, children cried, and shouts of panic rose into the night air.

Du Bao quickly ascended the watchtower. The noise came from a village in the hilly areas to the north of the city. Li the Bandit was attacking again.

"Shall we send troops?" Du's military commander asked.

"No," Du told his commander. He wanted to preserve his army for the defense of the city.

A fire started to burn in the village. Du and his soldiers watched silently on the tower. It was a fast, ferocious fire. Aided by high winds, it lit up half the sky, consuming houses, barns, animals and people.

The fire died down in about an hour, as suddenly as it had started. Darkness again gained control, and the only reminder of the fire was the acid smell carried by the wind from the village into the city.

Du descended the watchtower, dispirited and depressed. Although he knew his decision was a wise one in military terms, he felt terrible for the people in the village attacked by the rebels.

"Sir, it's time for you to get some rest," his army commander suggested.

Silently, Du Bao walked through the underground tunnel that connected the watchtower to his residence. When he emerged from the tunnel into a large meeting room, he saw his wife sitting at the long table in the room, gazing at Liniang's portrait.

"Why are you up so late at night?" he asked his wife.

"I dreamed of Liniang crying and calling for me. I woke up, and couldn't fall asleep again," Madam Du answered.

Du Bao sat down beside his wife and looked at his daughter's smiling face in silence for a long time. Then he told his wife, "It was not Liniang. It was the village people outside the city crying and shouting."

"Did you send your troops?"

"No. I didn't want them to get slaughtered again in the hills."

"But the village people got slaughtered."

Du did not answer. His heart was weighed down by his inability to help the villagers.

"I have been dreaming of Liniang all the time since I came here, but now it is getting worse," his wife told him.

Du lowered his head as painful memories came back to him. In Liniang's sixteen years of life, he had rarely spent time with her. He did not celebrate her birthdays, nor did he take an interest in her everyday life. Only in her last year of life did he start to pay a little more attention to her.

Du Bao felt especially guilty that he did not visit his daughter when the doctor he had sent to Nan'an had reported to him that there was no cure for his daughter's illness. How he wished he had gone to Nan'an and said "I love you" to his daughter in the last few days of her life.

He couldn't leave Yangzhou because enemy troops were at his door, he told himself repeatedly. But subconsciously, Du Bao suspected he could have made the trip to Nan'an if he had truly wanted to. He remembered he had been deeply disappointed by Liniang's amorous obsession. That might be the real reason, Du Bao reflected painfully, that had stopped him from going to Nan'an.

"Being love-sick was not a great sin," Madam Du knew what her husband was thinking and defended her daughter.

"I had always wanted to raise Liniang as a virtuous girl and to marry her to a young man with a bright future," Du sighed.

"Please forgive her," Madam Du pleaded. "She was our only daughter."

"I forgive her," Du Bao murmured to his wife sincerely.

"Please love her."

"I love her."

"Love her wholeheartedly."

"I love her wholeheartedly."

"Thank you, my dear husband," tears rolled down Madam Du's cheeks.

Du Bao gazed at his wife, an anguished expression on his face. For many years after their marriage, he had been cold and passionless toward her, disappointed that she had not been able to give him any sons. Then, for a brief period, before and during their trip to Hangzhou, his passion for her had rekindled.

After Madam Du arrived in Yangzhou at his insistence, their relationship became strained again. While his wife was tormented by memories of Liniang, his responsibilities and his own guilt overwhelmed him. He rarely had time to eat with his wife, sleep with her, or even talk to her.

In Nan'an, his wife seemed to have fared well despite his neglect because she had had Liniang with her and had a farm to manage. Now, without Liniang, and living in the heavily guarded residence with nothing to occupy her mind, she had become more and more depressed and grew thinner and paler by the day.

Du Bao asked his attendant for a pot of tea and sat over the tea for a long time.

"Go back to Nan'an," he finally told his wife. In Nan'an, she could at least visit Liniang's tomb anytime she wanted and have a farm to divert her attention.

"No," Madam Du shook her head. She would have considered her husband's proposal happily if Du Bao had asked her earlier, but now with the military situation worsening daily, she did not want to leave her husband alone in Yangzhou. She wanted to stay to support her husband.

"Please go," Du Bao pleaded.

"I will go to Nan'an with you when you finish your work here."

"I may never finish my work here. The rebels are too strong, so are the northern barbarians."

"You received reinforcements last month, and I'm sure more are on the way."

"Not likely," Du Bao was pessimistic. "The whole country is exhausted by the war."

"I will stay with you here as long as it takes," Madam Du said resolutely.

Du Bao was deeply touched. He knew his wife was not happy with her life, but she never complained. Instead, she bore it stoically, and she always put his career before her own happiness.

Du Bao was determined that her wife should leave for Nan'an before Li the Bandit's final assault on the city. If his wife did not leave now, she might not be able to leave the city for a long time, or she might never be able to get out of the city alive. If he was unable to give his wife more time and more attention, at least, he should make sure that she was out of harm's way.

"You must leave the city today," Du Bao stood up and told his wife firmly.

"Please let me stay with you," Madam Du pleaded.

Turning to his attendant, Du Bao ordered, "Select twenty best soldiers and prepare to leave at dawn."

Madam Du started to sob. "My dear husband, I haven't borne you any son. After I leave, take Fragrance as your concubine. There is still time." Her voice broke.

Du waved his hand. "No, you take Fragrance with you. You need her on the journey and in Nan'an."

"Then take any woman you like here to keep you company and to bear you a son."

"I'm not interested," Du Bao answered. "Get prepared. You will leave with Fragrance at dawn."

As dawn broke and as soldiers opened the South Gate, Madam Du knelt in front of her husband and bid him good-bye, "My husband, take good care of yourself."

Du Bao raised his wife to her feet, "Burn a bouquet of incense for me at Liniang's grave. I will join you in Nan'an once my work is finished here."

Madam Du, Fragrance, and the soldiers mounted the horses and left the city of Yangzhou.

Du climbed up the tower and watched the group gallop away on the highway toward the Yangtze River. In better times, they could have used the Grand Canal that connected the city to the big river. However, a few days before, the rebels had sunk a few supply boats, totally blocking the canal.

They almost disappeared on the horizon when, to his horror, Du Bao saw a contingent of rebel soldiers suddenly emerge from a forest at a hillside and swoop on his wife's entourage.

"Send reinforcements," he yelled an order.

His troops rushed out of the gate toward the hill, but they were stopped by a larger contingent of rebels before they were able to reach the hill.

Du watched the fighting anxiously. Soon, his wife's entourage succumbed to the attack. One by one they fell off their horses.

Closer to the gate, his reinforcements were engaged in a vicious battle with the rebel troops. As the fight went on, thousands more rebel troops rushed from nearby hills toward the city from all directions. They seemed to be intent on storming the city.

"Order the soldiers to retreat and close the city gate immediately," Du ordered.

A soldier beat the drum five times, a signal for retreat. His troops hastily turned back, dragging with them the dead and the wounded. The drawbridge was raised, and the gate was closed.

A few rebels from the ambush group rode to the edge of the moat surrounding the city, holding in their hands the heads they had cut off. They held up the bloody heads, cursing and taunting Du and his soldiers. Du's soldiers showered them with poison-tipped arrows, driving them away from the gate.

Not far from the gate, along the highway, the rebel troops started to dig trenches, put up tents, and set up attack positions. Soon, messengers from the other three city gates came to report that the enemies had cut off the roads and surrounded the gates as well.

"How much food do we have in the city?" Du asked.

"Enough to last for a year," his army commander answered.

"The enemy has laid siege to the city," Du addressed his officers, "but if we remain vigilant and defend the city until winter, the rebels will have to retreat."

"Yes, sir. We will remain vigilant and defend the city to our death," the officers answered.

Then Du turned to his officers. "Can you leave me a few minutes to grieve?"

The officers and soldiers left him alone on the top of the watchtower.

Du Bao knelt and sobbed. He had meant to send his wife to safety, but instead of safety, he had sent her, Fragrance, and the soldiers into a deadly trap. He prayed that gods would find a resting place for the bodies of his wife, Fragrance, and the soldiers. And he promised that, if he survived the siege, he would look for his wife's bones, take them back to Nan'an, and bury them alongside Liniang's grave.

❀❀

Darkness fell. Two women crawled out from a marsh at the edge of the highway. They listened intently and searched the landscape with the help of the moonlight. There were no rebel soldiers near by, nor was there anyone else. The highway was deserted.

Madam Du and Fragrance did not die. When the rebels came out of the woody hill on the other side of the highway to attack them, the captain of the entourage pushed them off the horses and into the marsh. He and his soldiers then engaged the rebels in a fierce fight. While the fighting was going on, Madam Du and Fragrance scrambled in waist-high water, moving through reeds into the depth of the marsh to hide themselves.

Soon, the clanking of weapons and the cries of battle died down. They heard rebel soldiers coming toward the edge of the marsh in search of them.

"I saw two women in the group," one voice said.

"Me too," another voice agreed.

"I don't know why we bother," a third voice said. "Dame Li has orders that we should not rape or kill any women."

"There is no order saying that we cannot take their money," one rebel disagreed.

"Besides, we can do whatever we like with these women so long as no one in the group is telling," another rebel added.

So the rebels continued to search. They waded into the water several times. They threw stones into the marsh and shouted, "Come out, you women, or alligators will eat you alive."

Madam Du and Fragrance lowered their heads until water reached their chins, and they held their breaths. The dense reeds waved in the breeze, protecting them from the rebels.

After a while, the rebels gave up, cursing at the marsh and at the two women they could not find.

Madam Du and Fragrance stayed in the marsh for the whole day. They did not dare to come out, fearing more ambushes.

They waited until darkness fell and then picked their way back to the shore.

The road was littered with mutilated bodies of Du's soldiers as well as those of rebel soldiers. Their bodies had been stripped of their armor and of their clothes. Fragrance was frightened by the ghastly scene and vomited. Madam Du quieted her down and said prayers for the souls of the dead soldiers.

In the morning raid, Madam Du had lost the purse where she had put her gold and silver. The two women combed through the highway, turning over dead bodies and looking in the ditches. There was no trace of the purse. The only thing they found was the luggage sack Fragrance had dropped in the flight. The rebels had cut open the flex sack and stole the few silk dresses they had packed.

The two women sat down against a tree. They were hungry, tired, and frightened. They ate a few corns that were left in the sack. Then they counted the silver coins in Fragrance's small purse.

"We have only twenty-two *taels* of silver here," Madam Du said disappointedly.

"Let's go back to Yangzhou," Fragrance pointed at the dark silhouette of the city they had left in the morning.

"No, we can't," Madam Du reminded Fragrance. "The city is under siege."

"What shall we do now?" Fragrance was on the verge of tears.

"Let's go," Madam Du stood up.

"Go where?" Fragrance asked uncertainly.

"Nan'an," Madam Du answered, her voice resolute. She pulled Fragrance to her feet.

The two women began their journey eastward toward the Yangtze River.

As they trekked east, the deserted highway slowly came back to life. A few refugees joined them. Then more of them emerged from fields and burning villages. They walked in the darkness silently without talking to each other. Only the occasional cries of babies and small children broke the woeful silence.

Madam Du and Fragrance took a nap in a forest. When dawn broke, they were on the road again.

Although there were hundreds of refugees on the road, the journey was perilous. Bands of robbers took advantage of the chaos to raid refugees, especially refugees who seemed to come from well-to-do families. Madam Du and Fragrance had no attendants nor mules or donkeys, their clothing was coated with dried mud from the marsh, and their faces were brownish from the dirt they had smeared themselves. So they largely escaped the attention of the robbers and traveled unmolested.

At dusk, they finally reached a port on the Yangtze River. The usually quiet and peaceful town was swarming with refugees.

Madam Du started to look for a boat to go to Nan'an immediately. However, the boat people told her that her money was not enough for a trip upstream to Nan'an. It could only buy a trip to Hangzhou. One of them explained to her that a boat going upstream could only carry half the passengers but needed twice the workers. Besides, there was no one else who wanted to go to Nan'an.

"Please help us go home. I will pay you double once we get there," Madam Du pleaded with the boat people.

The boat people shook their heads one by one. "Sorry, madam. You have to pay first."

"What are we going to do?" Fragrance asked tearfully. She was frightened. Never, since her father sold her to Madam Du, had she suffered so much and seen so much suffering in the two days on the road. Young women were raped, young men were either killed or pressed into service for the rebel troops, frail old people dropped dead at roadsides, and babies and children screamed out of fear and hunger. She wanted to get back to the safety of Nan'an as soon as possible.

"We will beg here until we get enough money," Madam Du told Fragrance.

"People here are all refugees," Fragrance sobbed. "They don't have money to give us."

Fragrance was right, Madam Du told herself. She thought for a long time, then made up her mind. "Let's go to Hangzhou. When we get there, we'll go and see the emperor and ask him for some money."

"Are you sure the emperor would see us?" Fragrance asked doubtfully.

Madam Du was doubtful as well, but at least it was a hope, and there was really no other choice.

The crowded boat started for Hangzhou. The boat ride was not as dangerous as their escape from Yangzhou, but it was very unpleasant. The food was poor. They had to sit in the cabin day and night since the boat had no sleeping quarters. Mosquitoes swarmed all over them, eager for blood.

Their hearts were filled with joy when the boat finally docked at the shantytown outside the North Gate of Hangzhou after four days on the river.

But their joy only lasted for a short time. As they watched the passengers from the boat disperse into the night, they realized that they had no money for lodging, nor relatives or friends who might offer help.

"Where are we going to stay for the night?" Fragrance asked anxiously.

Madam Du looked around. She saw a large lodging house near the dock site with a lantern hanging on its door.

The large house had a corridor in the middle and nine or ten rooms on each side of the corridor. The rooms were only separated from each other with straw sheets hanging down from joists, and the rooms had no doors. With the dim light from a lantern hanging in the middle of the corridor, they could see all the rooms were packed with people sleeping on the floor.

Men snored loudly, a few people were coughing, and a mother was humming softly, trying to get a crying baby to sleep. Madam Du and Fragrance could smell the stifling stench in the air.

The attendant, a short man with a big belly, told them that all the rooms were full. And even if he had vacancies, he could not accommodate anyone who could not pay up front. The owner would fire him, he told them apologetically.

"Could we sleep on the corridor please?" Fragrance begged.

"No," the man answered.

The two women looked at each other in desperation.

"Go to Main Street," the short man pointed in the easterly direction. "Opposite the public bathhouse, there are several rental houses. Someone there might be willing to put you up for the night."

Madam Du and Fragrance looked in the direction of Main Street. In the moonlight, the town was a dark mass of bamboo houses and narrow byzantine mud lanes. The lanes had no lights. Neither did the houses.

"Why are there no lights in this town?" Fragrance asked fearfully.

"By the order of the emperor, no private residences are allowed to have candlelight."

"Why not?"

Candle lights were dangerous, the short man explained. With bamboo houses so close to each other, an inadvertently knocked-over candle could lead to a fiery inferno. In fact, the short man added, a fire a few years before destroyed most of the town and killed thousands of people.

Madam Du and Fragrance thanked the short man and left for Main Street. They navigated the mud lanes in the darkness, avoiding collision with locals who scurried by like ghosts and walking around the drunk and the homeless who took refuge in the privacy of the lanes.

They sighed with relief when they finally reached Main Street and located the public bathhouse. Fragrance hesitantly knocked on the first house.

A man opened the door. "Sorry," he closed the door on them as soon as he had heard their request.

They knocked on the second house, the third house, and the fourth house. People opened doors, but they all refused to put them up.

"We have to sleep in the lanes," Fragrance gave up.

Madam Du knocked on the fifth house. "Is anybody in?"

There was no answer.

Madam Du knocked again. This time, she heard some steps inside the house.

"Who is it?" a young woman's voice answered from inside the house.

"We are two lady travelers looking for lodging."

"The lodging house is at the dock site," the young woman told them.

Madam Du explained how they ended up at her door looking for help.

"Please come in," the young woman lifted some metallic object inside and opened the door, a loose sleeping gown draped over her shoulder.

Madam Du and Fragrance thanked the young woman profusely. They were relieved that they had finally found a place to spend the night.

Although the house was unlighted, with the help of the moonlight from the night sky, Madam Du was struck by the uncanny resemblance of the young woman to her daughter, Liniang. Even her voice sounded like Liniang's sweet and vivacious voice.

"Don't be ridiculous," Madam Du told herself. "I must be thinking too much about Liniang. Now my eyes and my ears start to play tricks on me."

But the young woman was staring at her as well. "Madam, where are you from?" she asked in a strangely intense voice.

"I am from Yangzhou."

"Yangzhou? May I ask why you travel without your husband?"

"He is still in Yangzhou."

"May I know who he is?"

"His name is Du Bao, and he is Pacification Commissioner for Yangzhou."

"You are my mother," the young woman burst out crying. Abruptly, she grabbed Madam Du and embraced her. "Mother, Mother, I am Liniang."

Madam Du froze. Cold sweat broke out all over her. "Ghost!" she stammered.

"Ghost!" Fragrance jumped out of the house and ran back into the street.

"Please, mother. Look at me. I am your daughter," Liniang cried, holding her tightly.

"Let me go please," Madam Du pleaded.

"I am not ghost, mother."

"My child, I know you are not happy with me. I never visited your grave after I left Nan'an. But I was away in Yangzhou with your father. I never had an opportunity to visit Nan'an."

"Mother," Liniang started to cry.

"My child, when I reach Nan'an, I will arrange a great mass for you," Madam Du promised.

At that time, a door of a bedroom opened, and a middle-aged woman came out and demanded in an annoyed voice, "Liniang, who are you arguing with in the middle of the night?"

"Sister Stone, it's my mother. Please tell her I am not a ghost."

Sister Stone walked over and inspected Madam Du closely. "What a surprise, Madam Du!" She greeted her old friend happily. "This is your daughter, Liniang."

"Sister Stone, I am glad to see you here. But my daughter died three years ago," Madam Du stuttered.

"I came back to life, mother," Liniang explained.

"You came back to life? How is it possible? I buried you in the back garden."

"A young man opened my tomb and brought me back to life."

"I witnessed it with my own eyes, Madam Du," Sister Stone confirmed.

Madam Du stared at Liniang and Sister Stone incredulously. In her whole life, she had never heard that a dead person could come back to life.

"It is impossible, it is impossible," she mumbled and muttered to herself repeatedly.

"Let go of your mother," Sister Stone told Liniang. Then she led her friend to a chair, seated her, and tried to calm her down. "Why are you here, Madam Du?"

"It is impossible," Madam Du muttered, her eyes still fixed on Liniang.

"Get your mother some tea," Sister Stone told Liniang.

Liniang went to the kitchen.

With the young woman leaving the room, Madam Du calmed down a little and explained the situation in Yangzhou, and how she had intended to go to Nan'an, but ended up here in Hangzhou.

Sister Stone then explained to Madam Du the whole story. How a young scholar, Liu Mengmei, came to stay at the estate on his way to Hangzhou, how he dug up the grave to bring Liniang back to life, and how they came to Hangzhou to avoid the trouble in Nan'an and to take the royal examination.

"How was it possible?"

"It was a miracle, Madam Du."

"A miracle?"

"Why don't you stay here for a few days?" Sister Stone suggested. "Then you'll see that everything I told you is true."

Madam Du hesitated.

"Even if Liniang is a ghost, she is not going to hurt you," Sister Stone continued.

Madame Du nodded her head. She knew that her daughter, ghost or not, was not going to hurt her.

"Young Mistress," Sister Stone called, "your mother had agreed to stay with us for a few days."

"Thank you, mother," Liniang came out of the kitchen, knelt before her mother, and wept happily.

Chapter Thirteen

AFTER CROSSING the Yangtze River, Liu Mengmei doggedly headed toward Yangzhou despite warnings from refugees. Sneaking around several rebel checkpoints on the highway, he managed to reach within a mile of the city. Then he realized that the city was totally encircled by rebel troops.

Liu Mengmei, however, had no intention of turning back. He did not want to disappoint his wife. So he hid in a burned-down farmhouse during the day. At night, he came out of the house to scavenge for food and look for an opportunity to break into the city.

As the siege went on, Liu's search for food became increasingly difficult. Very often, he had to sleep with an empty stomach. Once he vomited violently after he feasted on some pig feed he had discovered in a pigsty.

In desperation, he decided to take a chance. According to his plan, he would wait until midnight. Then he would crawl his way toward the South Gate, swim across the river, and knock on the gate. Hopefully, Du's soldiers inside the gate would be able to open the gate before he was shot to death by rebel arrows.

Unfortunately, about two hundred yards away from the gate, a rebel patrol dog spotted him and started to bark. Liu tried to dash toward the river, but caught his feet on some debris and fell on the ground. The rebels arrested him and dragged him to the largest tent in their camp.

In the middle of the tent, there were two large chairs draped with the skins of Siberian tigers. The chair on the right belonged to Li the Bandit and the one on the left to his wife. To their left and right, two large makeshift wood stoves were burning, giving out warmth and light.

The tent was eerily silent in the wee hours of the night. Dame Li sat slumped in her chair, sleeping. Li the Bandit paced the tent with a flask of wine in his hand. A few attendants stood at the entrance of the tent, yawning.

Li's troops had been encircling the city for many days now, but the city was heavily fortified and Du's soldiers defended it vigorously, so the siege was going nowhere. He was worried about three possibilities. Number one, the southern court might send fresh reinforcements. Number two, even if the reinforcements did not come, he would have to abandon the siege when winter came. Number three, the northern barbarians might accuse him of not fighting hard enough for them. After all, they might think that, as a native of East China, he was not one of them.

He had ordered the execution of two generals who had failed to take the city. What else could he do? He could not kill all his generals.

A rebel officer came into the tent and whispered to Li the Bandit, "Your servant beg to report. The soldiers captured a southerner sneaking toward the South Gate."

"Did you find any letters on him?" Li asked the officer.

"He tore a letter to pieces before we arrested him."

"Anything else on him?"

"We found a portrait of a pretty girl."

"Cut his head off," Li the Bandit waved his hand.

"Wait," Dame Li suddenly woke up from her sleep. "He may be useful to us."

"Any man is useful to you," Li the Bandit retorted drunkenly.

"Bring him in and tie him to the post," Dame Li ignored her husband and ordered the officer. She watched as the soldiers carried out her order.

"You have drunk too much," Dame Li reproached her husband. "Now get some sleep."

Angrily, Li the Bandit finished the flask in one draft, threw it at the prisoner, and slumped down on his chair. He soon started to snore loudly. Dame Li went back to sleep as well.

Tied to the post and scorched by the heat from the stove, Liu sweated profusely. He knew his end was near. Once Li the Bandit and his wife woke up from their sleep, he would very likely be interrogated and executed.

Liu thought about his wife. How pretty she was, how loving she was, and how unusual their union was. Now he would never be able to see her again. His body would rot in the open unburied, and his bones would scatter in the fields, licked clean by scavengers.

Liu Mengmei fell into a tormented sleep. When he was awakened by a loud voice, it was already morning. He opened his eyes and saw a soldier rushing into the tent.

"Your servant beg to report," the soldier bowed to Li the Bandit, who sat up in his chair and looked irritated that the soldier had interrupted his sleep. "A few Tartars are making a commotion at the gate."

Li the Bandit stood up and went out.

"Stop fighting," Liu heard him bellow.

"Great Prince," one of the guards yelled, "we told them to wait outside the gate for your order, but they got mad and started thrusting their swords at us."

"Let them come to the tent," Li the Bandit yelled back.

A big Tartar with red whiskers soon came into the tent with Li the Bandit.

The Tartar's bodyguards tried to come into the tent as well, but Li's soldiers stopped them at the entrance.

"Who are you, my Tartar friend?" Li asked.

The Tartar was angry. "I Tartar envoy. I hungry." He pointed at Li's guards, "They bad. They made I wait."

"You are an envoy from the northern court?"

"I Tartar envoy," the Tartar pointed at himself and pointed in the northern direction.

"Sorry I did not know you were coming."

The big Tartar pointed at his mouth and at his stomach impatiently, "All night, I rode. I hungry, hungry."

Li ordered his attendant, "Bring wine and roast mutton."

The attendant came back with big flasks of wine and huge chunks of roast mutton and gave them to the envoy and his bodyguards at the entrance. The Tartars gulped down the wine and ripped at the meat with knives. The wine and the meat were gone in a minute.

The big Tartar with red whiskers gave a satisfied belch, wiped his greasy hands on his robe, and pointed at the empty wine flask.

"Get more wine," Li the Bandit ordered.

The attendant got another flask of wine. The big Tartar finished it in a few drafts.

He started to sway in his seat, and he started to sing with wild gestures. His eyes rolling, he soon noticed Dame Li, who was sitting on her chair on the left hand and watching his movement with amusement. The Tartar envoy pointed at Dame Li repeatedly.

"Envoy from the North," Li the Bandit introduced, "this is my wife, Princess Li."

"Welcome, envoy," Dame Li greeted him. Turning to her attendant, she ordered, "Get another flask of wine as my welcoming gift for the honorable envoy."

The Tartar gulped down the wine in one long draft, spilling the wine all over his robe. Dame Li watched him, giggling. The Tartar envoy started to point at Dame Li repeatedly again.

"What does this clown want?" Li the Bandit asked his wife, annoyed.

"I think he wants me to dance for him," Dame Li answered. Still giggling, she came down from her elevated chair and started to sing and dance.

Whirl and spin,
Twirl and shake,
Twist my hips,
Show my legs.
The princely husband
Red with jealousy.
The moorish Tartar
Wild with desire.

The Tartar roared with laughter and fell to the ground. Li's attendant helped him to his feet. Swaying unsteadily, he grabbed Dame Li by the sleeve.

"You hairy I want," he shouted.

Li the Bandit pushed the Tartar to the ground. Turning to his wife, he asked, "What does the clown want from you?"

"I'd rather not say," Dame Li answered coyly.

"Tell me, what is it he wants?" Li demanded angrily.

"He wants a private part of mine that has hair on it."

Li the Bandit flew into a rage. "You stinking barbarian. How dare you insult my wife! I'll wring your filthy neck and cut off your smelling head!" He jumped on the Tartar, who was still roaring with laughter on the ground, and started to pound him with his fists.

The attendants and Dame Li pulled Li the Bandit off the Tartar. The Tartar rolled on the ground for several minutes, yelling some incomprehensible curses. Then he jumped up, grabbed his sword and thrust it at Li.

Li the Bandit dodged it and ran for his broadsword. With a loud yell, he chopped the Tartar's head off his neck.

The Tartar fell, blood gargling out of his neck. His body-guards, who had been standing at the entrance to the tent, grabbed their horses, and galloped away.

Looking at the Tartar's severed body and head, Dame Li was distressed, "My prince, you shouldn't have done it."

"But, but," Li stammered, "he was after that hairy part of yours."

"What would be the harm if he had got it? Now we are in big trouble with the barbarians."

Li slowly gained his composure. "Don't worry, old lecher. Remember they made me a prince? What are they going to do to a prince for killing a lowly envoy?"

"A prince?" Dame Li chortled sardonically. "How much is it worth? They gave it to you, and they can take it away from you. Remember, you are not a Tartar, you are just an eastern bandit they have been using."

Groaning, Li the Bandit collapsed into his chair.

Liu Mengmei, who had watched the whole incident, saw his opportunity.

"Sir," he addressed Li the Bandit, "I think it is time for you to switch your loyalties."

"Who are you?" Li the Bandit stood up and asked him fiercely.

"I am a messenger from the southern court," Liu answered calmly.

"What is your message for Commissioner Du?" Dame Li walked up to Liu and asked him nicely.

"A large army is on its way to attack your base in the mountains, and the emperor wants Commissioner Du to hold you here as long as possible."

The Tartar fell, blood gargling out of his neck.

"You are a lying vagabond," Li the Bandit picked up his broadsword and raised it over Liu Mengmei's head, blood from the dead Tartar dripping onto him.

"You are free to disregard my message now, but you will soon regret it."

"Let's withdraw to our base immediately," Dame Li told her husband, a hint of panic on her face.

"You can retreat to your base, Madam," Liu Mengmei continued, "but without the help of the barbarians, and with Commissioner Du on your heels, you will have little chance to survive the attack."

Li the Bandit turned to his wife, and the couple whispered to each other for a while.

"What would the southern court give me if I give up the rebellion?" Li the bandit finally asked.

"I can get Commissioner Du to make you a prince and Dame Li a princess in her own right."

Li and his wife whispered to each other again. "Get a map," Dame Li ordered an attendant.

Opening a map an attendant handed her, Dame Li pointed to a large island about fifty miles off the mainland, "Young man, tell Commissioner Du we want to be prince and princess of this island."

Li the Bandit drew his wife aside, "Old lecher, I know you are a strategist, but I don't understand why we want to lord over an island cut off from the mainland."

"Great Prince, we have relied on the Tartars for support in the past. Now we are turning against the Tartars, the southern court can wipe us out any time they want. But on this island, with the sea as a barrier, we can more easily defend ourselves."

"Brilliant, brilliant."

Turning to Liu Mengmei, Dame Li said, "I also want a headpiece made of gold and decorated with precious stones, modeled in the latest fashion, and befitting a princess."

"No problem," Liu assured Dame Li.

"Untie our new friend and get him some food," Li the Bandit ordered a soldier.

Liu Mengmei was very hungry, but he did not want to tarry too long in the rebel camp. Wolfing down a piece of mutton and a flask of wine, he bowed to Li and his wife and took his leave.

Liu almost reached the gate when Li the Bandit caught up with him with a sack in his hand. "Young man, I have a gift for Commissioner Du."

Looking inside the sack, Liu saw the bloody head of the Tartar with red whiskers. He almost vomited.

Liu Mengmei first soaked himself in a stone tub in the public bathhouse. He then relaxed on a sleeping chair as darkness slowly gathered outside. Liu was happy with himself. With the help of a lucky turn of events, he had been able to arrange Li's surrender and lift the siege of Yangzhou.

But before he went back to Hangzhou, Liu Mengmei wanted to tell Du Bao that his daughter had come back to life and married him. That was why he had come to Yangzhou in the first place.

Liu had destroyed Liniang's letter to her parents before his arrest by the rebels. Now he had to think of a way to convince Du Bao. The task seemed much harder than convincing Inspector Miao to sponsor his trip to Hangzhou and convincing Li the Bandit to give up his rebellion. How could he persuade anyone that a dead person could come back to life? But Liu was determined to try.

At that time, a soldier rushed into the bathhouse. "I have been looking for you throughout the city," he told Liu Mengmei.

"Why, my brother?"

"Commissioner Du invites you to a farewell party."

"A farewell party?"

"The emperor has summoned him to the capital, and he is leaving tomorrow."

When he got to Du's residence, Liu Mengmei saw numerous carriages parked in the street and their drivers chatting with one another.

Inside the courtyard, a large banquet was going on in the open air. Huge lanterns illuminated the air, hundreds of guests clank their cups and gulped down delicacies, and a dozen young girls sang and performed on a platform.

"Come here, my young hero," Du Bao called out to Liu Mengmei when he saw him. He appeared to be happily inebriated. Filling a cup with a strong millet liquor, he gave it to Liu. "This is to your valor and intelligence."

"Thank you, Commissioner Du," Liu downed the liquor. Immediately, he felt the hotness from the liquor scorching his esophagus and his stomach.

The crowd cheered.

"I want to show my appreciation as well," Du's military commander filled a cup and came up to Liu.

"We all do," the crowd agreed noisily, and they lined up behind the officer with their filled cups.

Very soon, Liu Mengmei was drunk. His head spinning and his speech blurring, he pleaded with the crowd, "Thank you all, but please no more."

"It's the night to get drunk," the crowd clamored.

Liu took a few more drinks. Then he collapsed.

Laughing, Du Bao's military commander dragged the young man from under the table and into a chair. Turning to two soldiers, he ordered, "Escort the young man to his room."

"No. I'm fine." Liu struggled up from his chair and wobbled to Du Bao's seat. "Sir, in the excitement of the past few days, I almost forgot that I came here to deliver a personal message to you," he blurted.

"A personal message from whom?" Du Bao looked surprised.

"From your daughter, Liniang."

The noisy crowd suddenly became silent. They looked anxiously at Liu Mengmei and Du Bao.

"What did you say?" Du Bao's face clouded.

"I have a message from Liniang."

"Go back to your room," Du Bao told Liu Mengmei sternly.

The military commander dragged Liu Mengmei away from Du and whispered to him. "You'd better shut up. Commissioner Du's daughter died three years ago."

"But I brought his daughter back to life and married her," Liu replied.

"Don't play with my feelings," Du Bao controlled his anger and warned Liu Mengmei.

"Every word I say is true, Commissioner Du."

"Get out of here," Du exploded.

"Sir," his commander tried to calm down Du Bao, "please don't be too offended. The young man is obviously drunk."

Turning to Liu Mengmei, he said, "Apologize to the commissioner."

"There is nothing to apologize for," Liu answered. "I am his son-in-law."

Du Bao flew into a fury. "Throw this impostor out of here."

When Liu Mengmei woke up the next morning, his head ached from the alcohol in his blood and the memory of his confrontation with Du Bao the previous night.

He had to try again, Liu told himself. So he quickly washed and went to Du Bao's residence.

Du's soldiers were packing, but Du Bao was sitting in a chair, sipping a cup of tea. When he saw Liu Mengmei, he pointed at a large leather purse on the table, "This is for you, young man."

Liu opened the purse; it was filled with silver bars. He closed the purse and said, "Thank you, sir, but I don't want it."

"I will ask the emperor to get a job for you."

Liu shook his head. "I don't want you to do that either."

"What do you want then?"

"I want you to believe me," Liu Mengmei answered sincerely.

"Look, young man," Du's voice took on a hint of impatience. "You were drunk last night, and I was drunk too. Let's forget it ever happened."

"Everything I said last night is true."

Du Bao stood up from his chair abruptly and turned to leave the room.

"Before you leave, sir," Liu Mengmei pleaded, "please take a look at a portrait of your daughter in my possession." He then took out the rosewood box from his sleeve, opened it, and gave the scroll to Du Bao.

On the scroll, Liniang was smiling innocently and sweetly. Gazing at the portrait for a long time, Du's expression softened.

Encouraged by the change in Du's mood, Liu tried to explain, "Your daughter gave it to me as a gift of love."

"Nonsense," Du Bao suddenly woke up from his reverie. "My wife told me she had left this portrait in my daughter's room. You must have broken into my house."

"Sir, allow me to tell you the whole story."

"I don't have time for your story now," Du answered coldly. Turning to his soldiers, he ordered, "Arrest this thief and send him to the royal prison in Hangzhou."

The news of Li's surrender spread quickly. Hangzhou, the capital city, was in a festival mood. For the first time in a long time, people smiled, waved, and chatted in public.

Liniang also rejoiced in the turn of events. It meant that her father was safe, and her husband would be back very soon with news of her father. After his return, Liniang decided, the three of them should go to Yangzhou immediately. With Madam Du finally accepting her resurrection, the prospect of a whole family reunion excited her.

Every day, Liniang spent her time doing needlework by the window. Her eyes, however, focused on the street, expecting her husband to turn up any minute. Every night, she slept half-heartedly, sitting up at every little noise, hoping to hear a knock on the door.

A few days passed, but her husband had yet to return. Liniang grew anxious. One early morning, Liniang woke up feeling particularly distraught. She had dreamed of her husband crying for help in a deserted forest. Hastily, she put on an old dress and walked out of the rental house.

"Liniang, where are you going?" Her mother got up in a hurry, came to the door and asked in a worried voice.

"I am taking a walk down the street, mother," Liniang answered.

"The sun is not up yet," Madam Du pointed to the pale gray of the pre-dawn sky in the east.

"I like the quietness of the morning," Liniang tried to sound upbeat, but her mother could hear despair in her voice.

"Let me walk with you, young mistress," Fragrance called out from her room.

"No. I will be back very soon."

"Come back before the sun burns your skin," Fragrance tried to cheer Liniang up. "You want to look pretty for Scholar Liu."

Liniang walked to the canal. Several dozen boats lined the loading area. However, there was not a single passenger boat. Laborers were unloading bags of rice from the boats. They carried the heavy bags on their backs, stepped on and off the boats, chanting rhythmically and in unison. They paid little attention to Liniang. Nearby, the big lodging house was still asleep, the tiny light of the lantern rendered indistinct by the on-coming dawn.

Liniang went back to Main Street. She wandered toward the city gate. The gate was already open. A tired-looking guard sat on his haunches against the gate, yawning. When he saw her, the lonely soldier stood up and greeted her.

Liniang greeted back.

Inside the gate, a sonorous voice was walking slowly toward them, announcing, "The night is over. The new day starts. Today is the twelfth day of the eighth month. The emperor has no meetings with his ministers today. There is a charity event in the Temple of Peace for the refugees this afternoon."

He was a monk with a small bamboo drum slung over his shoulder. He beat on the drum rhythmically with a bamboo stick. When he reached the North gate, he turned and went back toward the South Gate.

Liniang turned back toward her house.

The street had little traffic. Tea-houses were open, but not restaurants and stores. The only people Liniang saw were lone farmers who were carting their vegetables, meats, and eggs into the city.

"Want some meat for your family? Best quality and best price," one farmer greeted her.

Liniang told him that she was not interested.

The man continued on his way, but looked back several times. It was rare for a young woman to walk alone so early in the morning.

In the distance, a one-horse carriage was driving toward her. When it came near her, the carriage stopped, and the driver, a man wearing a black cap, asked her, "Are you looking for a ride, young lady?"

"No," Liniang shook her head. "I'm looking for my hus-band."

"Where is your husband?" the driver seemed to be very interested.

"My husband left for Yangzhou about a month ago. He is supposed to be back by now."

The driver looked Liniang up and down closely. Her dress was plain, and she wore no make-up, but she surely was one of the prettiest women he had ever seen. He looked around him. There was nobody else around. He smiled and said in a low and confidential voice, "Your husband is in the city now."

"Where in the city?" Liniang was surprised to hear the news.

"Just get on the carriage. I'll give you a ride to the hotel where your husband has been staying."

"Let me tell my mother first."

"No, no, no," the man shook his head urgently. "I don't have time to wait. If you want to go, just get on."

"I need to get some money for you anyway," Liniang pointed at the rental houses opposite the public bath, "I live just a block up the street."

"Don't worry. I'll give you a free ride. Come on now."

Liniang thanked the driver and got on the carriage. Before she had time to settle into her seat, the driver started the carriage. Waving his whip, the driver hurried the horse into a trot.

Liniang was both elated and angry. She was elated that her husband was sound and safe. She was angry because he did not return to the rental house first. Why was her husband staying in the city? How did the driver get to know her husband?

Liniang asked the driver amid the clanking noise the metal wheels of the carriage made on the stone-paved street.

"Ask your husband when you see him," the driver answered.

Liniang looked out of the carriage window. They had entered the North Gate of the city and the boulevard they were traveling on was called Imperial Way. The boulevard had four lanes paved with granite stone and separated by flower beds of various colors.

On her right side, the famed West Lake glistened in the morning sun. On her left side, big estates with ornamental iron gates lined the boulevard. This was the first time Liniang had been inside imperial Hangzhou since she and her husband arrived here more than a month ago. Its beauty and opulence contrasted sharply with the squalor and the poverty in the outer town she had been staying. Liniang was impressed.

Ahead of them, about two miles away, a hill rose at the end of the boulevard. Amid the splendor of fall colors, the imperial palace, a cluster of elegant red brick buildings with golden roofs, stood on the top of the hill, overlooking the boulevard, the lake, and the whole city.

Before reaching the hill, the driver turned east into a side street. Along the street, two-storied brick houses nestled in lush gardens. Lanterns with the words "Guest House" painted on them hung at the doors of many of the houses.

The driver stopped at a gray brick house with a long half-circular driveway bordered by carefully cropped trees and bushes. A small marble stone stood at the entrance of the driveway with the inscription "Happy House."

"Wait for me in the carriage for a few minutes," the man told Liniang before getting off his seat. He walked up to the house and knocked on the door.

The door opened. A big and heavily made-up woman came out. The driver whispered to her. Then the big woman came up to the carriage.

"I am Wang the Big Sister. Your husband left a few minutes ago, but he said he would be back this afternoon. Please come in and wait for him inside."

Liniang got off the carriage and went with Big Sister into a huge reception hall. One end of the hall was a raised stage. A dozen mahogany tables and cushioned chairs stood between the stage and the windows looking out to the driveway. On the wall to the left, there were landscape paintings and calligraphy by famous artists. On the wall to the right, there were several portraits of very beautiful young women.

"Who are they?" Liniang asked curiously.

"They are my hostesses. They sing, dance, and they entertain hotel guests in other ways," Big Sister answered casually.

Liniang felt angry again. She had heard about pleasure places men liked to frequent, but she had never imagined her husband would come to visit such a place while leaving her worrying about him in a rental house.

"Take a seat, honey," Big Sister told Liniang pleasantly.

"Where did my husband go?"

"He didn't tell me, but he said he would be back this afternoon," Big Sister answered. "Honey, do you know how to play musical instruments?"

"I know how to play *Shen*," Liniang answered. "Why?"

"I am just curious," Big Sister continued, "Can you sing?"

"I never took any lessons, but I can hum a few notes."

"Very good," Big Sister was impressed. "Honey, why don't you wait for your husband in one of my guest rooms?"

Big Sister took Liniang to the second floor. The staircase was made of carved hardwood and painted dark red. The hallway was carpeted. Big Sister led Liniang into one of the rooms on the second floor. The room was not big, but it was tastefully furnished. The furniture was handmade and in a classic style. The window overlooked the front garden.

Big Sister opened the wardrobe, went through it, and picked a bright red dress with a deep cleavage. "Honey, take off your old dress. Put on this one. Your husband will be pleased."

"I don't want to please him anymore," Liniang told Big Sister.

Liniang waited forlornly for her husband in the hotel room. She could not understand why her husband, who had married her even though she had been a ghost, would so soon forget her and abandon her. How could he change his heart so quickly? As the day dragged on, Liniang asked again and again why.

The sun was setting, splashing the sky in the west with brilliant colors, but Liniang did not have the peace of mind to appreciate it. She paced the room impatiently. She had been waiting for her husband the whole day. Now, she must go back to her house. Her mother, Fragrance, and Sister Stone must be worried that she had disappeared without leaving a word.

Her mother must be especially worried. Since their chance reunion about half a month ago, Madam Du had gradually come to accept her story of resurrection and had grown closer to her. Liniang had shared with her mother stories about her life in the underworld and her love for Liu Mengmei while Madam Du in turn had told Liniang her life in Yangzhou with Du Bao.

Outside her room, Liniang heard some giggling. She opened the door and saw two young women in the corridor. "Hello," she greeted them.

"Hello," they greeted back. "What's your name?" one of them asked.

"I am Liniang."

"I am Rose. I live next door to you."

"I am Spring Leaf. I live further down the corridor."

"Who sold you here?" Rose asked Liniang.

"No one sold me here," Liniang was surprised by the question.

"Then how did you end up here?"

"I'm waiting for my husband."

"Why are you waiting for your husband in this place?" the two girls looked at each other incredulously.

Liniang explained to them why and how she came to the hotel. She told them what her husband looked like and asked them whether they had seen him.

The two girls became silent. They looked at each other as if they did not know what to say to Liniang. Finally, Rose told Liniang, "I have never seen your husband here." Spring Leaf shook her head as well.

"Then why did Big Sister lie to me?"

"I'm afraid she wants to keep you here like us."

"What treachery," Liniang strode down the stairs in anger and ran into the big woman in the hallway. "My husband has never been here," she told her. "I'm leaving right now."

"You can go if you pay me back the five hundred silver coins I paid the driver this morning," Big Sister answered coldly.

"What?" Liniang could not believe her ears.

"He said you were a vagabond, and he sold you for five hundred coins."

"Let me go home and I'll pay you back," Liniang pleaded.

"Give me the money now, or you have to work for me just like the other sisters," Big Sister was getting impatient.

"No way," Liniang yelled at the big woman furiously. She ran toward the door and pulled it hard. But the door was locked.

A big and fat man came out from a small room behind the stairs, grabbed her, and dragged her upstairs. "Stay in your room," he growled, "or I'll smash your face."

"I'm so stupid," Liniang sobbed piteously.

"You're not," Rose and Spring Leaf tried to comfort her.

"Yes, I am."

"I was lured here as well," Rose told Liniang.

"How?" Liniang raised her head.

"I was playing with my friends in a street corner," Rose told Liniang. "A man with a carriage stopped and told me that he wanted to take me to a candy store."

"How old were you?" Liniang asked.

"I was eight."

"You were eight, but I am nineteen."

"But you were anxious for your husband."

"Why don't you run away?" Liniang asked Rose.

"The fat man strangled a sister two years ago for trying to run away," Rose's face darkened. "Besides, I don't even know where my parents live."

"I know where my parents live, but I don't want to go back," Spring Leaf told Liniang.

"Why not?" Liniang was puzzled.

"My father sold me here," Spring Leaf answered, tears in her eyes. "He said he got too many daughters and couldn't afford to marry me off."

Soon after dusk, the hotel came back to life. From her window, Liniang saw carriages pulling up in front of the house. Men, some old, some young, and some in-between, but all well dressed and well mannered, exchanged greetings with Wang the Big Sister, and were welcomed into the house.

Music started. A woman started to sing. From the voice, Liniang could tell that it was Spring Leaf.

> *It is night,*
> *Time for delight.*
> *Forget your wife,*
> *Enjoy your life.*
> *Be happy,*
> *Have fun.*

Men applauded, and more women started singing. The smell of food, alcohol, and excitement drifted upstairs and into Liniang's closed room.

The revelry lasted for hours. Then the center of activity seemed to shift to the second floor. Liniang heard men and women coming upstairs, giggling and laughing, the doors opening and closing.

Then she heard a tap on her door. Alarmed, she asked, "Who is it?"

"Honey, it's me." Wang the Big Sister entered the room. Two men, one young and extremely tall and the other middle-aged with a slight hunchback, followed her into the room. The young man stood awkwardly in the doorway eyeing Liniang sideways while the middle-aged man ogled Liniang in an openly lascivious manner.

"Honey, I have two visitors for you." Big Sister pointed to the two men, who nodded their heads in greeting.

Liniang was frightened and outraged. She stood up and moved away from Big Sister and the two men. "Please let me go home."

Big Sister came up to her and put her arm on Liniang's shoulder. "Don't be a fool. At this moment, your husband may be having fun somewhere. Why don't you have some fun and earn some money as well?"

"Let me go home," Liniang threw off Big Sister's arm and raised her voice.

"Even if I let you, they will not," Big Sister pointed to the two men at her sides.

Picking up a porcelain rice bowl from the table, Liniang threw it forcefully on the floor. The bowl broke into pieces, and food splattered all over the floor. Liniang picked a sharp shrapnel and pointed at Big Sister. "Let me go," she demanded.

Surprised by the vehemence of Liniang's angry outburst, Wang ran behind the two men for cover. "You have to pay for it," she yelled at Liniang. Pushing the two men toward Liniang, she urged them, "Go on, you two. Teach her a lesson."

The middle-aged hunchback made a step toward Liniang.

Waving and pointing the porcelain at him, Liniang pleaded, "Go away, please."

The younger man stopped his companion by his shoulders. "Brother, we shouldn't force her. Let's go."

"But she is so pretty," the hunchback gawked at Liniang greedily.

"Let's go," the young man dragged him toward the door.

"Don't be a wimp," Big Sister blocked his way.

Angrily, the young man grabbed the big woman and threw her against the door. "Don't ever use the word again."

"Take it easy, big boy," the hunchback patted his friend on the back and eased Big Sister out of the grips of his friend. Then, without warning, he turned and rushed at Liniang, wrestling her to the ground.

"What are you doing?" The young man was shocked by the agility of his hunchback companion and by his single-mindedness in trying to get what he wanted.

"Stop asking questions. Get the porcelain out of her hand," the hunchback shouted.

The young man squatted down beside Liniang, who was struggling beneath the weight of the hunchback, "Give me the broken porcelain, young lady. I don't want you to get hurt," he cajoled.

Liniang waved the porcelain to warn him away, but the young man pinned her right wrist to the ground and wrestled the broken piece out of her hand.

With his body astride Liniang, the hunchback started to grope Liniang.

"Stop," Liniang shouted.

"It won't be long, my pretty lady," the hunchback told Liniang. "Just relax."

"Help me please," Liniang pleaded with the young man. But he seemed to be both repulsed and fascinated by the scene. Still squatting and holding Liniang's right hand tightly, he stared at Liniang without making any move.

"Help, help," Liniang cried out. The high pitched plea rang out of the room and into the whole house.

Doors opened, footsteps came, and people gathered at the door. Someone knocked. "What is going on in there?" It was Rose's voice.

"It is none of your business," Big Sister shouted. "Go back to your room."

"Leave her alone," Rose demanded.

"I'm going to break your neck if you don't go back," Big Sister threatened.

"Help," Liniang cried again, but Big Sister thrust her fat palm over Liniang's mouth.

People were whispering at the door, but no one knocked again.

Liniang sobbed through Big Sister's fingers. Then she spoke with resignation. "At least let me take off my clothes, please."

Big Sister withdrew her hand and stood up. Smiling, she said, "Now this is the right attitude. Be good, and I will treat you well."

Liniang pushed the hunchback away and struggled to her feet. She looked at the big woman and the two men in anger and contempt. Then Liniang suddenly dashed for the window. Without hesitation, she flung herself out of the window.

Liniang did not die. She landed on a low holly tree. The prickly leaves tore her dress and cut into her skin, and pain radiated throughout her body. Struggling with both her hands, she quickly disentangled herself from the plant. Then she ran into a cluster of bushes that separated the "Happy House" from the neighboring property and hid herself.

The house door flew open. Big Sister rushed out with a lantern in her hand, followed by the big, fat man and the hunchback. The fat man and the hunchback first inspected the shrubs below the window and then fanned out along the driveway in two different directions.

In a few moments, they came back to the door. "She must be hiding in the bushes. Let me get the dog and hunt her down," the fat man said to Big Sister.

Liniang was petrified.

"Fire," Liniang suddenly heard someone yelling with alarm.

Liniang looked out from the bush. From the window of Rose's room, a bright red fire billowed out amid black smoke.

"Fire, fire," a cacophony of frightened noise came from the house. Men and women, some of them naked, dashed out of the door.

"Get water, get water," Big Sister cried, trying to get into the house. But the panicked crowd rushing out of the house pushed her onto the ground and tramped on her.

Liniang ran away from the house as fast as she could. She ran and ran until her legs couldn't move anymore. Then she stopped and looked back. The bright red fire had already burst through the roof and was lighting up the nightly sky.

"All the gods in heaven, please help Rose and her sisters," Liniang prayed.

Chapter Fourteen

IT WAS noon. Du Bao came back from the imperial palace and plumped down on a chair in his living room. He felt tired and dispirited.

After he had arrived in Hangzhou, the emperor had appointed him chief minister of the cabinet. For a few days, Du Bao felt elated. He had always been ambitious, but he had never expected that he would become the highest-ranking government official under the emperor.

But the euphoria did not last long. Everyday when he came back from the palace and sat down alone in his living room, he missed keenly his daughter and his wife.

Du Bao reminisced about that memorable spring morning three years ago when he decided to spend a few days with his wife and his daughter on the estate. How happy he had made his wife and his daughter! Liniang's sweet smiles greatly warmed his heart, and his wife's passion and love excited his body and soul.

Then misfortunes struck. His daughter died, and his wife lost her life at the hands of rebels. How he wished that he could reverse the wheel of time and undo the cruelty of history!

"Sir," an attendant came into the room and announced quietly, "an old acquaintance of yours from Nan'an is here to see you."

"Who is it?" Du Bao was surprised.

"His name is Chen the Most Virtuous."

"Show him in immediately," Du Bao told the attendant.

Chen walked slowly into the living room. He had traveled first to Yangzhou and then to Hangzhou after learning about Du Bao's promotion. The traveling obviously took its toll on him. His face was gaunt, his eyes tired, and his hands were shaking.

"Welcome, Professor Chen," Du held the old man's hands to steady him. He then took the baggage off his back and sat him down on a chair. "Thank you for traveling hundreds of miles to visit me."

"Congratulations on your promotion, sir."

"Thank you," Du answered. Turning to the attendant, he ordered, "Bring tea."

Looking at Du Bao intently, Chen said, "It's just been three years since you left Nan'an, but your hair has turned completely gray."

"Government responsibilities and family misfortunes," Du sighed.

"Where is her ladyship?" Chen the Most Virtuous immediately sensed something tragic.

"She was killed by rebels on her way back to Nan'an."

"I'm sorry, sir," the old man's eyes became watery. Remembering the numerous acts of generosity Madam Du had bestowed on him, including giving him the accountant job after Liniang's death, the old man was genuinely saddened. "May she rest in peace," he prayed.

After Li the Bandit surrendered, Du Bao had personally gone to the hillside where his wife had been ambushed to search for her remains. Bones scattered everywhere, broken up by traffic and licked clean by scavengers. There was no way to identify which bone belonged to whom.

Du Bao took a pot of earth from the hillside and carried it to Hangzhou with him. He promised himself that as soon as possible, he would ask the emperor for a leave of absence and go to Nan'an to bury the pot at the side of his daughter's grave.

"Sir," Chen wiped away his tears, "I'm afraid I have some more bad news for you."

Du Bao looked at the old man, his eyes fearful.

"Liniang's grave was robbed."

Du Bao was silent for a long while, a pained and angry expression on his face.

"Sir, I have a pretty good idea who did it."

"Who?" Du demanded.

"Sister Stone and a young vagabond named Liu Mengmei."

"Liu Mengmei?" Du Bao remembered the young prisoner he had brought from Yangzhou. "Is he a young fellow with a strong southern accent?"

"Yes, he is."

After he had arrived in the royal prison, Liu Mengmei had tried first to contact his wife. The prison warden told him that he could not do that without special permission from Du Bao. He then made several pleas to Du Bao, but no reply came back from his office.

"What is going to happen to me?" a despairing Liu Mengmei asked the warden.

"You are going to rot here," the sadistic warden laughed.

Now, thank God, Du Bao had finally sent soldiers to summon him. As he walked down the Imperial Way, Liu Mengmei remembered he had walked the same boulevard many times before to the South Gate where the examination results were to be published.

For a brief moment, Liu almost felt that he was going to the South Gate again for the exam results. With the war in Yangzhou finally coming to a stop, the results might have been posted by now. Liu wondered whether he had made the list.

Then he realized that he was not going to the South Gate. He was a prisoner of his father-in-law, on his way to be interrogated. His hands were bound. One soldier walked in front of him, and the other behind him.

The three of them soon arrived at a large official residence. Two sculptured stone lions stood on each side of the gate looking menacingly down on him.

"Good afternoon, sir," he greeted Du Bao when he was led into a huge reception hall and saw his father-in-law sit at the head of a large table.

"I want you to meet an old friend of yours," Du Bao told him coldly.

"Who is it?"

"Chen the Most Virtuous."

"Professor Chen is here?" Colors drained from Liu's face.

"Don't you want to see him?" Du stared at him closely.

"Yes, I do," Liu closed his eyes with resignation.

When Liu opened his eyes again, he saw Chen the Most Virtuous coming out of the adjacent living room.

"Professor Chen, I'm happy to see you here. How are you?" he tried hard to be cheerful.

Without answering him, Chen walked up to him and looked him up and down for a few minutes. Then he responded coldly, "I am fine, thank you. But I can see, Scholar Liu, that you are not faring too well."

"Professor Chen, it was not what it looked like. I brought Liniang back to life and married her."

"You and Sister Stone robbed young mistress's grave. And yet you come here to tell me that you brought her back to life and married her! What a ridiculous lie! What a heinous crime!" Chen barked, his hands shaking.

Du Bao ordered an attendant, "Bring a writing brush and a piece of official paper."

When the attendant returned with the brush and the paper, Du Bao dictated, "I, Liu Mengmei, native of Guangzhou, hereby confess that I, together with an accomplice named Sister Stone, robbed the grave of Du Liniang and broke into the Du residence on..."

"On June 27th of this year," Professor Chen added.

"On June 27th of this year in Nan'an," Du continued.

"I did not rob Liniang's grave," Liu protested loudly.

The attendant soon finished writing and gave the document to Du. Turning to Liu, Du said, "Now all I need is your signature."

"Please believe me, sir. Your daughter, Liniang, is staying in the town outside the North Gate. If you allow me, I will bring her here immediately," Liu pleaded.

"Still refuse to confess and still persist in your lies? Officers, string him up in the courtyard and beat him hard," Du ordered.

The two soldiers dragged Liu Mengmei out into the courtyard and hung him up on a big tree. They began beating him with rods and sticks. Liu's already tattered gown fell to the ground piece by piece. His skin burst, and blood started to drip down to the ground.

Liu Mengmei wailed, "Stop please."

"They will stop if you sign," Du answered.

"What if I sign?" Liu asked.

"Desecrating a grave is a capital crime," Du Bao answered. "But considering your meritorious deeds in Yangzhou, I will exile you to the farthest border post in West China for twenty years."

"No, sir," Liu Mengmei refused. "I don't want to leave my wife, who happens to be your daughter."

"Beat him," Du was infuriated, "beat until he confesses."

Two middle-aged officials rode out from the office of the Commissioner for Royal Examinations. The taller one of the two was holding a big placard that read:

Liu Mengmei
First Prize Winner of the Royal Examination, Native of
Guangzhou, Twenty-six Years of Age, Tall, Without Defects.

"This is a joke. A southern beggar makes the first prize and never comes to claim it," he complained.

"How can we find him in a city this size?" his shorter companion echoed unhappily. "He may have gone back to Guangzhou, or he may have dropped dead."

As they rode down the boulevard, the shorter man started to shout, "Liu Mengmei, liu for willow, meng for dream, and mei for plum."

The noise soon attracted a small group of homeless boys who followed behind them. One of the boys, the oldest and tallest, called after them, "Give us a coin, mister. We'll shout for you."

The shorter man threw a coin to the boy.

"Why don't you hold the placard as well?" the taller man threw the placard to the boy and dug out a coin from his pocket.

The big boy pocketed the two coins and held the placard up over his head. The other boys started to chant as they followed the two officials down the boulevard.

"Liu Mengmei, liu for willow, meng for dream, and mei for plum."

The pain was intolerable for Liu Mengmei who had drifted in and out of consciousness. When he finally came to, he seemed to hear a cacophony of voices calling for him faintly but persistently, "Liu Mengmei, Liu Mengmei."

In his pain, Liu Mengmei remembered Liniang telling him that she had heard young male voices just before she died. The voices belonged to the fiends who had come to claim her spirit. Now they were here to claim his spirit. In a desperate attempt to fend off the fiends, he kicked his legs wildly, and he hissed violently at the invisible voices.

"Confess!" a soldier threw a bucket of cold water over him and shouted.

Liu opened his eyes and perked up his ears. He heard the voices again. This time they were much louder and much closer. "Liu Mengmei, where are you? liu for willow, meng for dream, mei for plum, where are you?"

"It is not the fiends," Liu suddenly realized.

"But who can they be?" Liu tried to rotate his body toward the gate to see who was looking for him, but he couldn't. He saw Du, Chen the Most Virtuous, and the soldiers were also looking in the direction of the street. They seemed to be as puzzled as he was.

When the chanting came closest to the gate, Liu cried at the top of his voice, "Liu Mengmei is here. Liu Mengmei is here."

The cacophony of young male voices suddenly stopped. Then came many loud knocks on Du's iron-gate. As a soldier opened the gate, several dirty-looking boys poked their heads through the gate curiously.

"Where is Liu Mengmei? Where is Liu Mengmei?" they clamored excitedly.

"I am here on the tree," Liu cried again.

Two men in drab official garment pushed the boys aside and strode into the courtyard. They came under the tree, inspected Liu Mengmei, and asked, "Where are you from?"

"I'm from Guangzhou."

"How old are you?"

"I am twenty-six years of age."

The shorter man turned to the soldiers and ordered, "Put him down."

Du Bao flew into a rage. During all his years as governor of Nan'an and commissioner for Yangzhou, no one had dared to dash into his official residence and to order his soldiers around.

Now he was chief minister, but two menial employees of some obscure government office dared to do both without even properly greeting him.

"Soldiers," he yelled, "throw these two out of here."

The soldiers wrestled the two men to the ground, kicked them viciously, and threw them out of the gate. Badly bruised, it took the two men some time to mount their horses and to gallop away. The homeless boys, seeing the situation had suddenly turned ugly, also disappeared into the bushes.

A soldier, while closing the gate, saw the placard on the ground. He picked it up, read it, and looked very surprised.

"How can this be possible?" Du Bao asked Chen the Most Virtuous after the soldier had shown him the placard.

"It must be a case of identical names," Chen answered.

"But the Liu Mengmei we have here is also from Guangzhou and is twenty-six years old."

"Then it must be a case of identical birth places, ages and names."

Du Bao was not so sure. He sat down on his chair, sipping a cup of tea and pondering what to do with the young man who had robbed his daughter's grave, but who had saved Yangzhou from Li the Bandit, and who might have also excelled in the royal examination.

He heard a knock on the gate.

When the gate was opened, Miao, Commissioner for Royal Examinations, came into the courtyard. The two men Du's soldiers had beaten and thrown out moments before stood at the gate.

"Please help me, Commissioner Miao," Liu yelled from the tree.

Miao ignored Liu and walked into Du Bao's reception hall and greeted him, "How are you, Chief Minister?"

"How are you, commissioner?" Du answered. "What can I do for you?"

"With your permission, I would like to see who you have strung up in that tree."

"Of course," Du answered, hoping that Chen the Most Virtuous was right.

Miao quickly walked to the tree and looked up at a bloody Liu Mengmei.

"Please help," Liu pleaded.

"Chief Minister," Miao turned toward Du Bao who had followed him into the courtyard, "this man you have strung up and beaten won the first prize in the royal examination."

"I won the first prize? I won the first prize?" Liu exclaimed excitedly.

"Shut up," a soldier growled at Liu.

"Are you sure?" Du asked Miao.

"Your Excellency, he is no other than Liu Mengmei, the first prize winner. I gave him an essay examination myself and I recommended him to His Majesty for the first prize."

"Then I have to tell you, Commissioner Miao," Du's voice was almost sorrowful, "the man you have recommended is a common criminal."

"What crime did Scholar Liu commit?"

"He robbed my daughter's grave in Nan'an."

"I did not rob the grave," Liu protested. "I opened the grave to bring your daughter back to life."

"You did what?" Miao turned to Liu Mengmei, stunned by what he had said.

"I brought Chief Minister's daughter back to life and married her," Liu repeated.

Miao stared at Liu, speechless. Has the young man he had sponsored and recommended for the first prize gone mad?

"You see what a lying criminal he is," Du Bao told Miao.

"Commissioner Miao," Liu pleaded calmly, "I beg you to fetch my wife, Chief Minister Du's daughter, as my witness. Her name is Du Liniang and she lives in a rental house opposite the public bath on Main Street outside the North Gate."

Miao was confused. The young man talked rationally and seemed to be in command of his senses. But how could a dead person come back to life? It was ridiculous. Was Liu Mengmei trying to cover up his crime with a widely improbable story?

"If you get my wife," Liu continued, "she will attest to everything I said."

"There is no need to waste time," Du Bao retorted impatiently. "His wife must be an impostor."

She must be, Miao agreed. There was no way a dead person could come back to life. But Miao wanted to save Liu Mengmei if it was at all possible. He had financed the young man's trip to Hangzhou, and he had been very impressed by his essay. In fact, Liu's essay was the only essay that had made sense to him.

The only hope of saving Liu from the capital crime, Miao decided, was to refer the matter to the emperor. Given Liu's talent and his rhetorical skills, he might be able to persuade the emperor to pardon him.

"Since Scholar Liu has won first prize in the royal examination," Miao told Du Bao, "I think we should let His Majesty adjudicate the case."

Du Bao nodded his head reluctantly.

"Can you release him into my custody meanwhile?"

"I am sorry," Du shook his head. "He remains my prisoner before our meeting with His Majesty."

"Please bring my wife to the court," Liu Mengmei shouted at Miao as he was leaving Du Bao's residence.

It was already noon. The sun splashed into the royal bedroom through half-opened windows, but the emperor was still in his huge bed. He had drunk too much the night before. In truth, he had been drinking too much every night in the name of celebration since Li the Bandit gave up his rebellion.

A eunuch was pacing anxiously in an adjacent room. It was very late. He had to wake up the emperor. So he started to make a bird-like sound. The emperor had made it clear early in his reign that he did not like to be awakened by any "abrupt, urgent, or unnatural sound," so all the eunuchs in the inner palace had perfected the skill of imitating some bird that sang in the morning.

The eunuch's song did not wake up the emperor. He was snoring like a pig. But it did wake up the two concubines who were in bed with him that day. One of them got up in her sleeping dress and walked to the door. "What is it?" she asked.

"His Majesty was to have an audience with Chief Minister Du and Scholar Liu for early this morning," the eunuch whispered.

The young woman went back to the bed and started to scratch the emperor's feet, "Wake up, you lazy bones."

"Wake up," the other concubine kissed his eyelids.

"No more games, you two lechers. I had enough last night." The emperor stopped snoring, but he was too tired to open his eyes.

"Some people have been waiting for you since early this morning," one concubine told him.

"What do they want?" the emperor whined. "Why can they leave me alone for a day with my women?"

"You have an appointment," the other concubine told him.

The emperor wiped his eyes with the back of his hand and sat up in the bed.

The eunuch walked into the room and reminded him quietly, "You have an audience with Chief Minister Du and Scholar Liu."

"Who is Scholar Liu?" the emperor asked.

"Scholar Liu won the first prize in this year's royal examination."

The emperor scratched his head, he remembered reading some essays a few days before, but he couldn't recall their contents. "What about him?" he asked.

"He has been missing since he took the examination, but Commissioner Miao found him yesterday," the eunuch reported.

"Did he find him in a brothel?" the emperor chortled.

"In his father-in-law's residence where he was being tortured."

"Why did his father-in-law do that?" The emperor's interest was piqued.

"His father-in-law accused him of grave robbing," the eunuch handed the emperor a document.

The emperor glanced at the document cursorily and threw it back to the eunuch.

"What a stupid father-in-law. Instead of celebrating, he is making trouble for his son-in-law and for me. Send my word that the father-in-law be beaten with the royal rod twenty-five times before the Imperial Gate." He slipped into the sheets, dragging his two concubines with him.

"But I can't," the eunuch told him.

"Why not?" the emperor sat up in his bed abruptly, mystified by the eunuch's rebellious answer.

"The father-in-law is Chief Minister Du."

"What a troublesome chief minister I have appointed," the emperor grumbled. "I have to take care of military affairs, civil affairs, love affairs, now I have to take care of my chief minister's private affairs."

But despite his complaint, the emperor walked with the eunuch to his audience hall. Along the way, he saw hills bathing in the glorious sunlight, trees changing colors, and the fascinating West Lake glistening in the distance. The beautiful scenery improved the emperor's mood.

❀❀

The audience hall was a large rectangular structure. The emperor's golden chair was at the north end of the room facing south. Two rows of seats were at each side of the audience hall extending all the way to the south end. In the middle of the hall, right in front of him, there were a few low seats. The emperor sat down on the imperial chair with a big yawn.

"Chief Minister Du and his witness, Chen the Most Virtuous, are waiting in the right wing. Scholar Liu and Commissioner Miao are waiting in the left wing. Which party would you like to see first?" the eunuch asked.

"Let me see Commissioner Miao and this young man who won the top prize first."

"Summon Scholar Liu and Commissioner Miao!" the eunuch called out.

Miao helped Liu Mengmei limp into the audience hall. The young man's right arm was heavily bandaged, and his face was cut and bruised in several places.

"May Your Majesty live ten thousand years!" they saluted him.

"What was the exam question?" the emperor asked Miao.

"Of the three policies, attack, defense, and appeasement, which one is the most appropriate policy in dealing with the barbarians?"

"And what was your answer, young man?"

"I advocated a combination of the three."

"How would you apply your triple strategy to the current situation?" the emperor asked curiously.

"With the surrender of Li the Bandit, I would first strengthen the defense of cities and towns in the frontiers. Then I would appease the population in the frontiers by stopping collecting taxes for a few years. Last, when popular support for Your

Majesty increases, I would start an all-out offensive against the barbarians."

"Very good, young man," the emperor was impressed. "Now tell me, why does your father-in-law accuse you of grave-digging?"

"Your Majesty, could you allow my wife to be my witness please?"

"Where is your wife now?"

"She is at the palace gate with her mother, waiting for your summons," Miao answered.

"Get Scholar Liu's wife and mother-in-law," the emperor told the eunuch.

"My dear husband," Liniang embraced her husband and cried inconsolably when she rushed into the audience hall.

"I missed you, my dear wife," Liu Mengmei kissed his wife on her face.

"I missed you too."

"What happened to you?" Liu saw a scratch on his wife's face and touched it gently with his finger.

"A minor accident," Liniang answered. "Did my father hurt you badly?"

"Nothing to worry about, my wife."

"I am sorry about what my father did."

"It's not your fault."

Sobbing, Liniang buried her face in her husband's chest. "I'm never going to let you out of my sight."

The emperor, Commissioner Miao, and the eunuch watched and waited patiently.

Madam Du was getting anxious. She tucked at Liniang's sleeve several times, but her daughter did not seem to notice. Finally, she whispered to Liniang, "His Majesty is waiting."

Freeing herself from her husband, Liniang saw the emperor sitting on his golden chair, looking down at her with an amused expression.

"I'm terribly sorry, Your Majesty, for not paying respect to you first," she prostrated.

"That's fine, my pretty young lady," the emperor answered in an avuncular voice. "Let's meet your father first. Then you can go home with your husband and enjoy yourselves."

"Thank you, Your Majesty," Liniang answered, blushing.

"Chief Minister Du Bao and Scholar Chen the Most Virtuous pay their respects to Your Majesty," the eunuch announced.

Liniang turned anxiously toward the waiting room on the other side of the audience hall. The door opened, and her father emerged from the waiting room. It had been three years since she last saw her father. Liniang noticed that his father's hair had turned completely white, his face had acquired deeper wrinkles, and his expression had become more severe.

Chen the Most Virtuous followed right after her father. With twitching face and unsteady steps, Chen looked like a man at the end of his life.

Du Bao came to the center of the hall. He was about to prostrate when he caught sight of Liniang and his wife, both of whom were gazing at him anxiously and tenderly. He stared first at Liniang, then turned to Madam Du, his eyes wide open and his nostrils flaring. He could not believe what he saw. Turning around abruptly, he sprang for the door.

"Ghosts, ghosts," he yelled as he fled.

"Father," Liniang called out after her father, her voice pained. "Come back, father, and hear my story." Her father, however, slammed close the door of the waiting room behind him.

Chen the Most Virtuous did not run. He seemed to be frozen on the ground. His hands shook, and his lips trembled. He stared piteously at Liniang, as if begging her not to move closer to him.

Liniang stood where she was. She did not want to scare the poor old man. "Professor Chen, what my husband told you and my father is true," she said softly.

Chen shook his head wildly. Then he fell backwards, hitting his head on the stone floor. Liniang, Madam Du, and Liu Mengmei all rushed to his side, trying to revive him. But Chen was not responding. His eyes went blank. His face was covered with sweat and his breathing was shallow and fast. In a few minutes, Chen started to spasm violently. His last breath was a long and gargling sound from his throat. Liniang closed his eyelids.

"Is this a show?" the emperor asked the eunuch. He found it amusing that his chief minister should call his wife and daughter "ghosts" and run away from them. Besides, who would have thought that an old man should suddenly expire in his audience hall without any apparent reason?

"I don't think so," the eunuch shook his head. He was confused as well.

"Bring back the Chief Minister," the emperor ordered.

Du Bao came back to the audience room and prostrated in front of the emperor. Glancing at the two women, he felt confused and disoriented.

His daughter Liniang died three years ago and was buried in the back garden. How could she be sitting in the royal palace?

He sent his wife out of Yangzhou with his soldiers and all of them were slaughtered at the hillside. How was it possible for her to come back to life as well?

"Where are the ghosts, Chief Minister?" the emperor asked.

Du pointed at his daughter and at his wife, "They are the ghosts."

The emperor laughed. It was so funny. The old man was losing his senses. "They are your daughter and your wife, my minister. Look at them closely."

Du Bao looked. He had never believed in the existence of ghosts and spirits, but now he was forced to accept it because there was no other way to explain what he saw. The more he looked, the more they looked like his daughter and his wife, and the more he was convinced that he was looking at two mischievous spirits who were playing a trick on him and on the emperor.

"They are ghosts," he insisted.

The emperor laughed again, so did his eunuch.

"Why do you think they are ghosts, old man?" He began to like his eunuch for waking him up.

"They died."

"If they died, how can they be here?"

Madam Du, pained by the spectacle, interrupted, "Your Majesty, can I ask my husband a question?"

"Go ahead."

"My dear husband, when did I die?"

Du Bao seemed to be calmed by Madam Du's quiet voice. "I saw you and all the soldiers who escorted you killed by the rebels in an ambush."

"The rebels killed all the soldiers, but Fragrance and I hid in a marsh and escaped to Hangzhou," Madam Du explained. "If you don't believe me, you can ask Fragrance, who is waiting right outside the palace gate."

Du looked at his wife silently, as if he did not know whether to believe her or not. Then he recalled that he had not been able to find the remains of either his wife or Fragrance. He may have been too hasty in concluding that they had been killed.

The emperor turned to the eunuch, "What do the classics say about testing for a ghost?"

"First, you use a mirror. A ghost shows itself a skeleton in the mirror. Second, you let her walk under the sun. A ghost has no shadows. Third, you hold his or her hands. A ghost has icy cold hands."

"Get me a big mirror," the emperor asked enthusiastically.

Two attendants carried a big mirror into the room. Smiling, Madam Du stepped before the mirror. She was smiling in the mirror as well.

"Now let's get out into the sun," the emperor ordered. They all went out and looked at Madam Du. There was a shadow on the ground.

"Now old man, do you want to touch her hands?" the emperor asked.

Du hesitated for a second. Then he walked up to his wife and touched her hands. They were warm.

"I beg your pardon, my wife," Du Bao felt ashamed. "I am sorry for my silliness. I am so happy to see you again."

"Congratulations, my husband. For victory at the frontier and for promotion at the court," Madam Du embraced her husband.

"Now let the father and the daughter reconcile," the emperor said.

"But my daughter really died three years ago."

"Are you sure, Chief Minister?" the emperor asked him mockingly.

"Your Majesty," Liniang said calmly, "it is true I died three years ago."

"You what?" the emperor almost fell off from his chair. The eunuch hastened to steady him.

"Don't be alarmed, Your Majesty. I died three years ago, but my husband," she pointed at Liu Mengmei, "opened my grave and brought me back to life."

"How is it possible?" the emperor asked incredulously.

"Sister Stone of the Purple Light Convent is an eyewitness. She is waiting outside the palace gate right now."

"It's impossible," Du Bao interjected. "No official histories have ever recorded such an event before. She must be a ghost."

"Ghost or not," the emperor said, "let's do the tests."

Liniang trembled. She knew she had returned to life, but in the deepest subconscious of her mind, she still had a little doubt. Her husband and her mother also watched anxiously.

Biting her lip, Liniang stepped in front of the mirror.

"As pretty in the mirror as outside the mirror," the emperor announced.

Liniang smiled at Liu with relief, and Liu smiled back.

The group then went outside. Liniang cast a long slender shadow on the ground.

"There is a shadow," the emperor announced again.

Liniang and Liu grinned at each other happily.

"Now touch your daughter's hand, old man."

"No, I won't," Du recoiled.

"Why not? You silly old man," the emperor was annoyed at Du's refusal. Turning to Liniang, he said, "Come here, my beauty. Let me touch your hand for your father."

Liniang stepped forward and extended her hands. The emperor held both her hands and inspected them admiringly for quite some time.

The eunuch made a little cough. The emperor released Liniang's hands, and said appreciatively, "Your hands are warmer than any of my concubines'."

"It can't be," Du blurted. He looked as if the world no longer made sense to him.

"You still think she is a ghost, despite all the tests?" the emperor asked Du Bao.

"Your Majesty, how can a dead person come back to life?"

"Let's say she is a ghost. What shall we do with a ghost, Chief Minister?"

Du Bao hesitated.

"As pretty in the mirror as outside the mirror."

Turning to the eunuch, the emperor asked, "According to the classics, what should we do with a ghost?"

"We should burn it on a wood pyre."

"Set up the pyre outside," the emperor ordered.

"Please no, Your Majesty," Madam Du knelt and cried.

"Burn me as well if you want to burn my wife," Liu Mengmei told the emperor.

"Father, touch me," Liniang pleaded. "I am not a ghost."

"The pyre is ready," an attendant came into the audience hall to report.

"Shall we go ahead?" the emperor looked at Du Bao.

Du Bao was quiet. Everybody watched him anxiously.

"Shall we go ahead, old man?" the emperor asked again.

Du Bao still remained silent. Then he shook his head slowly.

"Why not? She is a ghost."

"Ghost or not ghost, she is my daughter."

"Thank you, father," Liniang knelt before Du Bao and cried. Falteringly, Du Bao raised Liniang to her feet and embraced her. "I missed you, Liniang."

The emperor smiled. "Now let the father-in-law and son-in-law reconcile," he said.

Du Bao shook his head.

"Why not, my husband?" Madam Du asked in a pained and puzzled voice. "He won the first prize in the royal examination. Isn't that what you always wanted?"

"I know he won the first prize," Du Bao answered. "He also helped to bring about Li the Bandit's surrender. He is a young man with a bright future. But..."

"But what?" The emperor was becoming impatient with his chief minister. It had been a long meeting, and the emperor believed he had settled the matter satisfactorily.

"They married without my permission," Du Bao answered.

"That was a serious offense," the emperor agreed, "but surely there were mitigating factors."

"Your Majesty, obedience to parental authority, just like obedience to your imperial authority, is a fundamental principle of society," Du insisted. "I want the marriage annulled."

"No," Liniang protested. "I would rather die than separate with my husband," she told her father.

"So would I," Liu told the emperor.

"My dear husband," Madam Du turned to her husband. "They love each other. That's more important."

"What is love?" Du asked his wife. "All the classical sages talked about obedience as the foundation of family, not love."

Liniang embraced Liu Mengmei. "I dreamed of him, I pined for him, and I died for him. He married me while I was a ghost. He brought back my life and he risked his own life struggling all the way to Yangzhou to seek your blessing for our marriage. We are inseparable from each other and we are willing to die for each other. Father, this is love."

Du Bao's heart softened. He remembered how he had missed his wife after the ambush outside Yangzhou. He also remembered how his heart had been torn apart by Liniang's death.

"As a punishment for your marriage without your father's consent," the emperor told Liniang and Liu, "you forfeit your right to ask him for any dowry. Is that agreeable to you?"

"We don't need any dowry, but we want his blessing," the couple told the emperor.

"Very good. Now let the father-in-law and the son-in-law reconcile," the emperor urged.

"My respect to you, father-in-law," Liu knelt in front of Du.

Liniang turned to her father, "Please, please."

Madam Du took her husband's hands.

Stiffly, Du greeted Liu, "My son-in-law."

Liu then knelt before Madam Du, "My respect to you, mother-in-law."

Madam Du raised Liu Mengmei to his feet. Tears of happiness and gratitude streamed down her cheeks. "Thank you for bringing my daughter back to life."

"Note this story in the official history of the empire as the first known example of resurrection," the emperor told the eunuch. He then ordered an attendant. "Invite all the nobles, ministers, and generals for a grand celebration tonight."

Du Bao, touched by the happy atmosphere all around him, relaxed. "You owe me lots of grand children," he told his daughter and Liu Mengmei.

The young couple smiled at each. "We will try," they promised.

"Well," the emperor laughed, "I almost forget that I also owe my concubines lots of children. I'll get back to my work and see you tonight."

"By the way, Your Majesty," Madam Du stopped him. "Do you also owe my son-in-law a job since he won the first prize?"

"How about taking over your father-in-law's position in Yangzhou, my young strategist?" the emperor asked Liu.

"With pleasure," Liu Mengmei replied.

A loud thunder exploded over the West Lake. Liniang looked out of the window. The imperial palace was still bathing in the bright summer light, but a violent storm was fast approaching. Liniang turned pale as she remembered her interrupted dream at the peony pavilion three years before. Seized with fear, Liniang clutched Liu Mengmei impulsively.

"Is this all a dream?" she asked.

"It's not a dream, my love." Liu held Liniang tenderly.

Looking up at Liu, Liniang murmured, "My love, I'm not letting you go again, no matter what happens."

"I'm all yours," Liu whispered into her ear, "forever, and into eternity."

More fiction titles from Homa & Sekey Books

Flower Terror: Suffocating Stories of China by Pu Ning
(ISBN 0-9665421-0-X, Paperback, $13.95)

Acclaimed Chinese writer eloquently describes the oppression of intellectuals in his country between 1950s and 1970s in these twelve autobiographical novellas and short stories. Many of the stories are so shocking and heart-wrenching that one cannot but feel suffocated.

In "A Glass of Water," neighbors ignore a feverish old woman's pleas for water because her son has been denounced as counter-revolutionary. In "The Fossil," a wife does not speak to her writer husband for three years, because he is under suspicion. The title story portrays the absurdity of the period in which flowers seemed so alien to the oppressive political atmosphere that they evoked a sense of terror in people's mind and heart.

Butterfly Lovers: A Tale of the Chinese Romeo and Juliet by Fan Dai, forthcoming, (ISBN 0-9665421-4-2, pback, $16.95)

A beautiful girl disguises herself as a man and lives under one roof with a young male scholar for three years without revealing her true identity. They become sworn brothers, soul mates and lovers. In a world in which marriage is determined by social status and arranged by parents, what is their inescapable fate?

The novel is based upon a popular Chinese folktale that has moved millions to tears. There are various music, movie and drama adaptations of the story in the Chinese language, but this is the first English publication in original fiction form. The Chinese title of the story is *Liang Shanbo and Zhu Yingtai*.

Order Information: Please send a check or money order for each ordered book plus $3.50 shipping & handling to: Homa & Sekey Books, P.O. Box 103, Dumont, NJ 07628. New Jersey State residents should add sales tax.